DESERT GETAWAY

Also by Michael Craft

DESERT GETAWAY

MICHAEL CRAFT

ISBN: 1-954841-16-1
ISBN-13: 978-1-954841-16-1

Brash Books
PO Box 8212
Calabasas, CA 91372
www.brash-books.com

PART ONE
TROUBLE IN PARADISE

CHAPTER ONE

Palm Springs was *back*, baby!

Like a doddering, once glamorous diva, the town had limped out of the twentieth century in need of some serious dolling up. Gone were its glory days as a fabled getaway during Hollywood's golden age. Gone, too, was its later, seedier heyday when swinging crooners and affable mobsters held court from their corner booths at white-linen supper clubs.

The future, alas, was looking dim for the sunny desert oasis. But then, quietly at first, an influx of new settlers arrived, bringing along their stylish pizazz, a fresh outlook, and extravagant sass. Before long, the town grew into a gay mecca that would rise from its doldrums with a full-throated promise of fun, fun, *fun* for all—leathermen and bachelorettes alike.

I fit right in. Not only that, but when I moved here a few years ago (with the man who would later divorce me), I discovered a side of Palm Springs they don't promote to tourists—the darker side—where deadly sins take root in the sand and thrive in the warm nights. This so-called paradise does indeed have its serpents, and not all of them are reptilian. Others are metaphorical: the serpents of greed, betrayal, and murder.

But none of those unpleasantries were on my mind last February as I approached a rental house with my slim folder of paperwork. I rang the doorbell, then waited under the soaring, cantilevered roof of a boulder-lined entryway.

A voice crackled over the intercom: "Yes?"

"Dante from Sunny Junket."

A befuddled pause. "What?"

"My name's Dante. I'm from Sunny Junket Vacation Rentals."

"Oh. Just a minute."

This was one of our premier properties, up in the Palm Springs neighborhood known as Little Tuscany, where the bohemian feel of steep, winding streets and walled courtyards gave no hint of the million-dollar views enjoyed by residents. In the gravel parking court on that rare cloudy afternoon, my battered, used Camry looked especially pathetic—huddled next to an elegant champagne-colored SUV. When did Bentley start making those?

The party of two was registered under the name Edison Quesada Reál, booked for eleven nights, the entire duration of Modernism Week. It was a prime booking in high season, costing north of a thousand a day. The office said the guy was a bigwig art dealer from Los Angeles, and they wanted him happy, so they sent me out for the VIP treatment.

I'd intended to greet them when they arrived at the house, but they'd driven over early, letting themselves in with the keypad code we provided. The front door now rattled as someone fussed with the lock from inside. Then the door swung open.

"Well, *hello*." His Asian eyes widened with interest as he sized me up.

I grinned, returning the once-over. He didn't fit my picture of anyone named Edison Quesada Reál. And he was too young for a titan of the art world, maybe in his thirties. He had delicate features and a prettiness about him, like a twink who'd grown up, but he'd also hit the gym and was pleasingly buff, for a short guy. I've always had a thing for short guys.

I reached to shake hands. "I'm Dante. Welcome."

"And I'm Clarence Kwon. Friends call me Clark."

"Hi there"—I smiled—"Clark."

"C'mon in," he said, stepping aside and closing the door after me. He was dressed with the casual sophistication of fresh-faced,

3

moneyed LA—wispy calfskin loafers, skinny slacks, and a clingy, cream-colored cashmere sweater with its arms shoved up to his elbows. Nice pecs. Good guns.

By contrast, I had recently turned fifty-one after wasting too many years on starstruck dreams and the wrong men. I looked dorky in dad jeans and a yellow polo shirt embroidered with the Sunny Junket logo. Gesturing to myself, I told Clark, "They *make* me wear this."

He laughed. "You look great." And I half believed him as he wagged me along, leading me toward the back of the house.

As we entered the main room, the view opened up from a wall of glass. Although I had seen it many times, the elevated vista never failed to stop me cold. Even on that gloomy day, I caught my breath as the city spread out below, peeking through the crowns of distant palms. Sloping down from one side, granite mountains muscled into the scene to wrap around the city. Above, in a vast gray sky, clouds slowly roiled, snagged on the barren shards of the horizon.

"Edison," said Clark, "the guy from the agency is here."

Seated at the center of the huge window, facing out, mere inches from the glass, a man in a wheelchair remained dead still for a moment. Then he grasped both wheels. The rings adorning his hands clanged the chrome rims as he turned the chair to face me.

I stepped toward him.

"*Stop*," he said sharply. "Let me get a look at you."

I waited. He was older than me, well into his seventies, and way too heavy to be healthy. Though stuck in a wheelchair, he was smartly dressed—to the point of flamboyance—with a silk scarf of peacock blue poufed about his neck. I shot him a smile.

"Forgive me if I don't get up," he said. "If I could, I'd kiss you." He spoke with a worldly refinement and the trace of a Castilian lisp.

I moved to the wheelchair. "But I hardly know you."

He grinned as we shook hands. "You're quite the *cheeky* little cabbage, aren't you?"

"I've been called many things, Mr. Quesada Reál. But never a cabbage."

He let out a feeble roar of a laugh. "Please, please—it's Edison."

"And I'm Dante."

"Of *course* you are." His tone sounded skeptical.

Had he seen through my act, the stagey name, the swarthy tan? Unlike the tourists and well-heeled snowbirds who fled Palm Springs during the long summers, I had been soaking up twelve-month doses of sunshine, which not only gave me a bronzed glow but inspired me to stay fit.

Clark moved to the far end of the room, near the long dining table, where he fussed with several piles of art prints, all of them protected by plastic sleeves. While arranging them vertically in wood-slatted browsing racks, he called over to me, "Did you bring us something to sign?"

"No, I just need to snap a picture of the credit card you'll use for payment—and a driver's license to verify the name."

Edison noted, "I don't drive. Can you handle this, precious?"

The younger man stopped his sorting. With an impatient sigh, he pulled his wallet from a pocket, slid out his license and an AmEx, and plopped them on the table. "This what you need?"

"You bet." I went over and took pictures of the cards with my phone. I noticed that Clarence Kwon was thirty-four, which could not have been half Edison's age. I assumed they were a couple; even though their rental was one of our more expensive properties, it had only one bedroom. I explained, "For these pedigreed houses, we run the charges every other day."

Clark shrugged. "Whatever."

"Perfectly understandable," said Edison, wheeling himself in our direction. "You know I'm good for it, precious."

Clark said nothing as he resumed sorting the artwork.

Edison continued, "Truth be told, no price would be too high for *this*." He flung both arms, a gesture that embraced the whole house. Then he leaned forward, beading me with a milky stare. "Do you know who designed this, Dante?"

"Um, I've heard, but..."

Edison sat back, twining the plump fingers of both hands. "Alva Kessler designed and built this house for himself shortly before he died in the late fifties. He envisioned it as a pure, modernist vacation 'cabin'—a sleek exercise in glass and steel. Truly magnificent, yes? In its sheer minimalism, it's every bit as fresh and avant-garde as it was sixty years ago. And now, for a while, it's all mine." Edison paused, turning his head toward Clark. "I mean, it's all *ours*."

"Right," said Clark, looking peeved. "Ours, when I'm not at the convention center."

I asked, "The art sale? I know it's a big deal during Modernism. I went once."

"Once"—Edison sniffed—"is enough."

Clark added, "If you've seen one lava lamp, or one Noguchi table, you've seen'm all."

Edison explained that his Los Angeles gallery, Quesada Fine Prints—which dealt in original graphic art, no reproductions—had rented exhibit space where they would offer collectors a wide selection of lithographs, etchings, and screen prints from the mid-1900s. The bulk of their inventory had already been delivered to the convention center, with two of their staffers setting up for the show. The most valuable works, however, would remain here at the house, with Clark showing them by appointment or delivering them for consideration by high-end buyers.

Listening to these details, I stepped over to one of the racks to take a look and was instantly drawn to a smaller print, less than a foot high. "This is *great*," I said, breaking into a smile as I lifted it from the bin. "It would sure be at home in Palm Springs."

Bright and colorful, it was a blotchy depiction of a swimming pool.

"That's a David Hockney," said Clark. "Limited-edition lithograph, signed artist's proof, mint condition. At *this* show, it's our jewel in the crown."

Edison said, "Sell that one to the right buyer, precious, and you'll get the other Bentley." He turned to tell me, "Clark's been wanting the convertible."

Gingerly, I handed the Hockney to Clark, who said, "Edison is exaggerating." He glanced at the coded sticker on the back of the plastic sleeve, adding, "Or maybe not."

"I'm feeling peckish," said Edison. "Some trifle would help."

Under his breath, Clark told me, "He's been a bit much lately."

Edison reminded us, "I can hear you."

Seething, Clark turned to the wheelchair. "I'm *not* your coolie servant."

"But you *are*." Edison chuckled. "You can leave—if you want—but you won't. And I can't *divorce* you, can I? Far too costly. Face it, precious: we're stuck."

Rain began to spit against the expansive window and drip in long tendrils, streaking the glass from top to bottom, rippling the million-dollar view.

Hoping to defuse the tension, I asked, "Is there anything I can help you with?"

Edison gave me a lecherous look. "Like ... *what*?"

"I'd show you through the house, but you're already settled in. It's an older place, has a few quirks. The electronics are all new. Most guests have questions."

Edison said, "We'll figure it out." Then he blurted, "Pink fluff!"

Bewildered, I looked to Clark for guidance.

Still sorting prints, he spoke to me over his shoulder. "We brought a few things that belong in the fridge—including the raspberry trifle. Could you?"

"Sure." The galley kitchen opened into the main room from the street side of the house. While the A/V system was up-to-the-minute, the kitchen had retro appliances with a midcentury vibe. The vintage refrigerator was a hulking old Philco in red porcelain enamel; the doors of the top freezer and the main compartment both featured elaborate chrome-handled latches.

Edison wheeled in behind me, watching as I lifted five or six shopping bags from the floor to the countertop. They held a few canned goods and liquor bottles, which I set aside, but they were mostly filled with clear plastic containers brimming with a sludgy concoction that Edison had aptly described as pink fluff. Two bags contained ingredients to make more of it—box after box of fresh raspberries, jars of raspberry jam and melba sauce, several hefty packages of pound cake. A zippered thermal bag contained at least a dozen clanging cans of aerosol whipped cream.

"*Now,*" Edison barked with a wild look in his eyes. "Pink fluff!"

I removed the lid from one of the Tupperware tubs.

"*Smell* it," he commanded.

Whoa. The recipe had been lavishly spiked with Cointreau. The piercing boozy scent of orange melded with the tart perfume of crushed berries, making both my mouth and my eyes water.

"*Now,*" he repeated, reaching with trembling hands.

I gave it to him, then slid a drawer open. "Fork? Or spoon?"

"It doesn't *matter.*" He looked ready to slop into it with his fingers. I gave him a spoon.

He rolled a few feet back and gobbled the trifle. Between swallows, he groaned and gurgled.

I glanced over at Clark, who seemed unfazed by this behavior. In fact, he gave me a thumbs-up. So I returned to the task of putting things away. I had to tug at the Philco's heavy ornamental latch (which brought to mind the hardware on a casket) and soon had the beast filled. Its condenser hummed in earnest.

Edison was now banging his spoon on the sides of the plastic container as he scraped at the last of the trifle. I asked if he needed anything else from me, but he shook his head without looking up from his scavenging.

I stepped around the wheelchair, took my folder from the dining table, and told Clark I was leaving. He followed me toward the front of the house.

When I stepped outside, he went with me and gently closed the door behind us. We stood together on the landscaped walkway, protected by the jutting cantilever of the roof. It rained heavily now—straight down, with no wind to drive it—like a translucent curtain blurring the gray afternoon. Raindrops danced wildly on the windshield of the polished Bentley. In the hushed racket of the pelting water, the world was still.

"It's … exhausting," said Clark, his words no louder than a whisper as he gazed into the courtyard.

I asked, "Edison?"

Nodding, Clark turned to me. "Ten years ago, I knew what I was getting into, and I was sure I could deal with the age difference. He's always been pampered and fussy—that was part of his charm. But now, Jesus. It gets worse by the month, like he's regressing into childhood. You've seen the pink fluff; that's been going on awhile. As of last week, about the only *other* thing he's willing to eat is canned spaghetti, like a kid."

I'd noticed the SpaghettiOs while unpacking in the kitchen.

Clark asked, "What's next—diapers?"

"Maybe."

Clark was quiet for a moment, then laughed. Stepping near, he clasped my hand with both of his. "You've been super, Dante. Really helpful. Thank you."

I grinned. "Anything else, just let me know."

He moved closer still, brushing against me and lolling his head back to fix me in his stare. His dark almond-shaped eyes appeared black in the dusky shadows that hugged us. I could hear him breathing. I could almost hear his thoughts. Was he open to a fleeting kiss? Or did he want something less innocent— something more animal and lusty?

When his lips parted, he broke the spell. "Can you fix this weather?"

I backed off a few inches. "It'll dry up. We never get much, but they say we need it."

"Yeah," he agreed coyly. "We need it."

Which left me unsure if this was small talk—or foreplay. Either way, the time was right for a quick exit. I turned to leave but paused. "Enjoy your Sunny Junket."

Clark rolled his eyes. "Let me guess. They *make* you say that."

With a wink, I sprinted off toward my car.

■

When the office texted the next morning, it came as no surprise that the Quesada Reál party was having trouble with the cable and Wi-Fi. They had snubbed my earlier offer to explain things, and now they were miffed, so the office told me to return to Little Tuscany at once. I was driving down valley to inspect a property in Indian Wells—I'd nearly arrived—but I made a U-turn at the next light on Highway 111 and shot back toward Palm Springs.

Shortly after ten, I drove up the narrow driveway and parked in the courtyard next to the Bentley, which had been spiffed and detailed since the rain. More was on the way, but for now, tourists were getting the slice of winter paradise they'd paid for.

When I rang the doorbell, it took a while for someone to garble through the intercom. I said, "It's Dante."

Another long pause. "Let yourself in?"

"Sure." I tapped the code.

Inside, I walked back to the main room. "Hello?" Hearing no response, I stepped farther in and looked around. Everything seemed in order. In the kitchen, a few dishes were stacked near the sink, but the tenants clearly appreciated tidy surroundings. The print racks near the dining table had been rearranged, but the David Hockney was still prominently displayed. On the table, boxes and bulging portfolios contained more inventory.

I turned as one of the glass doors on a side wall slid open, and in from the pool deck strolled Clarence Kwon with a towel slung over one shoulder. He was otherwise naked—and far more buff than I'd imagined. He carried an empty Tupperware container of raspberry trifle, smeared pink.

"Morning, Dante," he said, crossing the room toward the kitchen. "Sorry to call you back. Edison got frustrated with the TV last night. He started punching buttons, and by the time he gave up, the Wi-Fi fritzed out." Clark set the towel on the counter and rinsed the Tupperware in the sink.

"Happens all the time," I said. "No two setups are alike. I'll restore the settings, then show him how to work the video."

"Fair warning: he'll never catch on." Clark stepped over to me while wiping his hands. "Can you tackle the Wi-Fi first?"

"Uh-huh." Looking him up and down, I managed to say, "Seems you had no trouble with the pool controls."

"Nope. But Edison was griping last night about the landscape lighting—said it was totally screwed up. I thought it looked fine."

"I'll check it out."

Clark wrapped the towel around his waist. "Gotta throw myself together. Someone's coming over from the convention center. Security—to help transport some of the good stuff. So go ahead and do your thing." He traipsed off toward the bedroom.

I gathered the remote controls and took them to a former linen closet, now overtaken by electronics. Resetting the Wi-Fi was easy, but rebooting the cable and restoring the streaming services was tedious. About ten minutes into it, I heard the doorbell ring. I also heard the spray of the shower from down the hall. Stepping out to the main room, I saw that Edison had not yet come in from the pool. The doorbell rang again, so I went to answer it.

When I opened the door, a Black woman stood there, locking eyes with me in disbelief. "What the *fuck*?" she said.

I froze, speechless, confronted by a nightmare from the past, which included my first encounter with this woman, a year earlier.

■

I had just started my job with Sunny Junket, which required several days of field training. On a Wednesday morning, while touring some of our properties with Ben, my supervisor, I began receiving messages from the office of Dr. Anthony Gascogne, ophthalmologist—the man who had recently divorced me and thrown me out of the house. His office was concerned because he had not shown up that day. He'd missed two appointments and could not be reached. Could I check on him at home?

Because I was with my boss at the far end of the valley, it was late afternoon when I finally drove back to the Palm Springs house I had once shared with Anthony. Letting myself in, I called to him. All was quiet. At a glance, there were no signs of trouble, but it was odd he'd skipped work—he had recently returned from a cruise—so I decided to do a walk-through.

When I entered his study, my knees went weak. I grabbed the doorjamb to steady myself as the room seemed to spin beneath me. Anthony had dropped face-first from the chair behind his desk, landing on the white shag carpet, which was puddled with the blackening ooze of his blood. His skull was bashed in. A lamp with a heavy crystal base, streaked red, had been thrown violently aside, cracking a cabinet door below the bookcase.

I knelt in the mess to check on Anthony, who was beyond helping. Stupidly, I picked up the lamp and set it upright. Then I phoned 911.

Among the first responders was a hotshot cop, a Black woman in her thirties with a street mouth and a chip on her shoulder. I assumed she was a dyke. Her name badge identified her, dubiously, as OFFICER FRIENDLY. I would later learn that her surname was indeed Friendly, that she was not a dyke, and that she was bucking for a promotion to detective.

That day at the crime scene, she must've figured she could grease her path to a promotion by arresting me on the spot. It sort of made sense: I'd had a messy breakup with the victim, there were no signs of intrusion, I still had a key, and I literally had blood on my hands. It was front-page news in Thursday morning's *Desert Sun*, though I never saw it, waking up behind bars.

By Thursday evening, the medical examiner released his finding that Anthony had died Wednesday around noon. My salvation turned out to be Ben at Sunny Junket, who had spent most of the day with me, providing a solid alibi. I was freed within the hour. Officer Friendly, however, was screwed.

■

And now, a year later, here she was, standing in the doorway at the rental house in Little Tuscany—wearing a rent-a-cop costume and running errands for the convention center. She sported a gun, a badge, and handcuffs, looking plenty pissed.

I smiled. "What happened? Lose your job?"

"None of your motherfucking business."

"Couth it up, Friendly. Our clients wouldn't approve."

"Go to hell, asshole."

"Aha," said Clark, strolling out from the bedroom, dressed for the day. "It seems you two have met. Morning, Jazz."

"*Jazz?*" I said.

She looked aside, mumbling, "Beats the shit out of Jasmine."

Nodding, I agreed. "Not quite your style."

Clark asked, "Get everything fixed, Dante?"

"Hold on," said Friendly. With a low chortle, she asked, "*Dante?* This asswipe lowlife? He's Danny O'Donnell."

We were interrupted by the rattle of the sliding glass door to the pool deck as Edison struggled to open it from his wheelchair. I rushed over and helped him inside.

"Dante, *dah*-ling," he said. "Too good of you."

"I've got the video up and running again. Can we take a few minutes to go over it?"

He heaved a weary sigh. "If we must. Later—when you come back to fix the lighting."

"I can take a look at that right now."

"Not in the *daylight*," he scoffed. "It has to be tonight."

Hesitating, I said, "I'll drop by around six." Not wanting to be stuck alone with Edison, I turned to ask Clark, "Will you be here?"

"Depends. I'll try." Clark was at the dining table, checking the inventory of prints against a list. As if he'd just thought of something, he looked up to tell Friendly, "I need a few minutes before we go. Make yourself at home. Check out the view."

Edison gave the Black woman a haughty, disapproving look as she sauntered out to the pool deck. I followed.

A mockingbird warbled as it swooped from the fronds of a palm to the scrub of an embankment that opened to the city below. Friendly stood at the railing, looking out. I approached from behind. With her back to me, she said, "You fucked up my life."

I stepped to the railing and stood beside her, looking out. "You didn't do *me* any favors, either. The few friends I still had after the divorce—they're *gone*."

"Shit happens, O'Donnell. It happened to me, starting with the murder of your ex. Still an open case"—she turned to look at me—"but I have my suspicions."

"Knock it off. You know I didn't do it. You were wrong."

"And *you* made a mess of that crime scene. My so-called partner—a racist prick—reported that the muddled evidence was *my* doing, that the arrest was wrongful and incompetent. So I was denied training for detective status. I lost overtime privileges. Got crappy shifts. Then my husband dumped me—said it was my drinking." She paused and looked away. Her voice dropped as she said, "Worst part, he got custody of our daughter. My little girl."

I blew a low whistle. "Sorry. That's rough."

The story had drained her swagger. I heard the tinge of fear in her words, in her uncertain future, as she explained how her standing with the police force had continued to sour. It was clear they wanted her out. Deciding to leave on her own terms, she quit. Trying to make a new start, she opened a private investigation service. "Not much business yet"—she shook her head—"so I'm doing security at the convention center."

I shrugged. "It's a plan."

"It sucks."

Clark appeared in the doorway. "Ready, Jazz."

With a parting smirk, she went inside.

So did I. Closing the glass slider, I noticed that the front door of the house was wide open, as if Clark had already trudged through with several batches of prints. But he was standing at the dining table with Jazz, telling her, "Light load today, just this portfolio. Take it in your van; I'll follow in the Bentley."

"Got it." After signing a receipt, she took the portfolio from Clark, and they headed toward the door.

"Pink fluff!" bellowed Edison.

Exasperated, Clark asked me, "Can you take care of him?" Before I could answer, Clark walked out to the courtyard with Friendly and shut the door.

"*Now*," said Edison.

I turned to him. "You just finished a whole tub of the stuff."

"And now I want *you* to try some. It's quite delicious."

I wanted to leave. But I'd been told to give him the VIP treatment. Plus, I'd been wondering if the trifle was as good as it looked. So I played along.

Edison wheeled himself into the kitchen and waited behind me as I tugged the refrigerator door open and removed one of the containers. I popped the lid, grabbed a spoon from a drawer, and gave it a taste.

"Get *out*," I said, amazed. It was fabulous.

"Didn't I tell you?"

I wolfed a few more spoonfuls, then stopped myself, returning the trifle to the fridge. "Thanks, really, it was great." I stepped to the sink to rinse the spoon.

"*Give* me that." He grabbed it, then licked it lewdly. When finished, he sat back, whirling the spoon. "Let me ask you something. What do you think of my Clark?"

"Nice guy. Seems attentive to your needs." I grinned. "And he's hot."

"Isn't he, though?" With an edge of bitterness, Edison added, "I'm not stupid, Dante. I *know* what you're thinking: I'm just a vapid old rice queen."

I assured him, "I would *never* say such a thing."

But that very thought had crossed my mind.

■

Driving back to Little Tuscany that evening, I hoped that Edison would not be alone at the house, that Clark would have returned from the convention center. He might be in the mood for a drink. He might ask me to join him. I was off the clock and felt no obligation to wear the insipid Sunny Junket uniform, so I wore tight black jeans and a leather jacket—surefire date bait.

February nights in the desert could be cold, and the bright, perfect day had already turned gray and windy. Clouds piled up beyond the mountains to the west, rushing the sunset. The dusk disappeared into a starless, moonless darkness.

As my Camry reached the top of the driveway, its headlights skimmed the parking court, which was empty. Peachy—I'd be solo with Edison. When I got out of the car, I took note of the landscape lighting and, finding no problems at the front of the house, checked along both sides, which also seemed fine. However, the most elaborate lighting could be seen only from the rear deck, and due to the embankment, the safest way to get there was through the house.

I rang the doorbell. After half a minute, I rang again. A minute later, I punched in the code and entered, calling, "Edison?" All was quiet.

The interior lights were on, as programmed. At a glance, there were no signs of trouble, and I thought Edison's afternoon nap might have drifted into the evening. But he had been expecting me, so I decided—with a chilling sense of déjà vu—to do a walk-through.

When I entered the kitchen, my knees went weak. I grabbed the doorjamb to steady myself as the room seemed to spin beneath me. Edison had fallen backward, crushed beneath the refrigerator, which had toppled onto him, covering his lower torso. The scene was a ghoulish shambles, with Edison pinned in his mangled wheelchair. The refrigerator was still running, its condenser humming, its door flung open. Raspberries, whipped cream, and tub after tub of pink fluff were scattered everywhere, oozing across Edison's chest. From his mouth, blood had gushed and begun to blacken, puddling with melba sauce on the hard white terrazzo floor.

This time, I knew better than to kneel in the mess and try to help.

This time, I knew better than to phone 911.

This time, I beat a path out the door and ran to my car.

Shaking, I fumbled to start the engine, then backed up to turn around, when I noticed headlights bouncing up the narrow drive. Running through my options—fuck me, there weren't any—I stopped the car and got out while Officer Friendly pulled her van in next to me, followed by Clark in the Bentley. The wind had picked up, rattling the palms in the black sky.

Friendly got out of the van with the portfolio she was guarding. With a flashlight, she swept the surroundings before proceeding. The beam slid up my backside. "Hngh," she grunted. "Nice ass, for a white guy."

Trying to keep things buoyant, I said, "I'll take that as a compliment."

"You damn well better."

Carrying a box of files from the Bentley toward the house, Clark asked, "Did you check out the lighting?"

"Uh, look," I said. "There's something you need to know. Inside. It's bad."

Clark and Friendly glanced at each other, then rushed into the house. I followed, telling them, "Kitchen."

"Holy fucking *Christ*," said Friendly, stunned by the grisly scene.

Clark dropped the files and gaped at his husband. "Jesus."

"No signs of intrusion," said Friendly, giving me a suspicious look.

I said, "Edison *asked* me here tonight. This *had* to be an accident. Why would I—"

"Then why didn't you report it? You were leaving."

Clark blurted, "I *knew* it." He had moved over to the print racks and held up one of the plastic sleeves, empty. "The Hockney. It's missing. It's worth more than this clown makes in a year—"

"Three years," I assured him.

"—and just yesterday, he practically *creamed* over it."

Turning to Friendly, I spread my jacket open. "If I took it, where is it? Wanna frisk me?"

"The car," said Clark, dashing out of the house with Friendly at his heels.

I took my time. In the courtyard, Clark had flung open the doors and trunk of my car, making a frantic search; Friendly assisted with her flashlight. While they trashed it, I watched calmly, secure in the knowledge that there was nothing to find.

"See?" said Clark. "I *told* you." And he withdrew the Hockney from underneath the passenger seat.

And Friendly was cuffing me and phoning it in and calling for backup and dreaming of salvaging her tattered career.

And I regretted that I had been so easily mesmerized by Clark's tight little body.

And I recalled that morning, when I came in from the pool deck, after talking to Friendly, while Clark was inside, fussing with prints, and I wondered why the front door was open.

And now, through the wind, I heard the first distant wail of sirens.

And I said, "Yes, indeed. This old house has state-of-the-art electronics. Surveillance in every room. Up under the eaves, too." I pointed vaguely toward the deep, dark recesses of the roof. "Back at the office, we can just scan through all the video. We'll see Clark planting the 'evidence' in my car this morning. Then we'll see him again, later, in the kitchen, killing his husband."

Clark froze, dropping the Hockney as the first cold spits of rain arrived on the wind. He hadn't planned on video—lying would be futile. With a convulsive heave, he said, "Edison was right. I couldn't leave, and he would never divorce me. We were stuck."

"Till death do you part," I said. "And I'll bet you're his heir."

Clark looked blindly into the rain. Beaten by the truth, he muttered, "There was … no other way."

Friendly released one of my cuffs and clamped it to one of Clark's wrists, saying, "We'll sort this out quick enough." The sirens grew louder. A gust of wind grabbed the soggy Hockney from the gravel and tumbled it through the courtyard, sending it over the embankment.

I laughed, saying to Clark, "You idiot. There's no *surveillance*. At Sunny Junket, we have a measure of respect for our guests."

Slowly, Clark's gaze pivoted to Friendly. With renewed fire, he stared into her eyes. "Some of our wealthier clients value their privacy and prefer cash transactions. I have forty thousand in the house. That could go a long way in the fight to get your daughter back. It's yours—tonight—if you forget what you heard."

Jazz Friendly, the ex-cop who'd accused me of fucking up her life, now studied my face while telling Clark, "But I'm not the only one who heard it."

Clark reminded her, "You've got a gun. Use it. If you say he tried to grab it, that's self-defense. Case closed."

Her eyes darted from mine to Clark's and back to mine.

Clark smiled. "Just shoot him."

Sirens screamed nearby.

CHAPTER TWO

Could it be said of someone who was gunned down point-blank—someone who had just turned fifty-one—could it be said that he had died "too young"?

Sure. If it's true that fifty is the new forty, then friends could mourn him for being felled in the prime of life by a needy ex-cop on the take, firing at close range with a Glock 19. On the other hand, if fifty is fifty, the shooting might be acknowledged with little more than a sympathetic shrug. "It is what it is," they might say of his fate, especially if his fifty years had been slipping away, without meaning or consequence, since he was forty. Or even thirty.

In that moment of niggling over the boundaries of middle age, in that split second of self-evaluation—and regret—as my life passed before me, I watched the slow, surreal movement of Jazz Friendly's hand. Just when headlights began lurching up the driveway, she drew her weapon. And she aimed it squarely at Clarence Kwon.

"Don't move," she told him. "And shut the fuck up."

■

Though my south-side apartment in Palm Springs was nothing special, I trained myself to think of it as not cramped, but "efficient." Not cheap, but "within my means." Not a month-to-month rental, but "home." I opened the front door while waiting for the morning coffee to brew. It was late May, about three months after Modernism Week, when, like clockwork, the snowbirds disappeared, shooed away by hotter days and the onset of summer in the desert. At dawn, though, there was still a cool breeze, allowing me to switch off the air conditioning and save a few bucks.

While sitting on one of the two stools at the breakfast bar in my kitchen—there was no separate dining area—I could look across the tiny living room and out the front door, which opened to a shared patio surrounded by the six units of our modest complex. At the center of the patio, a circular swimming pool reflected an orange-streaked sky that silhouetted black mountains, adding a touch of glam.

I heard the gentle thud of a car door, then approaching footsteps. It was a neighbor, an emergency-room nurse named Isandro, returning from his overnight shift. I gave a wave. Sometimes, if he wasn't burned-out, we would indulge in a bit of play—an occasional quickie to celebrate the end of his workday and to launch the start of mine.

"Morning, Dante," he said quietly, so as not to disturb our sleeping neighbors. Then he slipped through his door across the courtyard and closed it behind him. (It must have been a rough night.) The click of his lock was barely audible in the hush of daybreak.

My phone rang just as the coffeemaker began beeping the end of its cycle, which roused a yipping terrier in another neighbor's apartment. With one hand, I reached for the carafe to fill my mug; with the other, I picked up the call before the second ring. I didn't recognize the number, but I knew the voice.

"Christ, O'Donnell," she said, "why are you up so fucking early?"

"And a pleasant good-morning to you as well, ex-Officer Friendly. Were you *trying* to wake me?"

"I meant to leave a message."

"At *this* hour?" It was well before six. I was tempted to ask, Drinking again?

"The law never rests, O'Donnell."

"Yeah. *Tell* me about that." I let out a loud, rude laugh.

She paused. "That weird-ass *sound*. Is that a … dog?"

Trying to keep it down, I explained, "That's Mitzi. A neighbor's rat terrier."

"Cute." Friendly chortled. "Man's best friend, O'Donnell."

"Look. What do you want? And while we're at it—please don't call me O'Donnell."

"Why not?"

I shrugged, though of course she couldn't see it. "It just sounds so … *military*, I guess. Or athletic, or butch, which I'm not."

"I'll tell the world. Okay, Daniel."

"Actually"—I wasn't sure how far to push this—"my honest-to-God birth name is Danny, not Daniel. But lately, I've been Dante."

"How'd you come up with *that*?"

"I didn't. Before I started working at Sunny Junket, I had a bartending gig for a few months. When the manager hired me, he said they already had a Danny, so he rummaged through a drawer and found someone else's old name tag. 'There you go,' he said. 'Dante.'"

Clicking her tongue, Friendly noted, "A hand-me-down name …"

"Guess so," I admitted. "But it stuck. And I sorta like it."

"All *right* already. Dante."

"Thank you. So: Why'd you call?"

"Coffee."

I eyed the steaming mug that I hadn't yet tasted.

She continued, "Let's meet for a cup of coffee."

Incredulous, I held out the phone for a moment, giving it a wary look.

Her tiny, distant voice asked, "Still there?"

Drawing the phone near again, I said, "Yeah, I'm here." I paused in thought before asking, "And why do you want to meet?"

"To talk, of course."

"We're talking now. And you're making me nervous."

"Look, O'Donnell—sorry, *Dante*—nothing's wrong. In fact, I have a little proposition that might be of interest."

In spite of her reassurance, this did *not* sound good, but my apprehension was outweighed by curiosity. I asked, "Where? When?"

"Downtown somewhere. Seven?"

"How about seven thirty? I'm due at work at eight."

"Okay," she said. "There's that huge Starbucks, but maybe someplace quieter—Huggamug?"

"Sure. That's near the office. Seven thirty." And we rang off.

I sat there, perplexed, trying to drink a few slugs of coffee, which gagged me—it had leached the sour aftertaste of an unexpected conversation with someone I wanted to forget. Granted, she'd had the decency not to bump me off for an easy forty grand, but otherwise, our previous encounters had been grade A shitstorms. And now we had a *coffee* date?

The brew in front of me was undrinkable, so I stepped over to the sink and dumped it all, which drew a belch of protest from the plumbing. While rinsing the pot, I fretted over Jazz Friendly's call. What was she up to? She said nothing was wrong, but why should I trust her? She clearly had anger issues, not to mention the booze problem that caused her husband to ditch her and win custody of their kid. This morning, what could she possibly want to discuss that wouldn't spell trouble?

While drying the pot, I turned at the sound of knuckles rapping on the open front door. And there stood Isandro, my Brazilian neighbor, wearing silky gold gym shorts and brown leather flip-flops. His hair was wet and tousled.

"I needed a quick shower." He grinned. "All better now."

"C'mon in. And you can close the door."

.

We gave Mitzi plenty to yap about. In spite of Isandro's rough night in the ER, he found his second wind in my bedroom, and he wasn't shy about expressing his pleasure with noisy howls and laughter—a Latin thing? I wasn't about to shush him, so I responded in kind, with the dog next door whipped up by our frenzy.

Whenever we'd previously reached such an energy level, we finished within ten minutes—slam, bam, and out the door he went. But that Wednesday morning, we'd been at it for more than an hour when the woman next door, Mitzi's human, finally banged on the wall and shouted something. Her words were unintelligible, but her tone was pissed.

I answered, "Sorry, Mrs. Templeton."

Isandro tried but failed to stifle his laughter as we curled together in the tangle of damp sheets.

We rarely took time to talk about much, since our hook-ups were "just sex"—spontaneous and convenient. But this had been going on for a while, and we had the chemistry nailed, so I couldn't help wondering if there was a chance for something more meaningful. Something like friendship, at the least. Or even … a relationship?

I propped myself on one arm and looked down at his angelic features. With my free hand, I whisked a stray lock of his curly dark hair from his forehead. I knew he was in his thirties. I knew he'd come from Brazil for college here, then stayed. I wanted to know more about him.

With an uncertain smile, I suggested, "Maybe we could go out for dinner some night."

Those angelic features wrinkled with a momentary wave of apprehension. Then he traced a finger over my lips, saying, "It's a crazy job I've got, *coração*. Different schedule every week. Hard to plan a night out."

Either I was too old for him, or he just wasn't interested. Or both.

Isandro must have read the disappointment in my face. He raised his head and kissed the tip of my nose, then my mouth, mumbling, "Maybe. We'll see. Who knows?"

I knew it wouldn't happen. But I said, "Sure, we'll see, all in good time." I caught my breath. "Um, speaking of time, can you see the clock?"

He flopped over to look at the nightstand. "Seven twenty."

"Oops."

■

Showered but unshaven—and not looking my best—I waltzed into Huggamug Coffeehouse at ten minutes before eight, twenty minutes late for my meeting with Jazz Friendly. She scowled at me from across the room, drumming her fingers on the laminated pink tabletop. The rat-a-tat of her nails on the plastic pierced the morning hubbub of the crowd's chatter; it even cut through the hiss and explosive whoosh of an overworked espresso machine.

I acknowledged her with a sheepish wave, ducked over to the counter to place my order, and then plucked up the courage to approach her table.

Slouched in her chair, sizing me up with a sneer, she asked, "*What* happened to you?"

I bragged, "A horny Brazilian."

She rolled her eyes. "You are *such* a fuckup. And now you'll be late for work."

"Not if I leave right now." I turned to go.

"Stay." The word was spoken softly, but it had the ring of a command, as if training a puppy.

I sat in the chair across from her. "Besides," I said, "it's Wednesday. It's nearly June. The office is dead these days."

She wasn't listening. She was studying me. "Swell getup."

Deflated, I told her, "They *make* me wear this." She'd seen me in the Sunny Junket uniform before—the dad jeans, the acid-yellow polo—at the house in Little Tuscany. Stating the obvious, I added, "I hate it."

"Then don't wear it."

"It's part of my *job*. I have *bills*. And don't forget: I saw you in that rent-a-cop costume from the convention center, so who are you to talk?"

She flipped her hands. "Not wearing it now."

No, she wasn't. And she looked ... not bad, though it galled me to think it. She wore a dark suit, nicely tailored for her lanky, athletic build, with a silvery blouse that had a simple band collar. No jewelry at all, but she sported a black shoulder holster, peeking out from the lapel of her jacket. Her hair was shorter than I remembered; the tight Afro was all business, no nonsense. Her overall look managed to come across as both fierce *and* professional.

She said, "I quit the security gig at the convention center."

I allowed myself a smile. "Good for you. Does that mean the private-eye biz is starting to take off?"

"*Starting* to," she emphasized. "Still a long way to go."

The barista dropped off my iced tea in a tall plastic go-cup with a lid and a straw, then disappeared. I noticed that Friendly had the same cup, containing what appeared to be lemonade, half-finished. Odd coffee date, I thought. No coffee.

When I lifted the cup to sip from the straw, Friendly mirrored my action. With no expression whatever, she mumbled, "Cheers."

I nearly choked. It was the first truly civil word she'd ever said to me. "Cheers, Friendly," I said in return, then drank.

She drank. "Dante"—she paused—"you don't need to call me Friendly."

"I must admit, it sticks in the throat."

Ignoring that, she said, "So call me Jazz."

That wasn't much better. But I said, "Okay, Jazz."

Fiddling with her straw, which squeaked in the slit of the plastic lid, she seemed nervous—another first. She said, "Clarence Kwon is behind bars, awaiting trial for the murder of Edison Quesada Reál."

I reminded her, "I'm well aware of that."

"Of course. And the reason I quit the convention center—the reason my own business is picking up—is that I got some serious cred for Kwon's arrest. When the Palm Springs PD roared up the driveway that night, I handed over to them, without incident, a cuffed killer who'd admitted everything to two witnesses—me and you. That case went straight to the Riverside DA. The cops looked good, and so did I. And that's why, finally, I now stand a chance of making it on my own."

"I'm happy for you, Jazz."

"Thank you." She nodded. "And thank you for tricking Kwon into confessing. That crap about surveillance videos"—she laughed—"it was damn fucking *brilliant*. I never woulda come up with that."

"You already had the cuffs on me," I said, "but I knew something you didn't know: I *knew* I didn't kill Edison, and I *knew* I didn't hide the Hockney print in my car, so I *knew* it was all Kwon's doing. The song and dance about surveillance tapes— that part was easy."

Jazz said sternly, "You're being *way* too humble."

"Yes, I am."

"So here's the deal—"

"There's a 'deal'?"

"Shut up and listen. Your job with the rentals. You run into a lot of people, rich folks who like snazzy houses, who come out here to 'get away from it all'—right?"

I explained, "My job description is 'field inspector.' I check the condition of properties before guests arrive and after they leave. But my duties also include VIP check-ins and service calls for our top-end clients."

She nodded. "Got it. And I'll bet you see a fair share of weird shit, too—right?"

"Sure. Part of the job."

"And folks with money—with weird shit in their fucked-up lives—they're my target market."

Deadpan, I asked, "Huh?"

"*They're* the folks who sometimes need my services." Out of nowhere, she produced a business card, extending it across the table between two pronged fingers.

Taking it, I sat back to read it: JAZZ FRIENDLY, PRIVATE INVESTIGATOR. The office address was on North Palm Canyon Drive, not far from Sunny Junket. Noting the street number, I turned in my chair to compare it to the number on Huggamug's door. "Here?" I asked.

"Upstairs. It's not much, but sometimes I need a place to meet with clients. I mostly work from home and my vehicle."

"So what are you saying? You want me to leave your card on pillows?"

"No. Just do your normal job. But if you discover a situation where I might be useful, let me know. Clue me, and I'll follow through. You don't even have to *recommend* me."

"I dunno, Jazz. That's just not—"

"I'm not asking a *favor*, Dante. I'd pay you a finder's fee for clients who hire me." She named a figure.

I gave her my best poker face.

"I know, I know, it's chump change—not like you could quit the day job. But it's tough getting established, and with summer coming, it'll be worse. So I need the work. And I thought maybe *you* could use some extra cash, too." Pointedly, she asked, "That old Camry still running?"

"It gets me around."

"It's a shitbox."

She was right. I slipped her card into my wallet, telling her, "I'll keep you in mind."

"Perfect." She cracked the faintest smile. "So how was he? The Brazilian."

It hadn't been an hour. The sense memory of Isandro's sweat was still with me. "He was … great," I said with a shrug.

She studied me for a moment before asking, "Is this 'the boy-friend'? Mr. Right, maybe?"

"Just a neighbor." Winking, I added, "We're neighborly."

"Christ, Dante. Know what's wrong with you?"

"Plenty," I assured her. "But what's *your* theory?"

She crossed her arms. "You think with your dick."

Not nice, I thought. I would never have phrased it that way, but I couldn't deny it. Since my teens, I'd gotten by on what they used to call sex appeal, which made it sound almost wholesome, like those toothpaste ads. It worked for a while—still did, to a degree—but after so many years, where did it get me? Dorky jeans. A cramped apartment sharing a common wall with a deranged rat terrier. And a shitbox Camry.

I'd spent most of my adult life pursuing a so-called career in acting and modeling, relying on those same old charms, looking for fun where I could find it—and getting absolutely nowhere.

Jazz had already seen the results of my flirtation with Clarence Kwon. While I was drooling over Clark's tight little body, he was plotting to have me arrested for the murder of his husband—and then he tried to pay to have me killed.

If Jazz had known me longer, she would've been all the more justified in accusing me of faulty thinking, which was often driven more by base desires than by common sense.

Because she and I had first encountered each other a year before Clark killed Edison, back when she responded to a differ-ent crime scene, where she found me kneeling in a puddle of my ex-husband's blood, she was well aware of the circumstances of his death. But she knew nothing about the marriage itself—or why it had ended.

I looked up from my thoughts and watched her for a moment across the table. She eyed me with a blank stare, arms still crossed.

"Last year," I said. "In the spring. Dr. Anthony Gascogne."

Her eyes widened with interest. "Touchy subject. Unsolved murder. I assume you two weren't happy. I mean, you dumped him, right?"

"Wrong. Anthony and I were together nearly thirty years. We'd met in LA when I was in my early twenties, with high hopes for Hollywood. He was turning thirty, starting his ophthalmology practice. Much later—a few years ago—he decided to move his office to Palm Springs, thinking ahead to retirement. I wasn't interested, so I assumed that was the end of the relationship, and frankly, I wasn't broken up about it. We'd been leading separate lives for a long time by then—at least I was."

Jazz interrupted, "What does *that* mean?"

"It means: Anthony no longer 'satisfied' me. So I found satisfaction elsewhere. And often."

"Uh-huh. And he was *okay* with that?"

"No. But we never talked about it. I guess he was afraid he'd lose me."

"Did you love him?"

It was a simple, direct question, but it rattled me. I answered honestly, "I'm not sure. But when he offered me a job to make the move with him, as his office manager—why not? I didn't have any other decent prospects. And after we got out here, I discovered a very different sort of gay culture, not so youth-obsessed as LA. Which meant: I was suddenly a hot commodity again."

"How'd he feel about that development?"

"I could guess, but he never brought it up. Instead, he asked me to marry him. Gay marriage had just turned legal, and it seemed *everyone* was doing it. So again—why not? Rings, flowers, big swanky dinner—and *he* wrote the vows."

Jazz nodded. "Sounds like he was doing some wishful thinking. Sounds like he was expecting some changes." She laughed. "Did you fall in line and zip it up?"

"Of course not. So, after a couple of years, he finally *did* talk about it. Told me the marriage was over. Told me I was fired. Told me to get out. He even told me, and I quote, 'The only reason I hired you, the only reason I married you, was to keep an eye on you.'"

"Wow." Jazz grabbed her lemonade and sucked the last of it through the straw, making a racket.

I told her, "The marriage thing—and what it meant—that was *his* fantasy. But it wasn't *me*, and Anthony knew it all along. I was *never* that person."

"Mm-hmm," said Jazz. "Because you think with your dick."

I insisted, "It was not within my power to become the person he wanted me to be."

"Trust me," she said, "I get it. What you're describing—that sounds like an addiction."

Interesting. Her words, her tone, had the ring of experience. Out on the pool deck of the rental house in Little Tuscany, she had told me that her husband left her because of her drinking. I wondered, What about drugs? Was that part of the mix? And her all-too-evident anger issues: Was she merely short-tempered, or was there something much deeper at work?

This was all speculation, except the booze. With my elbows on the table, I leaned closer to ask quietly, "Did you quit drinking?"

Her gaze drifted to the ceiling. "Trying to." Then she looked me in the eye and shook the icy remnants in the bottom of her go-cup. "That ain't gin, honey."

■

When I arrived at the offices of Sunny Junket Vacation Rentals, less than a block away from Huggamug, it was well after eight.

During high season, the front desk was normally staffed by four of our "team members," but on that Wednesday after Memorial Day, it was down to a single clerk, Gianna, who sat there looking bored and tired, playing a game on her phone. Things had been busy over the long weekend, but that was the last gasp before the desert's summer slowdown. Plus, most guests now preferred our keyless check-in option, bypassing the office altogether.

"Morning, Gianna," I said while breezing past her.

She didn't look up from her phone. "You're late."

My job didn't involve much time at my desk. I was usually "in the field," driving back and forth around the Coachella Valley. But when I wasn't out on assignment, I was expected to be in the office, where there was never a shortage of paper that needed pushing. Or on a quiet day like this one, I might just answer the phones.

As I settled into my chair and began sorting through the desk debris that had accumulated over several days' absence, I noticed, from the corner of my eye, that Ben had emerged from his office, waddling in my direction. As managing director of the company, he was my boss. A year or so earlier, shortly before Dr. Anthony Gascogne was murdered, Ben had hired me. Ben also provided the alibi that proved I didn't kill Anthony. I was a few years older than Ben, but he treated me in a manner that seemed almost fatherly. In short, I could tell he liked me.

"Morning, Dante," he said as he arrived at my desk. "Hope everything's okay. Couldn't help noticing that you, uh…you came in late." His tone sounded more like an apology than a reprimand.

"Sorry, Ben." I flumped back in my chair. "Little emergency at home today."

He looked alarmed. "Nothing serious, I hope." He was from Minnesota, I think, or maybe Wisconsin. He was plump. He was nice.

"No," I assured him, "nothing serious. Needed to help a neighbor with something."

"Ah. Good for you." Ben rocked on his heels, smiling, hooking his thumbs in the pockets of his jeans. He wore the Sunny Junket uniform with pride. It suited him.

"And then," I said, "I got a call from Jazz Friendly. Remember her?"

Ben's jaw sagged. "How could I forget?" He knew all the details of my two prior scrapes with her. Rubbing his chin, he seemed lost in thought. "Do you, uh, have a moment?"

I looked at the mess on my desk and laughed. "Yeah, I do."

He waggled a finger, led me into his office, and closed the door.

The spacious room contained two desks. Ben's was cluttered but well organized. His job was second-in-command, covering information technology, hiring and firing, training and scheduling, the works—so there was plenty on his plate. The other desk belonged to Ben's boss, the owner of the company, Bob something, who was never around. The prior December, he'd hosted a holiday dinner for the staff at a mediocre restaurant, made a speech, and left. It was the first time I'd seen him, and I hadn't seen him since. His desk of chrome and glass was twice the size of Ben's—and immaculate—not a scrap of paper, not even a fingerprint, as if awaiting his Second Coming.

Ben motioned for me to have a seat while he dropped into the chair behind his desk. He said, "Jazz Friendly. She's not a cop anymore, right? She's a security guard?"

I made a *mezza-mezza* gesture with my hand. "No longer a cop. No longer a security guard, at least not for the convention center. Trying to strike out on her own—as a private eye."

"How is she? I mean, as a person. If you hate her, I'd understand."

I wasn't expecting such a question and had to give it some thought. "I don't ... *hate* her. God knows, I'm not exactly president of her fan club, and vice versa, but she's honest. Clarence Kwon tried to bribe her—and couldn't. Bottom line, she has some issues, but I think she's a straight shooter."

"Hmm." Ben mulled something. "You know, since the pandemic, cities are struggling with staff issues—who isn't? Most of the resort cities in the valley have vacation-rental ordinances and compliance hotlines. They want the bed tax, but they answer to the voters who *live* here. When they get a complaint, they send out a compliance officer, trying to keep the locals happy. But they've all cut their staffing, so they're in a bind."

"Meaning," I asked, "you want to add some code enforcement of our own?"

He nodded. "Might be a good investment—having someone on call, or on retainer, to respond to complaints and tamp things down before the city sends out the cops, sends us the bill, and fines the renter. Sometimes a warning call to the renter from our office isn't enough. But when someone shows up with a badge, they listen."

"They'd listen to Jazz Friendly," I said. "I would *not* want her pounding on my door."

"West Valley Rentals is already doing it." Ben was referring to our largest competitor. "They've hired someone. They're even promoting it. Maybe I should talk to this gal."

I fished the card out of my wallet and read the phone number to Ben, who made note of it. "No harm in asking," I said. "She might snap at the chance. Or, knowing *her*, she might just tell you to go ... jump in the lake." I was reluctant to be more explicit with Ben. He was not an f-bomb sorta guy.

■

Friday morning, I needed to check in at the office before lunch. Parking behind Sunny Junket, I then walked along the side of the building toward the entrance at the corner of North Palm Canyon.

During high season, cars would have been parked bumper to bumper in both directions on the side street, but on that hot, quiet final day of May, with the sun inching toward noon, the only vehicle at the curb, just a few yards from the office door, was a fierce-looking SUV, black, with fat tires and tinted windows—like something that had escaped from a Secret Service motorcade. Stripped of all badging, it had one of those menacing matte-black grille guards bolted to the front—you could almost smell the testosterone.

I stopped to gape at it just as Jazz Friendly emerged from my office with a bundle of something shoved under one arm, jangling her keys.

Hands on hips, I asked, "Now, *why* doesn't this surprise me?"

She pressed the fob; the vehicle let out a whoop as its doors unlocked and the windows opened. From the curb, she tossed in the bundle, which was wrapped in clear plastic.

I noticed a flash of Sunny Junket's acid yellow. "Are congratulations in order? As in 'welcome to the team'?"

Jazz strutted out to the street side of the vehicle and opened the driver's door. She whipped a pair of mirrored sunglasses out of her jacket and put them on. "I am *not* wearing that fucking clown shirt."

"Did you tell Ben that?"

"No. I thanked him *ever* so kindly—'for the opportunity to be of service.'" She hoisted herself up and into the SUV.

I strolled into the street and asked through her window, "Aren't you forgetting something?"

Her head turned in my direction, but I couldn't see her eyes behind the glasses. She inhaled deeply and paused before telling me, "Thanks. I appreciate the referral."

"Don't mention it."

I stepped aside as she fired up the engine and sped away from the curb.

When I entered the office, Gianna was working with a customer at the front desk, but she turned to tell me, "Ben wants to see you."

I gave her a thumbs-up and headed back to Ben's office. The door was open as he worked at something on his computer. Noticing me, he waved me in.

Big smile. "Guess who was just here."

"Ran into her outside."

With a satisfied nod, Ben said, "I think this'll work, Dante. Sometimes you just get a feeling. She's really *very* nice."

I flinched. Ben was nice. Minnesota nice. But Jazz?

"Nice," he repeated. "Polite. I like that."

I wasn't sure what to say. "Glad you're pleased, Ben." I turned to leave.

"Dante? You're scheduled for this weekend, right?"

I stepped back into his office. "Right. I was off three days for Memorial Day, so I'm on for Saturday and Sunday."

"Great. Let's plan on a VIP check-in tomorrow. The Ellinger House."

It was named after the dot-commer who built it twenty years earlier in Rancho Mirage, a few miles east of Palm Springs. He later got bored and moved to New Zealand, leaving us to manage the estate as income property, which we listed as part of our Luxury Retreats Portfolio. I asked, "What time should I be there?"

Ben scrolled his computer screen. "Mr. and Mrs. Kenneth Terry are driving over from LA, arriving around eleven."

"Fine. Who are they?"

Ben shrugged. "Beats me, but they booked online, opting for our 'concierge service.' They took the place for the entire month of June."

"*That'll* pay a few bills."

"Wish we had a dozen more like that. So let's make'm happy."

■

Having lived in Los Angeles much of my adult life, I was only too well acquainted with the coastal phenomenon known as June gloom, a weather pattern producing cool, cloudy mornings, often accompanied by fog and drizzle, sometimes lasting into the afternoon. June served as an ugly reminder that, even in sunny Southern California, nothing's perfect, prompting affluent Angelenos to get out of town for a while, seeking bluer skies and drier, hotter weather. A two-hour drive east on the 10 landed them in the desert environs of Palm Springs.

Some of them already had second homes here for extended stays or a more modest condo for the occasional getaway. But to rent a place like the Ellinger House for an entire month seemed over-the-top—houses in that league were rarely booked for longer than three nights, maybe a week. So I was eager to meet Mr. and Mrs. Kenneth Terry and curious to know more about them.

Saturday morning, June first, I decided to give myself plenty of time at the house before our guests' arrival, allowing me to spiff the place, crank the air conditioning, and skim the pool for an impeccable VIP welcome. I also had a bottle of champagne to leave in the fridge for them, along with a basket of snacks and breakfast items. After loading up the car at my apartment, I took off around ten o'clock and left Palm Springs on Highway 111, heading down valley.

Ten minutes later, I was zipping into Rancho Mirage, where the highway widened, the billboards and power lines disappeared, and the manicured medians brimmed with tasteful desert plantings. The pace seemed instantly more relaxed, more refined, without the tourist glitz.

The highway hugged the mountains to the south, the Santa Rosas, their shards of ruddy granite rising from the desert floor. I slowed the car as I approached the cove area, then turned, climbing the curving roads that rose toward a private mesa. Unlike most of the neighborhoods in town, this was not a gated club, though many of the houses on these public streets had gated driveways.

The Ellinger estate was at the top of the climb, where the road swung away from the mesa before descending. The property had a gate, and although I knew the code, I drove ahead, just beyond the curve of the road, and parked on the street. I figured that the esteemed Mr. and Mrs. Kenneth Terry would not appreciate arriving to the sight of my old Camry in their pristine courtyard.

I gathered my things from the car and walked back to the gate, opening it with the keypad. Crossing the courtyard, I left the gate open—one less hassle for our guests.

Ahead, glass walls sparkled in the morning sun. Lush plantings and meticulous rows of dwarf palms softened another wall of rough-hewn limestone, crisp and angular, rising near the entry like a dramatic sculpture, a whimsy.

I entered the house, set down my things, and keypadded another code—then watched as the monolithic slab of the front door retreated and disappeared, blurring the transition from the outdoors to the interior space, which was also spectacular, designed to take full advantage of the home's setting and its views. The main room was huge, with a ceiling some twenty feet high and a polished stone floor that descended several steps toward a glass wall to the rear terrace, which I opened.

Stepping outside, I circled the pool—immaculate, no need to skim it—and then made my way to the far edge of the terrace. The tips of my shoes touched a stone parapet, about two feet high, which separated the man-made fantasy of the house behind me from the handiwork of nature beyond, where green swaths of golf courses gave way to the open desert that stretched to the ring of surrounding mountains. The highest peaks, Mount San Jacinto and the more distant Mount San Gorgonio, were still decked out with caps of snow. A warm breeze swelled up from the arroyos—the gullies of the canyons below the house—and swept over me as I spotted the distant airport, where a plane raced along the main runway and slid silently into the vast, cloudless sky.

Reminding myself that I was there to work, not gawk, I went indoors and made my rounds, primping the beds, flushing toilets, checking drawers, and testing all the electronics—Wi-Fi, cable, streaming services, internet.

In the kitchen, I stowed the champagne in the fridge and made an attractive display of the gift basket on the center island. Conspicuously, I also arranged near the basket a set of brochures we always leave with our guests, detailing local regulations that govern short-term rentals—noise, parking, number of guests, and so on.

Glancing over the brochures, I was reminded of something and dashed out back to check. Yes, as required, a laminated sign issued by the city was clearly posted near the pool: NO OUTDOOR MUSIC ALLOWED! *Complaints can lead to citations and fines.* It struck me as overkill, but no one could claim they weren't warned.

Hearing the jaunty *toot-toot* of a car horn in the courtyard, I returned to the front of the house, grabbed my paperwork and Sunny Junket's welcome folder, then strolled out to the entryway, where I stopped in my tracks.

I'd expected an older couple in a hulking sedan, the sort of land yacht favored by moneyed grandparents. Instead, my eyes widened at the sight of a vintage Karmann Ghia convertible, graphite silver, top down, perfectly restored. And its driver, who was alone, was no grandpa, but much younger—in his thirties, I guessed—with wavy sandy-colored hair, some stylish bristle along his square jawline, and a classic pair of Ray-Bans. When he saw me emerge from the house, he broke into a drop-dead smile.

Flustered, I checked my notes before asking, "Mr. Terry?"

"Yeah." He stepped out of the car—khaki shorts, Top-Siders, and a dusty-gray polo, probably merino wool—a preppy style that was exactly right with the retro convertible. Clearly no stranger to the gym, he was in far better shape than I was. Still, he wasn't shy about sizing me up with evident interest. He said, "You're Dante, right?"

"Right." I extended my hand for a shake. "Happy to meet you, Mr. Terry."

Pumping my hand (great grip, strong and bony), he said, "My pleasure. Please, though: drop the 'Mr. Terry.'"

"Okay, Kenneth."

"He's my dad. I *am* a 'junior,' but when I was a kid, everyone called me Skip, and it stuck." He explained, "I was short for my age."

He still was—and to my eye, he was just right.

Glancing at my notes again, I said, "So you booked the house for your *parents*."

Skip nodded. "Kenneth and Claudia should be here any minute. They phoned from the road."

"Can I show you around? Want to make sure you're pleased."

He gave me a wry look. "Careful. I can be *very* demanding."

I laughed. "Good. Try me." Then, while leading him from the courtyard to the house, I said, "That car is flat-out fabulous. Always *loved* Karmann Ghias."

"Wanna drive it sometime?"

"Well, *sure*. What year is it—late fifties?"

"Fifty-eight. Good eye."

When we stepped into the house, he removed the sunglasses for a better look at the interior. "Stunning," he said.

"Yeah," I agreed, though I was staring at his face, not the decorating. Without his glasses, he looked familiar. I thought, Skip Terry. The name was familiar, too. I asked, "Have we met?"

"Maybe. I've been to a *lot* of charity galas."

I laughed. "Well, I haven't."

Skip shrugged. "I'm in the news quite a bit—society page, mainly. I guess you could say I hang around with a lot of the 'right people.' Fact is, though, I'm a lowly travel agent."

He may have been a travel agent—in fact, that rang a bell—but whatever he did for a living, I was certain there was nothing "lowly" about it.

I showed him through the house, explaining controls for the lighting, pool, and security. "It's a lot to absorb at once," I said, handing him my card. "If you have any problems, just call."

"Count on it," he said with a grin, tucking the card away. "But I won't be staying here—I live in town. The house is for Mom and Dad."

"Ah."

We ended up in the kitchen. While standing opposite Skip at the center island, I said, "I'll need to get photos of a credit card and driver's license. Should I wait for your dad, or will you be handling it?"

He fished out his license and a black AmEx. "There you go."

"Sorry to seem so finicky, but with a house like this, charges run up pretty fast."

"No big deal."

Maybe in his world. These charges would run into the tens of thousands. Taking out my phone, I snapped away. The license informed me that Kenneth Terry Jr. was thirty-six years old, five foot eight, living in Rancho Mirage.

When I returned the cards, he asked, "Anything else?"

Reluctantly, I said, "Can you check this out?"

He stepped around the island and stood next to me as I handed him one of the brochures detailing vacation-rental regulations. While he looked it over, I explained, "The city is damned tough about this. No noise, no crowds, no parking on the street. The house has four bedrooms, so that basically limits you to eight people and four cars. If neighbors bitch—and they will if they have cause to—you're in trouble, and so are we." Lightening my tone, I asked, "We wouldn't want *that*, now, would we?"

With a chuckle, Skip set down the brochure. "Dad's on the board of a museum, and he mentioned meeting with a few of the other trustees, but that's a minor item. My parents are coming here to relax, and let's just say they're not the rowdy type." He winked at me—looking up into my eyes.

I've always had a thing for short guys.

CHAPTER THREE

Kenneth and Claudia Terry arrived a few minutes later, and I found them delightful—it was easy to see where Skip had acquired his charms, not to mention his taste for wellborn attire. His parents, who appeared to be in their late sixties (and as flawlessly restored as their son's Karmann Ghia), had dressed for vacation, ready to relax in coordinating Brooks Brothers outfits. Kenneth's shorts were the color of lime sherbet, sporting a small embroidered pattern of crossed golf clubs; Claudia's were the color of raspberry sherbet, with flamingos.

They *loved* the house, *loved* the views, *loved* the quiet surroundings, the fresh air, the clear skies. "Skipper," said Kenneth, clapping an arm over his son's shoulders, "you chose well. Bravo."

I offered, "May I bring in your luggage?"

Answering for his parents, Skip said, "Good idea. I'll give you a hand." He took the keys from his father, and we headed outside.

Parked in the courtyard, dwarfing the little convertible, was an altogether different German car, a long, hefty Maybach, darkest blue. Its deep back-seat compartment was loaded high with a boggling array of Vuitton luggage. As we opened the doors, Claudia called to us from the house, "Boys? We packed some kitchen things in the trunk."

Skip said to me, "I'll take the clothes to their bedroom. Can you unload the trunk?" He pressed the fob to open it.

"You bet." I stepped to the back of the car and peered inside. A small shopping bag contained fruit and vegetables. Another held a few artisanal breads and cheeses. But mostly, the trunk was filled with heavy boxes—cartons of bottles. It seemed they'd brought a *lot* of liquor. Then again, I reminded myself, they were staying an entire month.

When everything was unloaded and brought indoors, the Terry family walked out to the courtyard with me. I told the parents, "Enjoy your Sunny Junket."

Claudia gave me a hug. Kenneth shook my hand. Skip said, "Thanks, Dante. You've been great."

Leaving, crossing toward the gate, then glancing back at Skip, I hoped for an opportunity to return to the house.

It didn't take long.

■

Next morning, I was scheduled to work at the office, starting at nine, an hour later than usual because it was Sunday. After unlocking the building, I stepped inside and switched on a few lights. I would be the only one there until noon, when Gianna would come in to relieve me for lunch.

I sat at one of the slots at the front desk, but there were no scheduled check-ins that day, and the few check-outs were all keyless, so I was little more than window dressing, in case someone strolled in to inquire about properties.

Beyond the window, the street scene was dead quiet. North Palm Canyon, much of it known as the Uptown Design District and populated mainly by showrooms, galleries, and offices, was never very hectic compared to South Palm Canyon, the central tourist destination, several blocks ahead. On Sunday morning at nine, however, the city's entire main drag—north and south—was deserted, except for the foot traffic into and out of Huggamug, just a few doors down the street.

Sunny Junket's phones, as expected, did not ring. After tiring of watching the cycle of the traffic lights, I decided to amuse myself on the computer, which eventually led me to type in a search for Kenneth Terry Sr. There weren't many in the Los Angeles area, and I was quickly able to identify Skip's father, confirmed by a picture.

Hmm. The source of his wealth became clear to me. Now sixty-eight, Kenneth Terry had taken Claudia Berquist as his wife forty years earlier. Shortly after marrying, they cofounded Terraquist Investment Corporation in LA, which grew into one of the area's largest privately held real-estate companies, specializing in commercial properties. Their ongoing success led both Kenneth and Claudia to become fixtures of the LA charity scene, with their most substantial philanthropy focused on the arts and culture. Most recently, their names were engraved over the entrance to the new library wing of a children's discovery museum in the coastal community of Santa Leona, which had been Claudia's childhood home.

Now that I knew the parents' background, I Googled their son.

Kenneth "Skip" Terry Jr., an only child, was born in LA and schooled "back east," where he graduated with a business degree from Cornell, his father's alma mater. Returning home after college, he eventually settled in the Palm Springs area, where he established an exclusive travel service, catering to the needs of the rich and famous.

As Skip had mentioned to me the day before, he'd received a good deal of local news coverage, mostly for his presence at big-dollar charity functions, where he dined with wealthy widows, served as the occasional celebrity auctioneer, and even strutted a runway, shirtless, at an annual fashion show. There was no shortage of pictures—photographers seemed irresistibly drawn to him—which is why I'd felt the jolt of recognition when he removed his sunglasses at the Ellinger House.

Transfixed by his face on the screen, I clicked and enlarged photo after photo, exploring the frozen moments, wanting to learn more about this beautiful man, hoping to know him better. I recognized some of the other faces—the handful of local donors who competed for the philanthropy crown by writing million-dollar checks—but most were just bodies in gowns and tuxes, with names that were lucky to merit mention as "also attending."

One of the unnamed faces seemed to pop up with greater frequency than the others, a mousy woman who was nicely dressed but looked uncomfortably out of her element. Younger than the moneyed matrons, she was sometimes near Skip's side but usually in the background.

Who was she—a secretary? Did she keep notes for him, whispering trivia he could use while schmoozing the elite and transforming mere acquaintances into clients?

.

After lunch, as I returned to the office and strolled through the door, Gianna waved me over to the front desk with a panicky look. Handing me the receiver of her phone, she said, "It's Ben. He needs to talk to you."

Lifting the phone to my ear, I asked my boss, "What's up, Ben?"

"We've got a problem, Dante. Over at the Ellinger House. Just got a call from the city hotline—bunch of complaints from neighbors—noise, crowd, cars. Seems there's a party going on, but it sounds more like a brawl. Lotsa shouting."

"Christ," I muttered.

"If the city sends out their compliance officer, it's double time on Sunday. If the neighbors call the cops, it's a worse ball of wax. I asked for thirty minutes to get it under control—and five are already wasted. Time to call Friendly."

"I'll handle it, Ben." With my free hand, I was already fishing for her card.

■

Jazz Friendly roared up to the curb in her SUV, stopping barely long enough for me to hop in—the vehicle was moving again by the time I closed the door.

"Thanks for driving," I said.

"We couldn't very well show up in your shitbox."

I checked my watch. "We need to be there in fifteen minutes. I don't think that's *possible*."

She laughed. "Wanna bet?" And she gunned it.

I tried calling Skip's cell phone again, the only number I had on file for his parents' booking, but no one answered. I left another message: "I'm on my way over with a security guard, Skip. If there's anything you can do to quiet things down—do it."

Jazz asked, "When we get there, what do you want me to do?"

Good question. "Depends how crazy it is. If there's no actual *danger*, just stay in the background and back me up—but look mean, okay?"

"Uh-huh. And if there *is* actual danger?"

I shook my head. "You're trained for that. Not me."

She patted the holster beneath her jacket. She wasn't wearing the Sunny Junket uniform—there'd been no time to insist that she change into it—and frankly, I was relieved. She wore the same dark suit she'd worn to our Wednesday meeting at Huggamug, but instead of the silvery blouse, she now wore a dressy black shirt, its cutaway collar buttoned by a single large pearl. With her Afro and sunglasses, not to mention the visible shoulder holster, along with other whatnot clipped to her belt, she looked like a bouncer—or a hit woman—someone the Brooks Brothers crowd would not ignore.

Barreling into Rancho Mirage, Jazz had somehow managed not to catch a single red light (with the exception of a couple she dismissed as "slightly pink"). I held tight to the door handle and the center console as the SUV lurched around a corner and into the cove neighborhood. Gears gnashed and downshifted as we rose through the winding streets. We didn't slow down until, approaching the mesa, we found the roadway littered with cars that didn't belong there, parked at slapdash angles in both directions.

Jazz pulled up to the open gate of the Ellinger House, switched on her flashers, and parked in the entrance to the courtyard, blocking other vehicles from coming or going. When we got out of the SUV, I cringed at the assault of noise, which grew steadily louder as we zigzagged through the packed parking court, approaching the house.

The huge disappearing entry door had been left open, and I could see, through the shifting silhouettes of the crowd inside, that the back wall to the pool terrace was open as well. The music was not happy—but raucous, blaring jazz. Nor did the guests sound happy—raised voices argued and bitched, shouting to be heard above one another.

Jazz and I exchanged a bewildered look, then stepped through the entryway and into the main room.

From where I stood, I could count at least thirty people inside; there were others on the pool terrace, most of which was beyond my view. Stretching on tiptoes to see above the crowd, I tried to spot Skip but could not. I couldn't see his parents, either. Everyone was drinking, and I didn't notice any food, so the boisterous behavior was clearly fueled by the booze. But what, I wondered, had caused the underlying anger?

The city had granted Ben a half hour to get this situation under control. Checking my watch, I saw that the grace period was about to end.

"*Skip*," I shouted, but my voice didn't travel far through the din. I tried again: "Mr. Terry? Claudia?" No one even glanced in my direction.

Jazz moved a step or two farther into the room, unclipped something from her belt, and aimed it high. I wasn't sure what it was—not a gun, but a small gadget with a nozzle. I realized it was one of those rape-deterrent safety horns when its sustained ear-piercing blast choked off all conversation and turned every head in the room.

Jazz shouted, "Turn *off* the fucking music!"

It abruptly ended. The rowdy crowd was speechless.

I checked my watch again and grinned: twenty-nine minutes, one to spare.

With a whoosh of the swinging door from the kitchen, Claudia Terry waltzed out with a tray of nibbles—too little too late—and asked, "What happened to the music? Anyone need a drink?"

"Mrs. *Terry*," I said. "What's going on?"

"Dante!" Her tone implied she was pleased as punch to see me. Setting down the tray, she said, "How nice of you to check on us—and you've brought a *friend*. Please, join the party."

Skip and his father made their way in from the terrace, parting the crowd. Mr. Terry wore a floppy white chef's toque and carried barbecue tongs with a giant oven mitt, telling everyone, "Got the grill going—won't be long. Drink up. Skipper? Maybe you could get me another gimlet." He waggled his free hand. "I seem to be missing something here. *Har-har.*"

Skip wasn't paying attention to his dad. From across the room, his eyes were locked on mine, and he looked mortified. He also looked good enough to eat. Wearing red Top-Siders and boldly striped pink-and-white swim trunks, he was quite the confection. For a moment, I forgot that I was there on a mission, focused instead on a fantasy that involved time alone with him.

Jazz pivoted her head in my direction. Though her eyes were hidden behind reflective glasses, I sensed a disapproving stare, as if she could read my thoughts about Skip. She had already warned me about that kind of thinking.

"Uh, Skip," I said, "what's going on here? We've had complaints."

Making his way toward me through the crowd, he said, "Really sorry about this. I had no idea that—"

His father interrupted: "My fault, Dante. I told the Skipper I wanted to meet with a few folks from the museum, but I must have understated my intentions."

Claudia asked anyone, "Were we doing something *wrong?*"

Jazz said, "Yes, ma'am. Local ordinances—several violations here."

"Oh, *my.*"

Jazz sauntered away from me, circling the perimeter of the room. I saw her pause near the bar, which concerned me. Then she pulled a can of Dr Pepper from an icy vat. With the house wide open—and crowded—the room was hot.

Skip now stood about eighteen inches away from me (within reach, so to speak, which forced me to tamp down another inappropriate thought). He told me, "I assumed Dad's 'little get-together' concerned some bit of board business. Instead, it was about...*me.*"

"You got *that* right," said a man from across the room, pouring another drink for himself at the bar. "This is *all* about Junior."

A disgruntled murmur rose from the crowd. "Yeah," said someone. I heard snippets from others: "fraud," "swindler," "restitution," "oughta be a law." Someone volleyed back, "There *are* laws—plenty."

Skip stepped near and touched my shoulder. He raised his chin to speak into my ear: "Help me, Dante."

"Huh?"

"I have this...situation. It might be dangerous."

I asked, "But why me? How can *I* possibly help?"

"I need discretion. And I think I can trust you—just a hunch." He smiled up at me.

Okay, that did it. I was in. I said, "If you need a private eye..." With a subtle jerk of my head, I directed his gaze across the room, toward Jazz. I told Skip, "She's a little rough, though."

"Good. I might need someone like that."

"Then I'll see if I can set you up."

Kenneth Terry Sr. removed his toque and set down his tongs. He walked through the crowd to the center of the room and cleared his throat. "Well, then," he said, "since things have calmed down now, perhaps the time is right to discuss this, but *rationally*, please."

Claudia said, "What a splendid idea, dear." With a chipper laugh, she added, "Maybe everyone would like to fill their glasses first."

No one else laughed, but they did line up to replenish their afternoon cocktails.

I said to Skip, "All right, fill me in."

He motioned for me to follow him out to the parking court. The car nearest the house was his Karmann Ghia, with its top down as before. He perched his rump on the top edge of the driver's door and crossed his feet at the ankles. His bare chest glistened with perspiration in the desert sun. Whatever he had to say, I was going to find it difficult to concentrate.

I said, "You mentioned danger. Why?"

He took a deep breath. "I've told you I run a travel service. Mostly, I organize high-end tours for groups. More often than not, I go along for the ride—not as a guide, exactly, but sort of a den mother and cheerleader. I like to say that I 'build relationships.'"

"Nice," I said. "You must be constantly on the move."

"Before the pandemic I was. Since then, the whole industry has been rebuilding. It won't happen overnight."

"Sure."

"Have you ever heard of the Museum of Anti-Academic Art in Los Angeles?"

"Can't say I have."

He laughed. "That's sort of a mouthful, so they usually go by M3A-LA. Or just M3A. I guess they think it sounds trendy."

"Sorry. Still haven't heard of it."

Skip shrugged. "You're not alone. But my folks are really into it, and Dad's on the board. Nonprofits are always on the look-out for fundraising opportunities, and M3A's executive director had the idea to organize an 'arts and antiquities' cruise of the Mediterranean and Aegean. Dad suggested that I could put this together for them."

"Sounds great."

"That's what I thought—highly exclusive, a private booking of a smaller luxury ship, custom itinerary, drop-dead cuisine from guest chefs. In short, the works, the voyage of a lifetime."

"Wow. Any takers?"

"Between the board and their top-tier donors and guests, we sold out in ten days. A hundred cabins at thirty grand each—that's three million bucks, with a sizable spiff earmarked for the museum."

"Congratulations."

Skip smirked. "With everyone signed up and paid in advance, we were all set to sail—departure was a week away—when the virus shut *everything* down. The cruise line, Sapphire Seaways, was registered in Greece, and before the wrangling over refunds even started, the company went belly-up. They no longer *exist*. So even now, we're dealing with insurance and lawsuits and bankruptcy regulators *in Greece*. The museum is fucked, the board is fucked, the donors are fucked. And me? I am most *assuredly* fucked."

I mumbled, "So much for 'building relationships.'"

"*Tell* me." He was steamed. He was hurt. I wanted to help make it go away. I wanted to—

"And *then*," he continued, flailing an arm toward the house, "Dad had the bright idea to throw this little powwow—with *me* as the surprise guest of honor. He wanted to smooth things over. But *they're* still livid." Even as he spoke, the noise level from the house was rising again.

I assured Skip, "They're not a mob. These are 'museum peo-ple.' They may be angry, but you're in no *physical* danger."

He raised a finger, leaned toward me, and tapped my chest. Under his breath, he said, "Don't be so sure. Noreen Penley Wade, the museum director—she's in there, and she's a ballbuster. Lots of folks are actually *afraid* of her." Skip hesitated, then leaned even closer. "There's a persistent rumor that she has connections with organized crime."

I broke into laughter. "You've *got* to be kidding."

"I'm serious."

His mother tootled from the entryway, "Time to come inside, boys. Your father's ready, Skip."

Skip turned to his car, leaned in, and pulled out a skimpy beach shirt—gray linen seersucker. He shrugged into it but left it unbuttoned, then cinched the hem around his waist while leading me into the house.

God, he was perfect. Where had Skip Terry been all my life?

Or was I thinking with my dick?

Yes … yes, I was.

■

Inside, Kenneth Terry stood next to a grand piano that was centered along a side wall of the main room. He hoisted a martini glass filled with a pale green liquid—presumably his gin gimlet—while gabbing with a cluster of his guests.

I stood with Skip not far from the entryway, which gave us a view of the entire room and most of the back terrace. Everyone had come indoors, with the exception of one young woman who lounged in the pool on a baby-blue inflatable raft, sunning herself. Her bathing attire was, in a word, scant, which seemed brazenly immodest among this button-down crowd.

Jazz approached me from one side of the room while, from the other side, I noticed a familiar woman—older than the gal in the pool, but younger than most of the guests—making her way toward Skip. It clicked. I had seen her in the photos I found online that morning, when I thought she looked mousy and uncomfortable. As I huddled with Jazz, telling her what I'd learned about the canceled cruise, I kept an eye on Miss Mousy, who now whispered something to Skip, looking as skittish and harried in person as she had in the pictures.

When she drifted off into the room, I said to Jazz, "That woman—can you check her out?"

Jazz peered over the top edge of her sunglasses for a moment, nodded, and wandered off in the same direction.

Skip stepped over to tell me, "The lady in red—next to my dad—that's Noreen Penley Wade, the museum director."

She could have been sent by central casting. An arty woman in her fifties, petite but wiry, with a pale, porcelain complexion, she wore a crimson jumpsuit of crinkly silk. Her hair was swept to one side in a severe asymmetrical style that defied gravity. Her features, though beautiful in a conventional sense, were pinched and fixed—as if it would kill her to smile.

"Next to her," said Skip, "that's Noreen's assistant, Riley Uba."

She was much younger than Noreen—late twenties, maybe—with Eastern European features that set her apart from the largely Waspish crowd. She dressed with a high sense of style, though she looked more hip and urban than her mentor, with a full-sleeve tattoo adorning her right arm. It depicted a whirl of manga characters. I couldn't hear Riley Uba's conversation with Noreen, but her manner projected self-confidence and—I caught a vibe—ambition.

A distinguished-looking older man with a rich mane of wavy silver hair had been swanning about the room with a camera—an actual, serious camera, not a phone—snapping pictures here and there, and now he was focused on Riley Uba and Noreen. Stepping near to capture the interplay of the two women's conversation, he offered direction while shooting, as if on assignment from *Vogue*. He was clearly a pro, and I could guess who he was. I said to Skip, "That's Rex Khalaji, right?"

"The one and only. My parents have known him forever."

Khalaji had worked in Los Angeles for decades as a fashion photographer, creating iconic images—mostly in black and white—of the industry's supermodels. Others rose to stardom *because* of his images, which came to be known for his signature "California style." Later, he retired to the desert, where his fame and connections ensured his A-list status among all the right people, who showered him with invitations to all the right events. If they were lucky, he brought his camera.

I noticed that Jazz had cornered Miss Mousy over by the bar. Jazz removed her mirrored glasses and pocketed them, smiling warmly. She then poured a glass of wine for the younger woman, who offered a tentative smile of her own. I wondered if Jazz would be tempted to grab a glass of the vino for herself—but no, she stuck with Dr Pepper.

Meanwhile, Khalaji finished taking his photos and stepped over to the bar. Setting down his camera, he browsed the selection of wines.

"If I could have your attention," Kenneth Terry said loudly, sounding a tad too formal. Conversation stopped as all heads turned to him. He continued, "I regret that today's festivities turned so rancorous earlier. That was not our intention. Claudia and I invited you—*and* our son, Skip—with hopes that we might achieve a meeting of minds regarding the canceled cruise and the best way forward. Seems I should have been more specific about the purpose of our gathering. But I figured that if I did that, no one would come. *Har-har.*"

His attempt to lighten the moment with levity fell flat. No one laughed. No one spoke as agonizing seconds slipped by.

Noreen Penley Wade broke the silence. "Kenneth," she said, "you've been a loyal and generous donor to M3A-LA over the years, and your current service on our board of directors is greatly valued. Our mission—to celebrate and preserve the anti-academic art movements of the nineteenth century—depends on the cultural passion demonstrated by so many of you in this room. But it also depends on funding. That's the hard reality. And M3A has been dealt a terrible blow by this cruise fiasco—measured not only by the dollar loss, but by the ill will."

"Noreen," said Kenneth, "I understand your disappointment. I share it. But the 'cruise fiasco'—that was no one's *fault*. The pandemic was a natural disaster."

Noreen snapped back at him, "So what does *that* mean? We just *lump* it? Throw in the towel, close our doors, call it quits?"

"Of course not."

"Howard?" said Noreen, turning to a man in a three-piece suit, which looked ridiculous at a pool party. "Can you explain to Kenneth the gravity of our situation?"

Skip told me, "That's Howard Quince, the museum's money guy."

Quince cleared his throat. "As chief financial officer of M3A-LA, I'm afraid the institution stands on shaky ground—very shaky ground, indeed. Our operating costs are just barely being met, with no cushion whatever for development or emergencies. The canceled cruise was the tipping point. The museum's financial future was once comfortably secure, but now? What lies ahead is anyone's guess."

The woman at his side—presumably his wife—wore a tweedy wool skirt and jacket. "Now, now, Howard," she said in a soothing tone, tugging at his sleeve, "it'll work out. Just do your best. Don't take it so personally."

"*Hannah*," he snapped at her, "how can I *not* take it personally? It's my job."

"Exactly," agreed Noreen. "It's my job, too. Christ, I *am* M3A. And I'll be damned if I'll let it fail on *my* watch. So here's the deal: The board *must* resolve the cruise fiasco. The board *must* make the museum financially whole again, and quickly. M3A doesn't hand out board positions as honorifics. It's well understood that the board's primary responsibility is to secure funding—either you *get* it, or you *give* it. And it's time to pony up. If you continue to ignore this crisis, I'll sue every damn one of you for dereliction of duty."

If her intention was to rouse some excitement, she succeeded. The room buzzed with angry dismay.

"*Jesus*, Noreen," said Kenneth Terry, slamming down his now empty gimlet glass, breaking the stem, "this high-and-mighty act of yours might work in *some* places, but not here. Do I really need to remind you that you serve at the pleasure of the board?"

With a defiant laugh, she told him, "So fire me. Or *try* to. You might regret it."

Skip, at my side, was shaking, trying to control himself, clenching his white-knuckled fists. He hopped a few steps forward and stood on the balls of his feet to shout at Noreen over the heads of the onlookers. "You fucking *bitch*. Did you just threaten my father—while a guest under his roof, drinking his liquor? Is that the way they do it in *your* circle? Is that the way the mob works?"

(God, he was cute when he was mad.)

With a collective gasp, the room waited for Noreen's response.

It did not disappoint. Her words were measured but incisive: "Careful, Skip—keep *that* up, and you'll piss off the wrong people."

"Now, hold on," said Kenneth. "This has gone *way* too far."

"I'm inclined to agree," said a new voice, sounding calm and sensible. The man speaking stepped out of the crowd and approached the piano. "We'd all like to get this cruise business worked out—for the good of the museum—but it won't get untangled anytime soon. Not here and now. Not with threats."

He was middle-aged, fifties maybe, sort of a bland-looking country-clubber wearing colorful shorts, like Skip's father and most of the men in the room.

I was standing at Skip's side with a hand on his shoulder, offering support and trying to calm him after his outburst. He said to me, speaking softly, "That's Jim Landon. He works in LA—banker or something—but he has a place out here, too. My parents know him through the museum."

Kenneth said to the banker, "Thank you, Jim. Always levelheaded."

"Nice job, sweets," said a woman standing at the back of the room, near the pool terrace.

Skip told me, "That's Fauvé Landon, Jim's wife."

"Of *course*," I said. "The real-estate bigwig. I've seen her commercials." She was dressed to dazzle, as always, and looked as if she was under the constant care of a hair-and-makeup artist. In stark contrast to her banker husband, bland she was not.

"Jim?" she said. "We should probably go. I think Cherisse has had too much sun."

As if on cue, the nymph from the raft appeared, still dripping and too red. Even with a towel hanging from her shoulders, she looked practically naked, drawing squeamish stares as she passed through the room with her parents.

Jazz said to Jim Landon, "Sir? If you parked in the courtyard, you probably can't get out for a while."

"No," he said, "we're on the street."

Jazz gave him a thumbs-up.

As the three Landons headed out the front of the house, Cherisse paused and turned to look me over with a hungry eye.

When they left, Skip leaned near with a gag-me expression, and we shared a low, conspiratorial laugh.

Someone else slipped past us, heading out to the courtyard. I had noticed him earlier, a Latino, probably in his forties, tastefully dressed for a warm day in a silk shirt, linen slacks, and huaraches, but the outfit was black—unusual for summer in the desert. His black hair contained sexy streaks of silver. He was clean-shaven and wore glasses with round black frames, which gave him a bookish air. I'd found him intriguing, and now he was gone.

I asked Skip, "Do you know that guy?"

"Don't know him, but I know who he is. That's Cameron Vicario, curator at the museum."

"Gay?"

"Seems like a reasonable guess," said Skip.

Over at the piano, Kenneth Terry said to Noreen, the lady in red who had threatened both him and his son, "I don't appreciate what you did here today." His tone, though miffed, was civil.

Noreen's tone wasn't civil. It was loud and badgering again: "And *I* don't appreciate the circumstances that forced this confrontation—the circumstances created by Skip. I lay this whole mess at *his* feet."

Kenneth let her have it. "You're full of shit, Noreen. Knock it off."

Noreen looked over her shoulder and said to someone, "I could use some help over here …"

"You're doin' just fine, babe." It was a Black man standing near the bar, watching with his arms crossed over his massive chest, which bounced as he chuckled. He looked like a quarterback—or an enforcer.

Jazz caught my eye. Simultaneously, we exchanged a curious shrug. Then I gave her a definite nod, and she sauntered over to check him out.

Skip explained, "That's Blade Wade, Noreen's husband. He's a painter—and 'significant,' as they say."

"Do tell."

■

Within an hour, the ill-fated party broke up. Jazz moved her SUV and directed traffic, helping the guests clear the courtyard and the street. I lingered indoors, confirming that I would set up a time for Skip to meet with Jazz about his concerns. I also spoke briefly with Mr. and Mrs. Terry, asking them to *please* review the rental regulations, and they offered profound apologies for causing trouble with the neighbors.

When I stepped outside, Jazz was waiting for me in the SUV with its motor running, just beyond the gate. Hopping in, I slammed the door, and we were off, heading back toward Palm Springs.

Once we were on the highway, I said, "I have a surprise for you."

With a skeptical laugh, she asked, "For real?"

"Seems you're going to owe me a finder's fee. Skip Terry told me he needs help. Says he has a 'situation,' and it might be dangerous. So I recommended you. Interested?"

"Hell yeah. Set it up."

"I assume the 'situation' is the trouble at the museum—with Noreen, the director. He told me people are actually *afraid* of her because they think she's connected to organized crime. I had my doubts, but then I saw her in action. We all did."

"Phew." Jazz shook her head. "Plenty mean. Snotty, too."

"What'd you learn from the guy at the bar? Skip said he's Noreen's husband."

"Mm-hmm. Salt-n-peppa. His name's Blade. Blade Wade—can you imagine? I asked, 'You make that *up?*' He says no—he's an artist—part of the gig. First glance, I thought he looked like a tough guy, but he's cool."

"Skip told me Blade's a painter. Apparently a good one."

With her hands on the wheel, Jazz shrugged. The SUV swerved. "Blade says his art thing is goin' real fine—got a agent. But that bitch wife of his can't be bothered. I mean, she's got this whole fuckin' *museum*. Wouldn't you think she'd help promote him?"

"I don't know," I said honestly. "Not sure how things work in that world."

"Yeah … different worlds … hard to tell."

"Plus," I said, "the biracial marriage."

Jazz glanced at me with an odd look.

I tried to clarify: "Don't get me wrong. That's great and all. But I wonder if sometimes there might be a gap in … expectations."

She gave a knowing nod. "You can ask Christopher about *that*."

I was thoroughly confused. "Who?"

"My ex-husband. Christopher is white."

"Oh." It really was time for me to shut up.

After an uncomfortable lull, Jazz asked, "Don't you want to hear about Ashley?"

Stumped, I said nothing.

Jazz explained, "That gal you asked me to check out today. Kinda nervous."

"Oh, of *course*—Miss Mousy."

"Yeah, her. She didn't seem to wanna talk, but once I got some wine in her, she opened right up."

"Well?" I asked. "Who is she? What does she do?"

"Like I said, her name is Ashley. I don't think she works."

"I mean, who *is* she? Why was she there?"

Jazz slowed the vehicle and turned to look at me. "Her name is Ashley Highsmith Terry. She's Skip's wife."

CHAPTER FOUR

lindsided by the news of Skip's marital status—to a woman,
no less—I was forced to consider some serious readjustment
of my fantasies. The ride back to Palm Springs involved no further chitchat with Jazz. I felt removed from my surroundings,
and time seemed to stand still while I questioned my indiscreet
lust for Skip.

My attraction to him was only too real. But the signals of
attraction being sent in return—were they imagined? Was I now
getting what I deserved for such crazy thinking?

These questions followed me back to the office that Sunday
afternoon. They followed me home that evening. Then they
followed me to bed. When sleep finally came—far later than
usual—it was not the reward of rest for the weary, but merely an
exhausted response to the weight of my foolishness.

Oddly, though, when I awoke on Monday morning, during that moment of return to consciousness, when memory of
the past meets the blank slate of a new day, I did not groan with
despair and burrow back into the bedding. Rather, I sensed that
I had already paid a sufficient price for my delusions of torrid sex
with a hot, but married, man. I was no longer ashamed of—or
aroused by—that pipe dream, which I could now simply dismiss. And by setting aside the craving that had gnawed at me
the entire weekend, I could begin the day with a fresh focus: I
wanted to find out who Skip Terry *really* was and what motivated
his strange behavior.

And I had a good idea where to start.

It was barely dawn when I hopped out of bed, threw on some shorts and a T-shirt, padded out to the kitchen, and started the coffee. Then I opened the front door, sat, and waited while the cool, quiet daybreak blended with the warm gurgle of brewing Sumatra.

Pouring my first cup, I heard the thud of a car door, then the approach of footsteps on the patio. I stepped outside to greet my neighbor, returning from his night shift at the hospital. "Morning, Isandro."

The other neighbors were sleeping. So was Mrs. Templeton's rat terrier. From the far side of the pool, Isandro said quietly, "Hi, Dante."

"Got a minute?"

"I, uh … this morning's not quite right."

I suppressed a laugh, assuming he meant "not quite right for a quickie." I explained, "No, I want to ask you about something."

He stepped around the pool and approached my door. "I won't have my schedule till the end of the week."

He must have been thinking I would pump him again for a dinner date, which he'd shot down when I first suggested it. Rather than let him squirm about this, I told him, "I was just wondering: Do you happen to know Skip Terry?"

He nodded. "Seems everyone knows him. Don't you?"

"We've … met," I said obliquely. "Want some coffee?"

"Sounds good. *Smells* good. Sure."

I brought him inside, poured a second mug, and settled with him on the sofa, better described as a love seat—nothing bigger would fit in the tiny living room. We angled ourselves to face each other, each drawing a leg onto the cushions. Our knees touched, prompting me to wonder, Where might *that* lead? Then I reminded myself to stay on topic.

"So," I said, "how do you know Skip?"

Isandro shrugged. "It's not as if we pal around or anything. He's just one of those guys you run into a lot—if you socialize much."

"I'll have to take your word on that. You're the party boy."

"Not like I used to be—I'm thirty-*three*."

I rolled my eyes. "Trust me: you're not at death's door."

"But Skip—*he's* the party boy. He must be out and around every night."

"Where do you see him?"

"Events. Restaurants. You know, *everywhere*."

I asked, "Bars?"

"Sure, all the time." Isandro laughed. "Not that he drinks that much. He just sorta works the room."

"Skip *is* gay, then. Right?"

With a sly grin, Isandro said, "Depends."

"Explain."

Isandro hesitated. Getting up from the sofa, he stepped a few paces into the room, as if needing to think out his response. Turning to me, he said, "Well, just *look* at the guy—way hot, great personality, lotsa money, friends, connections. Plus, he's such a flirt. We're passing acquaintances, but every time I see him, he asks me—kinda joking—'When are we gonna do it?'"

"Have you done it?"

Isandro smirked. "I may be a tramp, but I don't throw myself at just *anybody*."

"I'm highly complimented—you've tramped with *me* more than once."

"With pleasure, Dante." A warm smile spread across his face.

Skip faded from my thoughts.

"But Skip is married," said Isandro, jerking me back to the moment. "Married to a *woman*—at least that's what they say."

"Yeah. I've heard that."

"If it's true," said Isandro, "I've never seen her around. Everyone thinks he's 'conflicted' or whatever. But that's weird, right? It's not as if he's a closet case; he's as out as they come. Anyone who meets him just assumes he's gay as a goose—till they hear about the wife."

I admitted, "That was my experience. And the wife is not a myth. I've seen her—in the background. I thought she might be his secretary, but he never introduced us. I later learned her name is Ashley."

Isandro seemed impressed that I'd actually seen this woman. Sitting down next to me again, he asked, "What's she like?"

"Unworthy. Don't mean to be cruel, so I'll just leave it at that."

Nodding, Isandro reached for his coffee mug and drank a few swallows.

I summarized: "As far as you know, then, everyone thinks Skip is gay—until they learn he's married—and meanwhile, he doesn't actually have sex with men. Right?"

Coffee, I feared, would spray from Isandro's nostrils as he choked back a laugh and set down the mug. "I never said *that*. I said *I'd* never had sex with Skip."

"Are you aware of others who have?"

"Oh, *honey*. Think about it. Despite all his posturing and fancy connections, Skip's essentially a travel agent. Every year, he puts together one of those gay cruises that draws a thousand men from Palm Springs to LA. You and I have *joked* about this."

True. Isandro and I were both members at the same crowded gym, where the clientele was largely gay and the vibe was beyond campy. Whenever a gay cruise set sail, those of us who weren't on it enjoyed having the place to ourselves, telling one another, "I thought those rich bitches would *never* leave."

But Isandro had saved up for a blowout vacation and booked a stateroom on the most recent voyage of a queer party boat nicknamed the SS *Decadence*.

"It didn't surprise me," said Isandro, "that Skip himself was on the cruise—he arranged it, and the passengers were his customers. What did surprise me, though, was his extreme dedication to 'servicing' his clients."

"Oh?"

"Mm-hmm." Isandro scooched closer, touching my leg. "Skip may have been on that boat as a matter of business, but he made plenty of time for pleasure—with plenty of guys. I mean, people *talk*, and they were all telling the same story. Out there in international waters, Skip Terry was *not* a man with a wife. He was a man with a dance card, and it was always full. They say he was busy four or five times a day. And he always wanted more."

I gulped.

Isandro leaned near and hooked a finger under the hem of my shorts. His angelic features twisted into a devilish grin. "You make a fabulous cup of coffee."

■

Mitzi's yapping shot the mood—the sun was up, the day had begun. So Isandro went home to shower and nap while I put myself together for the workday.

When I arrived at Sunny Junket that Monday morning at eight, Gianna had already opened the office. She sat at the front desk licking from her fingers the frosting of a half-eaten cinnamon roll. With her clean hand, she wagged a pink message slip in my direction. "You just missed a call," she said. "Someone at the Ellinger House."

Snatching the note from her, I paused before heading over to my desk. I asked, "Was it Kenneth Terry? What'd he want?"

"Said his name was Skip. Said you should call him."

"Ah." I knew what he wanted. I'd promised to get back to him about a meeting with Jazz. He was apparently getting antsy for some follow-up—and I couldn't help wondering what to make of his fears about Noreen Penley Wade's rumored mob connections. In the bright, cleansing sunshine of a new week, that theory now seemed shaky at best, if not downright ludicrous.

My normal routine was to check in with Ben to get my marching orders for the day, but he would not be in that

morning—visiting a few properties we might add to our roster—
so I settled at my desk and returned Skip's phone call.

"Dante!" he said on the line. "That was quick."

"Just walked in. Sorry I didn't get back to you yesterday. After
what happened, I was running sort of ragged."

"You're not the only one," he assured me.

"But I talked to Jazz Friendly. She'll be happy to discuss your
needs for some private investigation. She suggested tomorrow
after lunch. Maybe one thirty?"

"Sure."

"She has an office in Palm Springs, or she could drive over
to see you."

"That might be better—at the rental house. My schedule's
sort of iffy, but I can be there at one thirty."

"All set, then. Glad to be of help, Skip. If there's—"

"Actually," he said, "the meeting with Jazz, that wasn't why
I called."

"Oh? Let me guess: you just wanted to hear my voice again."

"You're getting warmer." He laughed. "My parents are having
trouble with some of—all of—the electronics. I'm sorry. You ran
me through everything, but when I tried to explain it, I blanked,
and now I think they've screwed things up. No TV. Phones don't
work. Security system …"

"Say no more," I told him. "Happens all the time. When
should I come over?"

"Sooner rather than later, please. Eleven?"

"I'll be there. No problem." I wasn't just being polite. These
issues, although frustrating, were the reason I had a job—especially when guests were paying for the likes of the Ellinger
House.

Before ringing off, Skip told me, "Dad asked if I could help
with some errands today. If no one's at the house when you arrive,
just let yourself in. We won't be long getting back."

"Got it."

■

Later that morning, about a half hour before I was due in Rancho Mirage, I left the office, stepping through the doors to the street, where I felt the full assault of summer. It was just a few minutes past ten thirty when I checked my phone and found the temperature nudging a hundred—not horrible for June in the desert, but it served as fair warning to toughen up, as July and August would be much worse.

Although my old Camry was nothing special—as Jazz had so bluntly pointed out—it still got me where I needed to go, and the air-conditioning worked just fine, thank God. I had added an aftermarket remote starter, controlled by a phone app, which allowed me to cool down the car before getting in—a wise investment, even for a guy scraping to get by.

That morning, before walking around to the back of Sunny Junket's building, where I had parked in an unshaded lot several hours earlier, I paused to start the car with my phone.

When I arrived in back and opened the car door, the handle burned my fingers, so I stood there for a moment, wagging my hand as the hot air escaped the interior. Reaching inside, I held my hand to the vent and waited for the rush of air to feel cold. Only then would it be bearable to settle into the cracked vinyl seat.

There was little traffic that day as I drove out of town, heading down valley, and I found myself running a few minutes early as I crossed the line between Cathedral City and Rancho Mirage. A mile or two later, I turned into the cove neighborhood and climbed the winding streets toward the mesa.

When I arrived at the entrance to the Ellinger House, I saw that the gate was open. Though I was expected, I didn't want to leave my shabby car in the refined surroundings of the courtyard, so I parked it, as before, around a bend of the roadway, then walked back.

Entering the courtyard, I found that Skip's Karmann Ghia was the only car there; his parents' Maybach was gone. Skip had told me that he might need to run errands with his father, so I assumed they had left together in the big car. Although Skip said I was welcome to let myself into the house, I didn't know whether Mrs. Terry was still at home or not, so I rang the bell.

While waiting to see if anyone would answer, I stepped over to the Karmann Ghia, parked with its top down in the shade of a cluster of palms. The car was just flat-out beautiful—a timeless, sensuous design, built with precision and impeccably restored—but that's not what drew me to it that morning. That's not what prompted me to touch it. I ran my fingers over the steering wheel, which Skip had grasped countless times. I patted the leather upholstery of the driver's seat. I swept my hand along the rear fender, as if stroking the flank of an animal.

I shook my head, dismayed by the jumble of emotions I felt about Skip—his sham marriage, his cockeyed mob theories, his vacuous party-boy lifestyle—but I could not deny that my overwhelming response to the guy was blind, mindless attraction.

Returning to the entryway of the house, I gave the bell one more ring, then used the keypad to open the door. Stepping inside, I closed it behind me. All was quiet.

I noticed at once that the expansive main room was absolutely clean and tidy, with no evidence of yesterday's rowdy gathering. I had wondered if the office would need to send a housekeeping crew to put things back in order, but no, everything looked magazine-perfect. Tentatively, I called, "Mrs. Terry? Anyone home?"

No response.

I ducked into the kitchen, thinking she might be fussing with something, but no one was there, and that room, too, was sparkling—not even a stray glass near the sink or a misplaced towel.

There was nothing for me to do but wait, so I returned to the main room, and I noticed that a section of the sliding glass wall that led to the pool had been left open a couple of feet. I went over to close it, but first poked my head out to make sure there was no one on the terrace.

"Hello there, Dante."

The bland banker's nymphette daughter, Cherisse, who had sprawled her oiled body on the baby-blue pool raft the day before—she was long gone.

Lounging on it now, floating at the deep end, was Skip. My eyes drank in the sight of him, with his sandy hair and stubbly beard, wearing those classic Ray-Bans and nothing else. His arms were splayed like wings, with his head resting in both palms.

I stepped out to the terrace. With a shameless grin, I said, "Pardon the intrusion. I thought no one was home."

"You were right," he said, lifting his head with his hands to get a better look at me. "It's just us."

"Ah. Well, then. I'll go take care of the electronics—those issues you phoned about."

He made a shushing sound, then told me softly, "There are no issues."

I asked, "TV? Phones? Security?"

"All good."

"What about the Wi-Fi?"

"Working fine."

"Great." At an awkward loss for words, I told him, "Nice tan, by the way. But it's not just the tan—you look fantastic."

"You do, too."

"Uh, thanks," I said, "you're kind."

"I'm *serious*."

Frustrated once again by the awful Sunny Junket uniform, I gestured to it, telling Skip, "They *make* me wear this—I hate it."

"Then don't wear it."

Five days earlier, Jazz had told me the same thing, verbatim, when I complained to her about the uniform. In the context of her lecture, she was telling me to start asserting myself. Now, of course, Skip was simply telling me to get naked.

I hesitated. "When will your parents be back?"

He chuckled. "They drove to LA this morning. Gone for a few days." He started playing with himself. "So get in the pool."

During the frenzy of undressing, I ran through a mental checklist of the property's service schedule, hoping we'd have no embarrassing interruptions. Gardener, pool boy, window guy—nope, all clear till tomorrow.

Last to go was the acid-yellow polo, which I threw aside. Then I stepped to the edge of the pool and made a clean dive.

The water felt icy for a moment as I plied the depths, then it caressed and refreshed me as I glided below the baby-blue raft, where Skip floated like prey on the high seas, out in international waters, where he had no wife.

Surfacing at his side, I blew water from my mouth and flung my head, whipping a long arc of droplets from my hair. The raft squeaked as I gripped its edge, pulling Skip near. "Technically," I told him, "this is a service call."

He broke into that perfect smile. "Nice."

"Long as I'm here, anything else need attention?"

"Mm-hmm." It bobbed and waved at me.

CHAPTER FIVE

Because I'd worked over the weekend, I had Tuesday off and slept later than usual. Getting out of bed around eight, there was no need to be careful about rousing the neighbor's neurotic rat terrier. Mitzi was already yapping her head off on the other side of my bedroom wall—which is why I didn't snooze till nine.

I wondered if Isandro had glanced at my door earlier, returning from his hospital shift at dawn. Not that our morning hookups were an everyday thing—far from it, usually a week or two apart. But I couldn't help pondering that even if Isandro was raring for action that morning, I was not. The prior day's encounter with Skip Terry had left me, in a word, spent.

Skip seduced me, and I was ready. The whole setup was masterful on his part, a surefire fantasy he had choreographed for my benefit. The setting, the circumstances, the timing—he knew what he was doing, and I was powerless to resist—not that I was even remotely inclined to brush him off. On the contrary, he had saved me the humiliation of begging for it.

Boy, did he deliver. And it wasn't "just sex," at least not after our first round. Our tempest in the pool was merely the beginning. With the urgency of those pent-up needs satisfied, we moved to a double-wide chaise longue on the terrace. Then we went indoors to one of the guest rooms, where we tangled the sheets. Exhausted and hungry, we ended up in the kitchen, where we never got around to lunch, putting the center island to an unintended use.

Our mutual attraction felt like more than lust. I'd be a fool to call it love, but I couldn't deny that the joy of it felt more like love-making than tricking. It went on for hours. So Tuesday morning, yeah, I was spent.

Good thing I had the day off.

It was going to be a hot one, so I nixed the routine of opening the front door to cool off the apartment—better to leave the air-conditioning on. I was checking the news on my phone while the coffee brewed, and by the time it was ready, I noticed that the temperature in Palm Springs was already in the mid-nineties.

A few minutes after nine, the phone rang in my hand. I connected and said hello.

It was Jazz Friendly. "Just called your office and talked to Gianna. You've got the day off?"

I reminded her, "I worked over the weekend."

"Gianna says you weren't worth shit after you came back from a service call yesterday, late. Said you looked all fagged out." Jazz laughed merrily.

"Is there some *reason* you're bothering me at home?"

"Yeah. Just wanted to confirm that I'm meeting with Skip Terry today at one thirty. Thought you might come along and fill me in about this guy. I mean, you're not *doing* anything, right?"

"Nothing in particular." Truth is, I had a dozen errands to run that day, but they could wait. I told Jazz, "Sure, I could tag along. Pick me up at one?"

"Well, duh," she said. "We can't show up in that Camry."

I gave her my address.

■

So my lazy morning at home was now consumed with an urgent, burning question: What to wear?

Logically, this didn't matter in the least anymore. Skip had already seen me three times over the last three days—most recently naked—so it was a tad late to be fretting over first impressions. But it's often said that clothes make the man, and Skip's sense of personal style was spot-on, so I wanted to make the most of this opportunity to be seen wearing something other than Sunny Junket's dad jeans and dorky yellow polo.

Naturally, a quick scan of my closet convinced me that I had *nothing* to wear that day, and I even considered rushing out to buy something, but what? I realized that if my goal was to dress *like* Skip, I was doomed to fail. His look was his alone. If he'd found me attractive (as he apparently had) even in my work clothes, then he wasn't looking for a clone of himself. My best bet was simply to show him *my* personal style. I could do this.

Today's meeting had a business purpose—Jazz and Skip were considering each other for a possible sign-up as investigator and client. In spite of the heat, then, I couldn't show up in shorts and flip-flops.

I set out a pair of tight black jeans, perfect for any occasion (and I knew from experience that I looked good in them). I chose a cool but dressy camp shirt, white linen. And a stroke of luck: I found at the back of my closet an old pair of deck shoes, black leather. Those, with no socks, were a perfect nod to Skip's preppy instincts. Examining the shoes, I found that they were in fact Top-Siders.

■

Around one o'clock, Jazz texted: "I'm here."

I locked up the apartment, crossed the patio, and approached her SUV at the curb, which had been spiffed and polished for the appointment. When Jazz looked up from her phone and saw me coming, she lowered the passenger window and blew a wolf whistle. "Lookin' sorta studly there, Dante. Hot date?"

Thinking it best not to answer that, I got into the vehicle. While buckling up, I asked, "Find the address okay?"

She snorted. "Couldn't miss it—not with your shitbox parked on the street."

So much for pleasant chatter. A rap station thumped on the radio, droning low in the background as Jazz drove us over to Highway 111 and turned east, heading out of town. The constant beat of the music took on a lulling, hypnotic quality. I reacted with a startled jerk when Jazz broke the monotony, saying, "Tell me about Skip Terry. What do I need to know?"

"What do you *want* to know?" I wasn't sure where to begin. Jazz had been with me at the Terrys' party gone bad on Sunday, so she already knew plenty.

She said, "I know that Skip's a privileged white guy without a care in the world. Except he's in trouble with Mummy and Daddy's rich museum crowd. I also know that he's married to a pale, nervous woman named Ashley—she's a Highsmith, no less. Very la-di-da. Except he doesn't quite strike me as the marrying type. Any insights?"

"None," I said truthfully. "I can't claim to understand Skip's circumstances, but I've known many other guys—closet cases—who marry for appearances. They don't want to upset the family or hurt the business or 'sin' or whatever. I've known others who got married because they grew up never questioning that a wife, house, and kids were the natural course of things, only to figure out *later* that they weren't wired that way."

Jazz shrugged. "Marriage of convenience."

"Right. But that was *way* more common a generation ago. Skip doesn't need to play those games. His parents are cool, and his job's not at risk—everyone assumes he's gay anyway."

"Plus," said Jazz, "just *look* at that guy."

"You noticed, huh?"

"Mm-hmm. Holy Christ, he's not *ugly*. I bet a guy like that could land any man he sets his eyes on."

"*I'll* say…"

The SUV seemed to be losing speed as Jazz glanced over at me, then returned her eyes to the road. She reminded me, "Gianna said you weren't worth shit yesterday when you got back late from a service call. What happened?"

"Nothing," I said lamely. (I wouldn't have bought it, either.)

Jazz swerved the SUV into the parking lot of a strip mall along the highway in Cathedral City. She slammed on the brakes, whipped off her sunglasses, and turned to look me in the eye. "Don't *tell* me," she said, fuming. "Don't tell me you're fucking my *client*."

"Technically," I said, "he's not your client—yet."

"Jesus, Dante"—she pounded the steering wheel—"zip it up! You're too *old* for this shit."

"Says who? Skip had no complaints." After a day like yesterday, I could almost believe that age was just a number.

She tossed her hands. "You could drive a person to *drink*— you know that?"

Concerned by her reference to booze, I said softly, "Don't go there, Jazz. You've been doing so well."

Clenching her jaw, she paused to calm down. "Do *not* patronize me. Okay?"

I nodded. "Okay. But I don't want your high-hat moralizing, either. You're not my mama."

Jazz put on her sunglasses, shifted into drive, and returned to the highway.

■

By the time we got to Rancho Mirage, we were laughing about it, cracking "yo' mama" jokes. "Seriously, though," said Jazz as we started up the winding streets of the cove, "your mom—see her much?"

I shook my head. "She died a few years ago. Never left Indiana. Born and raised there. Me, too."

"Indiana," said Jazz—slowly—as if trying out a word she'd never used before. "Lotsa corn there?"

"Yes." I did not elaborate. "How about *your* mother?"

"Mama's still around, still doin' good. Still back in LA, where I grew up."

When we arrived at the entrance to the Ellinger estate, the gate was open, so I assumed Skip was already there, waiting. I grinned, wondering how he would react when he saw that I had accompanied Jazz. Would he blow me a wolf whistle, as she had? Would he find it a turn-on that I'd worn Top-Siders for him—or would he not even notice?

But when Jazz drove past the gate and into the parking court, I saw that Skip's Karmann Ghia was not there. Nor was the Maybach, which came as no surprise, as I knew that Skip's parents had returned to LA for a few days. What did surprise me—or at least confuse me—was the presence of a hefty Lexus sedan, a newer model, silver, like a thousand others in the affluent resort cities. Except, it was not spiffed. Spattered with the bugs and grime of highway travel, it also showed the wear and tear and dings of LA, where it could be difficult to keep a car pristine.

Jazz cut the engine of the SUV and sat looking out the window at the Lexus. "Who's that?"

"Good question. This house has a few service calls on Tuesdays—pool and windows, I think—but those guys drive trucks. So maybe it's Skip's 'other' car. His little convertible might be just for fun."

Jazz shrugged. "*Someone's* here. Let's find out."

We got out of the SUV, crossed the courtyard, and walked up the entryway to the house. Arriving at the massive front door, I rang the bell.

We waited. I checked my watch—on the dot, half past one. I rang again.

Jazz asked, "When you talked to him, what did he say?"

"He wasn't sure of his schedule, but he'd get here by one thirty."

Jazz reached past me and jabbed the bell. "Do you know how to get in?"

"Of course."

"Do it," she said. When I hesitated, she told me, "It's not like breaking and entering—we're expected."

"Maybe *you* are," I reminded her. She planted her hands on her hips, spreading her jacket, exposing her holster and the butt of a pistol grip. I tapped in the entry code.

When we stepped inside, I closed the door behind us and called, "Skip? Anyone here?"

No response. In fact, the house was oddly hushed. The lack of typical background noises—air conditioning, refrigerator, fans, pool pump—left my ears ringing. I wondered for a moment if the power had gone out, but no, the security panel by the door was lit, and I'd heard the doorbell before we entered.

I told Jazz, "I'll try calling Skip, but he hasn't been good about picking up calls."

Looking out the window beside the door, Jazz said, "Just for kicks, let's run the plates on that Lexus." And she went to work on her phone.

While leaving a voicemail for Skip, I poked my head into the kitchen. As expected, no one was there, but my gaze lingered on the center island where, twenty-four hours earlier, Skip and I had forgotten about lunch.

I took a quick walk through the bedroom wing, finding nothing unusual. Then I returned to the main room, walking along the rear wall of windows, where the drapes had been pulled to block the afternoon sun. Unlike yesterday, none of the glass panels to the terrace had been opened—everything was shut tight—so I had no reason to think Skip might be waiting out there, lounging naked in the pool.

Even so, I had to take a look. The memory of discovering him on that baby-blue raft filled my mind's eye as I slid back the curtain, then the glass.

Jazz was still standing by the front windows, phone in hand. "Well, whataya know," she said. "That Lexus? It belongs to—"

"*Jazz,*" I yelled, tossing my wallet and phone on a chair, "out here."

She was on her way as I raced across the terrace to the apron of the pool, kicked off my shoes, and dove in, stroking toward the fully clothed woman who floated, facedown, near the deep end.

"Holy *shit,*" cried Jazz as I tugged the corpse—it was clearly a corpse, beyond rescue—to the edge of the pool. Jazz squatted on the terrace and pulled while I stretched and pushed from the water, till the body came to rest on the flagstones, faceup, staring blindly into the full sun.

It was Noreen Penley Wade, the contentious executive director of the Museum of Anti-Academic Art, whose Lexus was parked in front of the house. Sunday's lady in red now wore basic black. Had she sensed that this day might not end well? Her severe asymmetrical hairdo, which had defied gravity on Sunday, now drooped and puddled on the wet pavers.

Jazz tried reviving her, mouth to mouth, then sat back, exhausted. "Too late."

Toot-toot.

The jaunty car horn signaled Skip's arrival in the courtyard.

Moments later, he waltzed through the front door just as Jazz and I trudged into the house from the terrace.

"Well, look at *this,*" he said, beaming that perfect smile, "a welcoming party. I didn't know you were bringing company, Miss Friendly." Approaching us from across the room, Skip added with a laugh, "And you, Dante—you are *way* too sexy when wet."

PART TWO
SMITHEREENS

CHAPTER SIX

Jazz was already phoning it in.

I asked Skip, "Where *were* you?" My tone conveyed that I was in no mood for joking and was not feeling sexy, even when wet.

"I, uh"—Skip seemed unable to comprehend the situation—"I was running late from lunch with a client. Sorry. Then I needed to pick up some groceries for the folks."

Jazz was nattering into the phone, "... a body in the swimming pool ... could not resuscitate ..."

"*What?*" said Skip.

I asked, "Were you *here* this morning?"

"No. I mean, I did swing by to open the gate—in case Miss Friendly got here early for our meeting. I didn't know you'd be with her. You could've opened it."

Jazz continued, "... yes, extremely suspicious circumstances ... local law enforcement ..."

Skip stepped around me and looked out to the pool terrace. "Jesus *Christ*. Is that Noreen?"

"None other."

"Jesus *Christ*," he repeated. "What's *she* doing here?"

Jazz pocketed her phone and turned to Skip. "I was about to ask you the same question, Mr. Terry. Did you or your parents invite her this morning? Did you know she was coming?"

"Of *course* not. You saw what a scene she made on Sunday. You heard her crazy threats. I didn't want to see her *here*—or anywhere else—ever again."

"Uh-huh," said Jazz. Her tone was inflected with a meaningful lilt.

Alarmed, Skip said, "I didn't mean it like *that*, Miss Friendly. I just meant: whatever Noreen was doing here today, it wasn't because she was invited."

Jazz nodded. "Look, I'm not 'Miss' Friendly. And I'm not exactly a 'Mrs.' either, cuz we're recently divorced. God's honest truth—I'm not sure who the hell I *am* anymore. So just call me Jazz."

"Sure, Jazz."

"Things are gonna get busy here real soon. And they'll be asking you questions. If you've got groceries you don't want to leave in the car—take care of that."

"Oh. All right." He made a few tentative steps toward the front door.

I said, "I'll give you a hand, Skip."

He was quiet while leading me out to the courtyard.

When we arrived at the Karmann Ghia, I saw no groceries inside. Skip made no move to open the trunk space under the hood. I gave him a puzzled look.

With a weary shake of his head, he admitted, "No groceries. Not sure why I made that up—just needed an excuse for being late. Pretty lame, huh?"

"Well, *yeah*. But worse, it makes you sound like you were lying about an alibi."

"Alibi?" said Skip. "An alibi for what?"

■

"Murder," said Jazz to the sheriff's detective who first responded to the scene. Jazz explained, "The victim was fully clothed, so she wasn't here for a swim. The front gate was open, but the house was locked up. Why did she drive from LA this morning? And how did she end up in the pool?"

The sheriff's detective, Arcie Madera, was a woman of fifty or so—older than Jazz, but they were dressed similarly, each in a dark suit with a light blouse. Rancho Mirage, along with several other resort communities, contracted for police services with the Riverside County sheriff's department. Madera explained that she was stationed in nearby Palm Desert. She and Jazz hunkered near the body on the terrace while a forensics team compared notes with the medical examiner.

My clothes still felt clammy, but thanks to the intense afternoon sun, they were no longer dripping wet. The victim's clothing had also dried in the heat. I now noticed that her outfit, which had appeared black when wet, was in fact navy blue. Either way, she had looked better in red.

When the photographer was finished and the forensic pathologist completed his initial exam, Noreen Penley Wade's body was covered and removed. Eventually, the entire investigating unit packed up their gear and left the crime scene, leaving only the sheriff's detective.

Arcie Madera had been taking notes and asking nonstop questions, but the terrace was sweltering, so Skip suggested moving indoors. Good idea—Jazz and the detective followed Skip and me into the house. Skip offered iced tea, another good idea, so we settled around a breakfast table in the kitchen. A large window, shaded by a deep overhang of the roof, provided a view of the pool, a symbol of paradise that now looked decidedly sinister.

My eye, however, kept drifting to the kitchen's center island. I had to blink away visions of yesterday in order to stay focused on today's conversation, the opening salvo of a murder investigation. Skip stood behind me for a moment and placed a hand on my shoulder while leaning to fill four glasses from a pitcher. Then he set the pitcher on the table and sat in the one vacant seat, next to mine.

The sheriff's detective said to Jazz, "Now, explain to me: When you discovered the body today, why were you here?"

"I came for a meeting with Mr. Terry. His parents, from LA, are renting the house for a month."

Skip provided their names and contact information, adding, "My legal name is Kenneth, like my father, but I've always gone by Skip."

The detective assured him, "I know who you are, Mr. Terry." Her neutral tone made it impossible to interpret her words as deferential—or suspicious.

Jazz continued, telling the detective, "Skip's parents invited some people to the house on Sunday, including Noreen, the victim. Things got rowdy, and the rental company sent me over. I do some security work for them, and I'm a licensed private investigator." Seemingly as an afterthought, Jazz added, "I'm an ex-cop. Quit the Palm Springs force."

The detective grinned. "I also know who *you* are, Officer Friendly. Or should I call you Inspector?"

"Just call me Jazz. That's my name, Detective Madera."

"Just call me Arcie. That's my name, Jazz. Actually, it's Arcelia, but Arcie's fine."

I sensed an unsubtle bonding—a sisterhood thing in the male-dominated profession of crime solving—a Black-and-Latina sisterhood that stemmed from an understanding of each other's challenges.

Skip must have sensed it, too. His eyes slid in my direction. They seemed to sparkle, as if smiling. Was he thinking that the forces of justice were already stacking up in his favor? I hoped so. But I wasn't so sure.

Jazz picked up her story again, telling Arcie, "On Sunday, the gathering was supposed to iron out some difficulties between Skip and Noreen." Jazz detailed how the canceled cruise had imperiled the museum that was run by Noreen. Jazz concluded, "By the time the party broke up, Skip and Noreen were trading threats. Later, Skip asked to meet with me—to discuss hiring me."

"For what?" asked Arcie.

"Protection, I guess. Skip seems to think Noreen has mob connections."

Arcie winced while scratching notes. "So Mr. Terry is your client?"

"We haven't had that talk yet. Things got messy first."

Arcie paused to drink from her iced tea. Setting down the glass, she turned to Skip. "I'd like to ask you a few questions, Mr. Terry, but I'll understand if you need an attorney."

So much for any illusions Skip might have harbored about things stacking up in his favor. But he put on a brave face.

"Detective," he said, "I have nothing to hide. If I intended to harm Noreen, why would I ask Jazz to protect me from her?"

Jazz told Arcie, "Sounds reasonable—unless he's *really* clever." She laughed. Then, scrunching her features, she asked, "The victim's time of death—established yet? We pulled the body from the pool shortly after one thirty, and I thought the corpse looked 'fresh,' like she died within the last hour, maybe. Not, for instance, the night before."

"Definitely not the night before," said Arcie. "The medical examiner will establish an approximate time of death after weighing all the variables—body temperature, water and air temperature, and such. He'll take lividity into account. And of course he'll look for water in the lungs: Did she in fact drown, or was she thrown in after she died? But the short answer, Jazz, based on my own observations, is that I agree with you. The victim appears to have died shortly before the body was found."

Jazz nodded. "And what I was driving at is that Skip can account for his whereabouts before he came here to meet me. He was with clients, then did some grocery shopping for his parents."

Oops. I had not told Jazz that I'd learned there were no groceries. She had gone out to the pool in back of the house when

Skip and I entered from the front empty-handed. So the facts went conveniently unnoticed. Now, though, I faced a moment of truth.

Arcie asked Skip, "Can you give me follow-up information so I can corroborate the client meeting? And a receipt for the groceries would be helpful."

I sat there, numb, committing a lie of omission.

But Skip's lie was unvarnished, at least to my ears. He told Arcie, "Sure, the client meeting should be easy to verify. And the grocery receipt—I'll look for that, but I might've tossed it. Don't even remember if I took it from the checkout counter."

Arcie started a new page in her notebook. "Who first spotted the body?"

Jazz nodded in my direction. "He was first—Dante, my associate."

I wondered, associate? This was news. Was Jazz inflating herself in front of the *real* detective by claiming, in effect, that her fledgling private-eye biz already had a staff?

"Dante," said Arcie, writing it down. "Full name?"

"Dante is a name I picked up as a bartender. But my legal name is Danny—not Daniel. Danny O'Donnell."

Arcie nodded while scribbling. Then she paused, looking up. "Palm Springs. Out of my usual jurisdiction, but I see reports when they end up in the DA's office."

Jazz told her, "Good memory. February. Dante was with me when Clarence Kwon was arrested for the murder of his husband, an art dealer."

I said to Arcie, "I found *that* body, too. Crushed under a refrigerator. I work for the rental company that manages that house—and this one. Sunny Junket Vacation Rentals."

Arcie made note of it. "Well," she said, "Peter Nadig most certainly thanks you."

"Who's he?"

Jazz said, "The DA. We're making his job *way* too easy. Murder—first-degree—that's his red meat. Never thinks twice about going for the death penalty."

Arcie exhaled an odd sound, not quite a sigh, not quite a laugh. "It's a dubious distinction. Ought to be embarrassing. During most recent years, even during the pandemic, Riverside County led the entire nation in new death sentences."

Jazz reminded her, "But the governor put a moratorium on executions. So the convictions just sit there, piling up."

"Nadig doesn't care. For him, a win's a win."

Unless I was mistaken, this conversation was making Skip plenty nervous.

■

A few minutes later, Arcie wanted to return to the pool terrace. Skip said he'd join us soon, needing to tidy up the kitchen first, though it looked just fine.

I led Arcie and Jazz out of the kitchen and over to the back window wall of the main room, with its view of the pool.

"I was standing here," I told Arcie, "when I noticed the body in the water. Jazz was on the other side of the room, near the front door, checking the license plates of the Lexus. I gave her a yell, and we ran out to the pool."

Arcie nodded, then led us just a few steps onto the terrace. "Okay," she said, halting, pointing to the pool, "try to remember exactly what you saw out here. Sure, you were focused on the body, but did anything else catch your eye? Specifically, do you recall wet footprints—or splashed water—around the pool?"

"Umm," said Jazz, "not sure. The body had my full attention. Sorry."

"Ditto," I said. "But I *do* recall thinking, just as I opened the curtains—and before I noticed the body—how *gorgeous* everything was, as usual. This house is one of our primo rentals, and this setting is second to none. It's a routine part of my job to inspect these properties, and my first reaction was: perfection. I don't recall any splashed water, which I think I'd have noticed."

"Great." Arcie looked up from her notes. "That's helpful. It leads me to believe that whatever happened, it must have been at least, say, fifteen minutes before you got here." She stepped over to the edge of the pool, leaned over, and whipped a few handfuls of water onto the terrace. She checked her watch as the water spread and settled into dark puddles under the dazzling sunlight.

Jazz and I checked our watches as well—three minutes past three.

Jazz said to Arcie, "Manner of death. Murder, right?"

I asked, "Manner of death?"

Arcie explained, "A suspicious death is defined by the coroner or medical examiner in terms of its cause, its mechanism, and its 'manner.' The cause and the mechanism are determined by straightforward medical science—usually an autopsy and subsequent testing. In a garden-variety case of a body found floating facedown in water, the investigation might reveal that the cause of death was drowning and the mechanism of death was asphyxiation."

Jazz said to me, "But that doesn't tell us *how* the death came about."

Arcie said, "Correct. It's often self-evident, and the coroner supplies the manner of death. Other times, though, when the circumstances are *not* clear, that determination is made by a law enforcement investigation—and that's why I'm here."

"So," I said, "if the manner of Noreen's death wasn't murder, what are the other options?"

"Sometimes," said Arcie, "the investigation is inconclusive. Otherwise we're left with four classifications for the manner of death: natural, accidental, suicide, or homicide. Jazz seems to think this was a homicide."

"Well, *yeah*," said Jazz. "A 'natural' death is the result of old age, illness, or disease—and none of those seem to apply here. Could it have been an accident? Sure, *maybe*, if the victim was just out here enjoying the scenery and happened to trip at the edge of the pool and couldn't swim or went into shock or whatever—but that's a long shot at best. As for suicide, come on— totally bizarre to drive all the way from LA, all gussied up, and do a belly flop into someone else's pool. Which leaves us with option number four—homicide."

"Homicide," I repeated. "Murder."

Arcie agreed. "Looks like it. Which leaves us with a series of four questions to answer. First, why was the victim here in the first place?"

"Well," said Jazz, "we know she was here before, on Sunday. And we know she still had a score to settle with Kenneth Terry— Senior *and* Junior."

I said, "But Skip's parents returned to LA for a few days. Why would they invite Noreen *here* again?"

"Skip's still here," Jazz reminded me—while giving Arcie a meaningful glance.

Arcie's reaction, a barely perceptible nod, spoke loud and clear to me: she suspected Skip's involvement in what happened to Noreen.

I told both Jazz and Arcie, "Skip did *not* invite Noreen here today."

Arcie poised her pen on her notes. "You know that for a fact?"

My claim, of course, was groundless. So I rephrased: "He just *couldn't* have."

Wryly, Arcie responded, "I'll keep that in mind. Now, our second question: If the victim was murdered, how was the crime committed? By my reasoning, either the victim was subdued by an assailant and then drowned, or she was killed by some other means first and then put into the water as an *apparent* drowning."

Jazz said, "There were no obvious wounds to indicate she'd been shot or injured—no signs of strangulation or a struggle. Her clothes weren't even mussed."

"Right," said Arcie. "And the postmortem will reveal if the victim had been drugged or poisoned, but I think it's far more likely that someone just pushed her in and held her down. She wasn't very big. The assailant wouldn't need to be some burly thug. A woman could've done it—or a smaller man."

"Uh-huh," said Jazz with the trace of a grin. She seemed to be saying: Even a guy of five foot eight, even a hot little number like Skip Terry, could have pushed Noreen into the pool and forced her to inhale deadly waters.

Hoping they wouldn't dwell on that theory, I tried to nudge Arcie along. "Detective," I said, "you mentioned having four questions. What's number three?"

"It's a big one," she said. "Motive. The 'why.' Why did someone want Noreen Penley Wade to die? Why was someone sufficiently motivated to kill her?"

In the kitchen, we had already discussed the cruise feud between Noreen and Skip—and their volley of threats—so I kept my mouth shut.

Jazz planted her hands on her hips. "Why would someone want to kill Noreen? Okay, I'll say it: she had a habit of pissing people off. I saw her in action, along with a roomful of other folks on Sunday. Trust me, no tears will be shed."

In the spirit of things, I added, "No flowers will be sent."

Arcie smirked. "It's one thing to be glad she's gone. But it's something else to kill her. Who had *that* kind of motive? And that's question number four: Who did it?"

Jazz and I glanced at each other.

Arcie said, "I mean, besides the easy answer, where else do we need to look?"

Jesus. There it was. Not only had Skip made it onto Arcie's suspect list, but at that moment, he was alone at the top.

Although I was inclined to defend him, I had *no* inclination to start naming other suspects—accusing random strangers of murder.

But Jazz didn't hesitate. "First person *I'd* talk to is Noreen's husband—goes by Blade Wade. He's an artist."

Arcie was taking notes.

I was looking at Jazz in disbelief.

"*What?*" she asked me.

"You said he was cool, even though he looks like a tough guy. His wife has been killed—why make things worse for him?" I hesitated. "And he's Black."

"Dante." Jazz squared her shoulders and gathered her thoughts. "I appreciate where you're coming from. Honest. But trust me—I am *not* saying Blade should be hauled away and locked up because he was the only Black dude in the room. I'm saying he should be *talked* to because he told me he was fed up with Noreen. He wanted his wife to help promote his career, but she wouldn't. That's a possible *motive*. It needs to be looked at. Give me some credit."

I felt myself shrinking into my damp Top-Siders. I wanted to melt into the pavement. "Jazz," I mumbled, "I'm *really* sorry."

She gave me a curt nod—apology accepted.

Arcie said, "How about you, Dante? You were there. In light of what happened today, did you see or hear anything on Sunday that now strikes you as suspicious? Sometimes it's just a vibe."

And I recalled the vibe I'd gotten from a young woman who struck me as ambitious. She happened to be an underling to someone who had now been drowned. I said, "This is probably nothing, Detective, but I felt uneasy about Noreen's assistant— her name is Riley Uba. I got the impression she wanted her boss's job."

Arcie eagerly made note of this. "Was it something Riley said?"

"No. I couldn't hear a word of their conversation. From the look of it, there was no hint of trouble. In fact, Riley seemed cordial and professional. But I stood there thinking: She wants the top job."

Jazz asked, "Was she that gal with the tattoo?"

"The whole right arm."

Jazz nodded. "I didn't get a vibe, one way or the other. But career advancement—that's *always* a plausible motive."

Arcie said, "I'll check her out, Dante. Anyone else?"

I thought for a moment. Shrugged.

Jazz said to me, "How about Ashley?"

"*Huh?*"

Arcie asked, "Who?"

Jazz told her, "Ashley Highsmith Terry. Skip's wife."

"Hold on." Arcie chortled. "Skip is *married*? To a *woman*?"

"Not messin' with ya, Arcie. She's this mousy little snip of a thing. Always in the background, not much gumption. But I can imagine how she might be motivated to kill Noreen."

I laughed. Out loud. "You have *got* to be kidding."

Jazz raised a hand, bidding patience. "Hear me out." She turned to Arcie. "God only knows why Ashley married Skip, or vice versa, because it's clear enough what Skip is into. Maybe they had an 'arrangement' from the start. Or maybe not. But I have it on good authority"—Jazz looked at me—"on *damn* good authority that Skip likes to get down with anything in pants."

Deadpan, I told her, "Well, darn. And I thought I was special."

"Hold on," said Arcie, who seemed every bit as confused as I was. "What are you driving at, Jazz?"

"Just this: If Skip and Ashley did *not* have an 'arrangement,' an understanding, and Skip is so brazenly unfaithful, maybe Ashley got sick of feeling hurt. Maybe she snapped. Could you blame her? And maybe she decided to take revenge on hubby by setting him up as the prime suspect in a weird-as-fuck drowning case."

There it was again. Skip was the prime suspect.

Arcie looked up from her notes. "It's ... *possible*, I suppose."

While Arcie and Jazz continued to discuss this, I studied both women, who shared a similar calling. Having just met Arcie, I knew nothing of her past. I didn't know if her apparent success in climbing the ranks of the sheriff's department had been easy or hard-won, but as a minority woman, she must have faced hurdles. Surely, Jazz now saw in Arcie a model of the working professional that Jazz herself hoped to become.

She was saying to Arcie, "There was a *lot* of anger in that room on Sunday—and most of those folks, I have no idea who they were."

"I'll need to get the guest list," said Arcie. Glancing back at the house, she added, "Wonder what's keeping Skip."

Jazz laughed. "Maybe he decided to wax the floors."

"Let's find out." Arcie led us toward the house, but then paused, checking her watch.

Jazz and I also checked the time. It was three fifteen, only twelve minutes after water had been splashed from the pool. The terrace was bone-dry.

■

Indoors, the air felt icy after our conversation in the afternoon sun. While closing the drapes behind us, I called, "Hey, Skip?"

He emerged from the kitchen, wiping his hands with a towel, which he then set aside. "Get everything solved?" he asked, jolly as could be—as if the crisis of the day had been no more serious than a leaky faucet or a tripped circuit.

Ignoring his question, Arcie asked him, "Mr. Terry? Do you have a list of the guests who were here on Sunday? I need to talk to a few people."

"Sorry," said Skip, "I don't. They were my parents' guests—some of them I didn't even recognize. But my dad is *very* well organized. I'm sure he can pull that together."

"How can I reach him?"

Skip gave Arcie the information, adding, "I was just on the phone with him—told him what happened. So he probably expects to hear from you."

When Arcie looked up from her notebook, she said, "Once more, run me through your whereabouts earlier today, please."

"Well, I woke up around six, at home, of course—"

"Um," said Arcie, interrupting, "let me be more specific. You arrived here a few minutes late for your one thirty meeting, with groceries. But you had also been here earlier to open the gate, correct?"

"Yes. I dropped by on my way to a morning meeting with clients."

"What time was that?"

"About a quarter to nine. The meeting was at nine."

Arcie asked, "Did you go inside the house?"

"No, didn't need to. It was all locked up from the day before."

Jazz jumped in: "Other than *our* meeting, were you expecting anyone else at the house today—like service people?"

He shrugged. "My parents' rental period began three days ago. I have no idea when the house is serviced."

I reminded Jazz, "Sunny Junket takes care of that. Let me check the Tuesday schedule." Scrolling through my phone, I said, "The window crew gets here early, at seven, so they were gone by the time Skip opened the gate. And the pool service doesn't arrive until after four."

Arcie said, "All those guys have the gate code, right?"

"Sure."

"And the security system is monitored?"

"Of course. The owners of each property handle that, contracting with any security company they choose. But in the case of *this* house, we provide complete management services for the owner, who lives in New Zealand. The house was built twenty years ago, so the security system is pretty basic by today's standards." I gave Arcie the name of the monitoring service.

Jazz said, "No video, huh?"

I shook my head. "There's little crime in this area, and the only access to the house is through the gate, so—" I stopped myself, recalling, "The gate. You know, there *might* be a camera at the gate."

All four of us walked out the front door of the house and crossed the courtyard to take a look.

"Aha," I said. The designer of the estate apparently hadn't wanted the entrance to look like a prison guardhouse, so the camera had been hidden behind a small window in the stone pylon that held the keypad and intercom. The window faced through the gate and into the courtyard. Jazz and I stepped close to the window and waved. I noticed the faint flashing of a tiny red pilot light. I told Arcie, "It must be motion-activated. With any luck, the video might be recorded."

Arcie grinned. "Well, that's the first thing I intend to find out." We followed as she walked toward her car, an unmarked tan cruiser, telling us, "If there's recorded video, this case just got a lot simpler."

Skip said, "Good luck, Detective. Let me know if I can help."

"Count on it, Mr. Terry." She got into her car but paused before closing the door. "And I would *highly* recommend that you not leave the area for a while."

"Wouldn't think of it, Detective." Then he repeated, "Good luck."

If Skip was acting, he did a damn good job of projecting innocence and a spirit of up-front cooperation. I wanted to believe him. But Arcie and Jazz shared a quick look before Arcie closed the door, started the car, and shifted into reverse. Their lingering, stolid expressions said it all.

They didn't buy a word of it.

CHAPTER SEVEN

As I watched Arcie drive out of the courtyard, Jazz turned to Skip, saying, "With Noreen Penley Wade out of the picture, she's no longer a threat. Guess you won't be needing my services now."

"Now more than ever," he said.

Jazz glanced at me, then asked Skip, "Why's that?"

"Didn't you see that look on Detective Madera's face? I'm innocent, but I'm not stupid. She doesn't believe me."

"I'm not so sure myself."

"I noticed that, too," said Skip, "but *you're* not itching to wrap this up and hand someone over to the DA."

"I'd love to wrap it up. But no, I can't arrest you."

"What you *can* do is help find out who killed Noreen—that's the best way to satisfy Madera. I need someone working on this who's on *my* side. And you'll be well paid."

Jazz hesitated. "*If* I take you on, I'll keep an open mind. But if the investigation leads me back to you, I won't ignore the evidence. This will be a search for truth."

"I'm not afraid of the truth." Again, if he was acting, he put on a convincing show.

Jazz wanted some time to think about this, and she asked to meet with Skip again, preferably with his parents, at her office in Palm Springs. Tomorrow. Ten o'clock.

He agreed.

■

I wondered if Skip might phone me later that day to pump me for details of what was discussed between Arcie Madera and Jazz. If he did phone, I wondered how I would respond. Would I spill it all, hoping to demonstrate that I was on his side, which might be met with his gratitude and endearment? Or would I keep it professional, suggesting that he should refer his questions to Jazz? I was certain she would not appreciate my meddling behind her back.

But Skip did not phone later that afternoon. Or anytime that night.

When I awoke Wednesday morning and started the coffee, I stepped out to the patio just in time to hear the thud of a car door. Checking my watch, I concluded that Isandro had returned from his shift at the hospital. Approaching footfalls seemed to confirm this, but then I heard his voice in muffled conversation with someone else.

I retreated into my apartment, leaving the door open a few inches, and watched as Isandro walked along the far side of the pool with another man. He was taller than Isandro, and in the early half-light, he seemed older than Isandro—but younger than me. A moment later, Isandro opened the door to his apartment, and the two of them slipped inside. The door closed softly, but there was no mistaking the click of its lock.

Later, while I was dressing for the office, my phone rang. It was Jazz.

"Busy today?" she asked.

"I'm working."

"Thought you were getting your delayed 'weekend' off."

"That was yesterday. I don't always get consecutive days off—goofy schedule."

"Pisser. I was gonna ask if you want to sit in on my meeting with Skip. He reconfirmed, and his parents will be with him. They drove back from LA early—got in last night." After a pause, she asked, "Still there?"

"Uh ... yeah. Let me see what I can work out."

When I arrived at Sunny Junket, I asked Gianna, "Is Ben here?"

"In his office." She didn't bother looking up from the crossword puzzle in that morning's *Desert Sun*. "Nabob?" she said. "What the hell's a nabob?"

"Some sorta bigwig, I think. Look it up."

Gianna lifted her nose from the paper to inform me, "That's *cheating*."

"Forgive me—I must have lost my moral compass."

Her middle finger rose to adjust her glasses before she focused again on the puzzle.

I walked around the front counter, tossed a few things on my desk, and made my way back to the head office. Through the open doorway, I saw that the owner's chrome-and-glass desk was, as always, immaculate and unoccupied. At the other desk, hardworking Ben moiled at his computer amid stacks of papers and file folders that were shingled with layers of sticky-notes.

I said, "Hey there, Ben. Got a minute?"

He broke into a smile as he turned to me. "*Morning*, Dante! Sure, c'mon in."

Sitting in a chair facing his desk, I said, "Didn't think you'd be so chipper today."

He shrugged. "I'm always chipper." He frowned. "Too bad about that woman at the Ellinger House." He smiled again. "I doubt if this qualifies as news in New Zealand, so I sent an email to Ellinger. Told him it must have been an accident, but the police are looking into it. I won't mention murder till it's settled. Thought I'd break it to him kinda easy, you know."

"Sounds reasonable, Ben. But I hope you don't mind that I went there yesterday—on my day off—with Jazz Friendly. It puts me in the *middle* of things."

"I don't mind at all," said Ben. "Shows we're on top of the situation."

This, of course, was exactly how I hoped he would respond. "Then I wonder if I could spend a bit of office time with Jazz today. She's meeting with Kenneth and Claudia Terry, the renters, and their son, Skip. They want to hire Jazz to help get to the bottom of this, and she asked if I could sit in."

"And you thought you had to *ask*?" said Ben. "Go ahead— take whatever time you need to get this wrapped up."

■

Not much was happening at Sunny Junket that morning, so I didn't wait till the last minute to leave for the meeting with Jazz. Although I had never been to her office above Huggamug Coffeehouse, I knew I could walk there in ninety seconds flat. Instead, I strolled down the block at a quarter till ten.

From the street, I had never even noticed that Huggamug's building had a second floor, and now, as it came into view along Palm Canyon Drive, I saw no obvious access to the space above the storefront. Arriving at the building, I found a narrow walkway leading back along one side, so I ducked into the shadows to explore where it might lead. Toward the rear of the building, in the white stucco wall, next to a jumble of circuit-breaker panels and utility meters, was a single glass door. Taped to the inside of the glass was a makeshift sign that I recognized as a photocopy of Jazz's business card, which had been enlarged several times. The resulting lettering was just big enough to read, but its fuzziness rendered it nearly illegible.

I assumed Jazz didn't get many walk-ins.

I entered. The lobby—a charitable description at best—was a bleak little cubby of a room, dominated by a stairway. Taped to the adjacent wall was a second photocopy of the enlarged business card, to which a hand-scrawled arrow had been added, pointing up. Nestled beneath the stairs was a mop closet; I closed its trapezoidal door, hiding the clutter within. Wedged into a corner across from the stairs was an odd little elevator that looked like a recent addition to the older building, probably a concession to ADA requirements. It stood waiting with its door open. Inside, the fluorescent lighting blinked on and off in irregular spasms. I took the stairs.

At the top, another glass door, another photocopied sign. I stepped inside.

Good God. The space was clean. It was tidy, mostly. But it lacked any sense of style or planning. The room was seemingly intended as a reception area, but there was no one to greet me. The furniture was sparse, junky, and mismatched. White walls. Matted beige carpeting. A single wide window on the outside wall was hung with plastic curtains adorned with beach balls and swaying palms. These "drapes" might have been a funky nod to the Palm Springs mid-mod vibe, but in truth, I suspected, they were someone's leftover shower curtains. Telltale calcium stains near the bottom confirmed my theory. At least the air conditioner was working.

"What's wrong?" said Jazz, appearing in the doorway to a back office.

"I'm ... speechless," I said honestly.

She laughed. "I know, I know—the place needs a little work."

"A *little*?"

She tossed her hands. "You're gay. *You're* the one with the decorating gene."

"Well," I admitted, "I've often been said to have a certain ... sensitivity."

"Mm-hmm. So if you want to help with a do-over, go ahead, strut your stuff. Make it artsy-fartsy."

I was surprised she suggested it—an admission that I had at least *some* minor competence that she did not. "Sure," I said, "I can probably help. What sort of budget are you looking at?"

"*Budget?*" she asked, as if I were nuts. "I'm lucky when I meet the rent."

This would be a challenge.

She took me into the conference room. "I thought we could talk to the Terrys in here."

I cringed. Kenneth and Claudia Terry had just driven their Maybach to their multimillion-dollar rental house and would soon arrive to discuss a pricey protection strategy for their pampered preppy son—known to them as Skipper—in a dingy, windowless room furnished with a folding banquet table and vinyl-strapped aluminum lawn chairs. In the far corner of the room, a dusty fiddle-leaf fig tree, brittle and brown, sagged in its plastic pot.

"Works for me," I said agreeably. There was nothing I could do to improve the accommodations in time for the Terrys' arrival, and my only other option was to leave—but I didn't want to abandon Skip. What's more, I now realized, Jazz had asked me to attend this meeting because (she would never admit it) she needed some moral support. Unless I was mistaken, this opportunity with the Terrys was the first big break she might land for her new enterprise, and despite our initial encounters, which had been nothing short of rancid, I didn't want to leave her in the lurch.

She was organizing several packets of folders around the table—her proposal, I assumed. I asked, "Jazz?"

"Yeah, what?" She retrieved a six-pack of bottled water from the mini fridge on the floor and set five of the bottles next to the packets on the table.

"Yesterday with Detective Madera—you referred to me as your 'associate.' That surprised me."

Jazz pulled out a chair and sat; so did I. She said, "Sorry about that."

"Don't be. I was sort of ... flattered, I guess."

"Thank you." She hemmed. "I was talkin' fast, talkin' big. You know, puffin' myself up for Arcie. But today? Any halfwit can see you don't work for me."

I gave her a curious look.

She said, "You wouldn't be wearing that sorry-ass clown shirt."

"Yoo-*hoo*-oo," warbled Claudia Terry from the front room. "Anyone home?"

"Sweet fuckin' Jesus," said Jazz. "They're here."

∎

Skip's parents were surprisingly effervescent that morning. They had been called back from LA because their son was implicated in a suspicious death, so I was prepared for grim faces and somber conversation. But no. Standing there in the reception room, they acted as if this emergency meeting with a private eye was *quite* the adventure, a merry diversion from their humdrum world of finance and philanthropy. Claudia was downright giddy.

"So *this* is where it happens," she said. "*This* is where you ferret out the vermin of the underworld." Claudia took a deep, noisy breath, as if savoring the seediness.

With a halfhearted smile, Jazz told her, "I do my best." Turning to Kenneth, she said, "Sorry this place is such a shambles, Mr. Terry. Still trying to get organized."

"*Nonsense*, Jazz. We weren't expecting anything fancy. You're just getting started—nothing wrong with big dreams."

With a demureness not natural to her, Jazz said, "This way, then." And she led them toward the conference room.

Skip lagged a few steps behind, giving my shoulder a hug. "Glad you're here."

"Likewise," I said, sounding stupid.

He looked me up and down, then grinned. I was wearing the black Top-Siders. His were oxblood.

As everyone settled around the table, Jazz asked, "Would anyone like coffee?"

I offered, "I can run downstairs—anything you'd like."

"No, no," Kenneth assured us. "Water's fine." He felt the bottle. "Nice and cold."

Jazz said, "Good of you to drive out from LA on such short notice."

"Well, we *had* to," said Claudia. "Detective Madera seemed confused—as if she thought *Skip* might be involved with this. Which is nonsense, of course."

"Of course," I echoed.

Jazz shot me a sidelong glance.

Kenneth said, "Madera called us late yesterday, then again this morning. She said the medical examiner was able to estimate the time of Noreen's death."

"Oh?" I said.

Jazz nodded. "I talked to Arcie, too. Noreen died between noon and one o'clock yesterday. And she did in fact drown—water in her lungs. The toxicology report will take a while, but nothing suspicious turned up in her stomach contents. So we're back to the theory we discussed at the scene. Noreen was probably taken by surprise, pushed into the pool, then held under. Simple and effective. But god-awful."

"Who would *do* such a thing?" asked Claudia, at last reacting to the gravity of the situation.

Jazz said, "That's what we need to find out, ma'am."

Kenneth said, "We *know* that our Skipper didn't do it. But Madera made me nervous."

Jazz explained, "Your faith in your son is commendable, Mr. Terry, but Detective Madera has to take a more objective approach—I do, too, for that matter. Due to the circumstances of how and when everything played out yesterday, Skip's possible involvement needs to be investigated. Assuming your son is innocent, assuming he has nothing to hide or to lie about, you should have no worries. But you should be prepared."

"That's why we're here," said Kenneth.

"Got it," said Jazz. "But you should take the additional step of securing legal counsel for Skip. Whether he'll ultimately need representation or not, who knows? But it's a good investment, even if wasted."

Kenneth assured Jazz, "It's not a matter of the *money*. It's the appearance. Getting a lawyer involved could make the Skipper look guilty."

I jumped in: "Do it anyway, Mr. Terry. For your son's sake."

Mr. and Mrs. Terry looked at each other for a moment. Then they both nodded. He told all of us, "All right. I'll put Walt Gifford on it. We have him on retainer for Terraquist. Best in the business."

I doubted if the Terrys' corporate attorney was the best fit for Skip's needs. Still, Walt Gifford was better than nothing, and he might be able to refer Skip to a top-notch criminal lawyer— although I wanted to believe it would never come to that.

Jazz said, "Sounds good, Mr. Terry. I'll leave you to handle that. Meanwhile, I'd like to discuss some of the people who were at your pool party on Sunday. Detective Madera told me you sent her the guest list."

Kenneth reached into the breast pocket of his navy silk blazer. The outer patch pocket was embroidered with a nautical-themed insignia. "I brought a copy for you."

"Thanks," said Jazz, "but Arcie already sent me the list. You'll find it inside your folders, right on top."

Along with everyone else, I opened my folder.

Jazz said, "If I'm counting correctly—singles and couples and a few guests of their own—there were about three dozen people at the rental house last weekend."

Kenneth nodded. "Sounds about right."

Claudia added, "Including the five of *us*, of course."

Jazz and I nodded. She said, "I'd like to run through the list, focusing on several people in particular, plus anyone else who *you* feel might've wanted Noreen dead." After an awkward, silent lull, Jazz added, "Sorry if that sounded too blunt—but that's why we're here."

"Of *course*," said Claudia, sounding thrilled again—and more than ready to help ferret out vermin of the underworld.

Jazz led the discussion. Most of the names we considered were unknown to me, and they were eventually dismissed by both Kenneth and Claudia as having no strong motive to harm— let alone kill—Noreen Penley Wade. "That said," Kenneth added, "Noreen could be *such* a pain in the ass. I suppose any damn one of them might've simply had enough of her."

Jazz looked up from her notes. "How about Blade Wade? The victim's husband."

Kenneth and Claudia turned to each other and shrugged. "We've met Blade," said Kenneth, "but can't say we really know him. He had no involvement with the museum that I'm aware of. Were they having problems?"

"Not sure," said Jazz. But she knew, as I did, that Blade's lack of involvement with the museum, led by Noreen, had been at the root of some deep professional resentment.

Jazz then asked Kenneth about the various staff members of M3A who had attended the pool party: Riley Uba, Noreen's ambitious assistant; Cameron Vicario, the bookish museum curator, thought to be gay; and Howard Quince, the panicky CFO who, alarmed by the museum's finances, snapped at his tweedy, soft-spoken wife, Hannah, when she tried to calm him down.

Kenneth and Claudia considered these staffers one by one, concluding that each might have been dealing with personal issues, as well as on-the-job conflicts with Noreen, but none of them seemed to have sufficient motive—or temperament—for murder.

Jazz skimmed over her list, top to bottom. "The young woman who came in from the pool and left with her parents—it's not clear to me who that was."

With a soft laugh, Claudia explained, "That *charming* young lady was Cherisse Landon, just graduated from college. Her mother is Fauvé Landon—a tad flashy for my taste—but she uses it to sell *heaps* of real estate here in the valley. Her husband, Jim, is a longtime friend of Kenneth's, so we asked them to the party. Jim's a banker in LA, but their main house is out here."

Kenneth added, "Jim Landon has some occasional dealings with the museum—that's what keeps us in touch—but he didn't *work* for Noreen. If he had a problem with her, he'd just tell her off, and that would be the end of it. Levelheaded as they come."

I agreed: "He was one of the few voices of reason at the party."

Glancing over the list, I leaned close to Jazz and tapped one of the names, Ashley Highsmith Terry, Skip's wife. The day before, while meeting with Detective Madera, Jazz had voiced her suspicions of Ashley. Now, though, she gave me a subtle shake of her head.

My eye landed on another name. I said to Skip's parents, "Rex Khalaji—how cool that you know him. And he even brought his camera on Sunday."

Although this meeting had been called for Skip's benefit, it had by now dragged on for nearly an hour, and Skip had barely commented as we sifted through the thirty-odd names on the list. But at the mention of Khalaji, Skip spoke up.

"Rex," he said wistfully, "what a gentleman, as well as a talent. Mom and Dad have been close to him forever. He's been in my life since I was born."

Claudia picked up her son's story. "Rex and Irene never had children, but they tried. So Skip took on the role of a foster nephew—a win-win for everyone."

I asked, "Rex Khalaji was married?" It had never even crossed my mind he might be straight.

Claudia nodded. "Ten years. Then Irene died, too young. She was never very healthy, poor thing—which is why she wasn't able to conceive. When cancer came, she just gave up."

Jazz said, "How awful. I'm so sorry."

"And Rex," I said, "had no connection at all to Noreen Penley Wade. Correct?"

Kenneth answered, "Correct. We invited him on Sunday because he's a dear old friend—and because he adds considerable cachet to *any* party."

"I'm sure." I nodded. "Tell me, Mr. Terry: You're on the M3A board, so you must've worked with Noreen as closely as anyone. How do *you* feel about her death?"

He blew a long, low whistle. "Well, Dante, let's just say that I was damned annoyed with her—and I won't miss her—but no one should die like that." Kenneth turned to Jazz. He winked. "And just for the record, I was in LA when it happened. Hope you'll make a note of that."

I asked, "Now that you're here again, will you be staying long?"

Kenneth turned to Claudia. "We need to get back pretty quick, don't we?"

She nodded. "We're *booked* this weekend. The Jensens. The heart-clinic ball."

"Already?" He laughed. "It can't be a whole year."

"It is," she assured him.

I said, "I'm a little confused about something … but it's none of my business."

Kenneth shrugged. "Ask anything you want, Dante."

"Well, the Ellinger House. That's one of Sunny Junket's top-tier properties. Estates like that are rarely rented for more than a few days, and you took it for a full month. Trust me, we're delighted to have you. But it's *expensive*—and you don't seem to be there very much."

Claudia tittered. "Oh, *that*. That's easily explained. The rental house was Skipper's idea. He thought we might like to have it available so we could get away from the city now and then. June can be rather unpleasant."

Kenneth leaned in his chair to tell me in a stage whisper, "The Skipper has marvelous taste."

.

Our meeting was ready to break up, except for one important bit of business. Jazz said, "If you'll turn to the back of your folders, you'll find a detailed proposal of investigative services I can provide for you, along with standard fees and a payment schedule. If this is agreeable, Mr. and Mrs. Terry, I'll get to work on behalf of your son."

I looked over the document, several pages long, which confirmed that this job would indeed be Jazz Friendly's big break—if accepted. She wasn't bashful with her fees. And Kenneth Terry didn't blink.

"This is fine," he said. "May I borrow your pen?"

As Jazz handed him the pen, he gave her a credit card.

When the dotted lines were taken care of, we all got up from the table. Skip gave his father a hug. "Thanks, Dad."

Kenneth Sr. said to Kenneth Jr., "Don't worry about a thing, Skipper. We'll get this cleaned up in no time."

As we strolled out to the reception room, Skip told his parents, "I'm going to run ahead and cool down the car. I'll pull it around and meet you in front."

"Skipper, sweetie," said his mother, "we're not *that* old. We can walk a block. Don't bother."

"But I want to," he said with that drop-dead smile. And out the door he went.

I didn't have much experience observing the inner dynamics of wealthy families. I would have guessed they were often messed up, as if that was the psychological price they had to pay for their material comforts. But I found Skip's relationship with his parents enviable. I hadn't enjoyed that sort of easy, natural affection at home. Sure, Mom was great, and I still remembered her as a friend. But Dad—not so much.

Mrs. Terry said to Jazz, "If you have things to do, dear, Kenneth and I can wait downstairs."

"Nonsense," said Jazz. "I want you to feel right at home here."

I eyed the stained shower curtains framing the street window.

Jazz continued, "And in fact, there's something I wanted to ask you about. It's sort of sensitive."

Kenneth said, "We're family now, Jazz. We're in this together. What's on your mind?"

Jazz said, "Ashley."

A trace of concern wrinkled Claudia's brow as she asked, "Skipper's wife?"

"Yeah. To be honest, I'm not real sure what to make of that marriage."

Whoa, I thought. I would never have gone there—with Skip's *parents*?

Kenneth and Claudia seemed no less surprised, but not the least offended. Kenneth chuckled. "Truth is, Jazz, we've always wondered about that ourselves. Even while Skipper was growing up, we just assumed he was gay. Hell, *we* didn't care. We've always hobnobbed with the arts crowd and have plenty of gay friends."

Claudia added, "We felt that having a gay son was rather with-it."

"So," said Kenneth, "when the Skipper brought Ashley home from college one Christmas and introduced her as his fiancée, we were nothing short of gobsmacked."

I thought aloud, "So it wasn't just me ..."

"No," Claudia assured me, "it was not."

Kenneth shrugged. "But who were *we* to question it? It was Skipper's choice. Ashley's, too. Fifteen years later, they're still together. Whatever they've got going, it seems to work for them."

Jazz said, "I had a short conversation with Ashley on Sunday. Thought I might follow up with her. She and Skip do live together, I assume."

"Yes," said Claudia. "They have a place at Wasi'chu Hills." It was one of the oldest, toniest clubs in Rancho Mirage. Claudia gave Jazz the address and phone number.

I heard the throaty, melodious sound of a car horn—it was no Karmann Ghia—out on the street, so I glanced out the front window and saw the Maybach idling at the curb. "Skip's waiting with the car," I told the Terrys.

After a flurry of farewells and handshakes and then hugs, they headed out the door and down the stairs.

Jazz turned to me. "I want you to set up a time to have a talk with Skip's wife."

"Me?"

"Don't worry—you'll be paid."

"Nice. But why *me*? Wouldn't you rather talk to her yourself?"

"I *already* talked to her. And now I'm wondering if she had a motive to frame her bed-hopping husband for murder."

I rolled my eyes. "We've been through this. She's not the type."

"Maybe. But it's my investigation, and I want Ashley investigated—by an *obviously* gay man."

"Thanks."

"It might be just enough of a reminder that she's got a *big* problem in her life. Your very presence might tick her off. If we're lucky, she could really lose it and prove that she *is* the type to take matters into her own hands."

"Okay," I said, "I'll give it a whirl."

"Who knows?" Jazz smiled. "Maybe she's already figured out that you're banging her husband."

■

It was now well after eleven, and I thought I should get back to Sunny Junket. Before leaving Jazz's office, I ducked into the conference room and returned to the reception area with the dead fiddle-leaf fig. "I'll dump this in the alley."

"Be my guest."

I set the plant on the floor. "Do you happen to have a tape measure?"

"Nope."

After snapping a few photos of the window and its shower curtains, I grabbed a sheet of letter-size paper from the desk and set about measuring—in eleven-inch increments—the size of the window and its placement on the wall. While I was making note of these dimensions, Jazz pulled her phone from her jacket and answered a call.

"Hey there, Arcie."

I set aside what I was doing as Jazz put the call on speaker.

Detective Madera was saying, "… and I found out from the monitoring service that the gate camera does send video snippets to them every time someone drives into or out of the courtyard."

Jazz asked, "And the video is recorded?"

"You bet. So they sent me the clips of yesterday's activity—from the earliest, when the window cleaners arrived shortly before seven, until I arrived on the scene at ten minutes till two."

Jazz asked, "Can I get a look at this?"

"Yes. Soon as I get off the phone, I'll email you a secure link with a passcode. After you've watched the video, call me back."

"Got it." Pocketing her phone, Jazz told me, "Let's go to my computer."

I followed her into her office, which I had not yet seen (it needed work, too, but at least it had a window). A good-size laptop sat open on the desk.

Jazz had a big leatherette office chair with casters. As she sat in it and rolled closer to the desk, she said, "Pull up a seat." My only option was to grab one of the folding lawn chairs from the conference room across the hall. Returning with it, I planted it next to her. Just as I sat, her laptop sounded the *ping* of an arriving email.

"That's it," said Jazz. She opened it, clicked the link, and entered the passcode. Together we began watching the series of time-stamped video clips. The grainy black-and-white images, shot from the stone pylon outside the gate of the Ellinger House, looked into the courtyard, framed to capture most of the parking area and merely a sliver of the house itself. None of the clips lasted longer than thirty seconds—about the time it took to activate the gate and drive through.

We leaned near the laptop to view this sequence of recordings:

At two minutes before seven the prior morning, the window-cleaning crew contracted by Sunny Junket arrived at the house and parked in the courtyard. Two men and a woman got out of the van and began unloading their supplies as the clip ended.

At eight fifteen, with their job complete, the window crew backed up the van, turned around, opened the gate, and left. The gate closed behind them.

At a quarter till nine, Skip Terry arrived to open the gate. He drove his Karmann Ghia into the courtyard, turned around, and left with the gate open—exactly as he had reported to us.

Then it got interesting. Shortly after eleven thirty, a pool-service truck pulled into the courtyard and parked near the entryway to the house. I said to Jazz, "That pickup, that's not our pool service. And our guy wasn't due until four." We watched as the driver got out of the truck.

He was not young. He wore shorts, a muscle shirt, and a pith helmet, looking a lot like hundreds of other laid-back pool guys who serviced the resort cities of the valley. Unlike the others, though, this one had lost his right leg below the knee and walked reliably, but carefully, with a prosthetic limb attached at the joint. The prosthetic was the sort that made no aesthetic pretense of being a natural leg; rather, it had the machined, techy look of bionic hardware. And the guy's right arm was covered with a full-sleeve tattoo, wrist to shoulder—which instantly reminded me of Riley Uba from M3A. The fuzzy video made it impossible to see the tattoo clearly, but I doubted if it consisted of the cutesy Japanese manga characters that adorned Riley's arm. The video clip ended as the pool guy carried a long-handled skimmer toward the side of the house, where a walkway led to the rear terrace.

In the next clip, at precisely twelve noon, a Lexus sedan pulled into the courtyard and parked near the house, not far from the pool truck, which hadn't moved. Noreen Penley Wade stepped out of her car, looked around for a moment, and walked up to the front door of the house as the clip ended.

At twelve twenty, the Lexus was still there as the pool guy backed up the pickup, turned it around, and drove out of the courtyard, leaving the gate open, just as he'd found it. As the clip ended, I said to Jazz, "I've never seen routine pool maintenance take more than ten minutes. That guy was at the house for nearly an hour."

A minute or two before one thirty, Jazz drove her SUV through the open gate and into the courtyard, parking not far from the Lexus. She and I got out of the vehicle and walked to the front door as the clip ended.

At one forty, Skip arrived in his Karmann Ghia, a few minutes late for our meeting.

At one fifty, Detective Madera, the first responder to the murder scene, sped into the courtyard in her unmarked cruiser with its hidden strobes flashing wildly. I could recall a siren as well, but the series of videos, which then ended, had no sound.

Jazz sat back and called Madera, telling her, "Arcie, I've got you on speakerphone. Dante O'Donnell is here with me. We just watched the video."

The detective's tinny voice crackled through the cell phone: "What do you think?"

Jazz said, "The guy with the pickup—Dante tells me that's not their pool service."

Madera laughed. "Didn't think so. That truck was reported stolen around noon yesterday. A few hours later it was found abandoned within a mile of the house. The sequence of the clips leaves little doubt: the victim was almost certainly drowned by the driver of the truck."

I spoke up. "In other words, all the possible suspects we've considered so far—they're off the hook." I felt relieved for Skip. As for Ashley Highsmith Terry, Blade Wade, and Riley Uba? Good for them as well.

"Not so fast," said Madera. "I've shown the video to the DA, and we've compared notes. Peter Nadig agrees with me that the drowning of Noreen Penley Wade has all the earmarks of a professional hit."

"Exactly," I said. "The hit man did it, right? Case closed?"

Jazz looked at me as if I were dense and answered my question with a simple question of her own: "Who hired the hit man?"

"Oh."

CHAPTER EIGHT

Back at my own office, things were quiet. Ben had driven down valley to meet with the owners of a property they wanted us to represent. Gianna was itching to go to lunch, so I relieved her and answered phone calls—there weren't many—from my desk. The four other desks in the room would all be busily occupied when temperatures cooled down in October, but on that sleepy Wednesday afternoon in June, I had the whole place to myself.

That morning's meeting with Skip and his parents had left me with mixed emotions, and I kept tussling with my attraction to him, which was intense but also superficial. Our romp on Monday seemed to confirm that the attraction was mutual, in spite of the fifteen years that separated us—an ego boost that only heightened my interest in Skip. But, really? I'd have to be nuts to think he had potential as The One, the achingly beautiful man who might be different, the whole-person guy who saw in me the answer to his gnawing need for a lover and soul mate. Forever.

There were, of course, some big obstacles to this fantasy. For starters, he was the product of wealth and privilege, while I was not (not even close). He was married (to a woman). He had a reputation for being promiscuous (with men at sea). Plus—even though I was unwilling to consider it seriously—he happened to be an active suspect in a murder investigation. How's *that* for a conversation starter? Years down the road, we might laugh about it, doling out delicious gossip at cocktail parties: Have you *heard* how we met?

And perhaps the most ironic twist of all was that I had now agreed to some subterfuge with Skip's wife, with the purpose of baiting her about Skip's infidelities.

Jazz had given me one of her business cards; jotted on the back were the address and phone number of Ashley Highsmith Terry. I turned the card in my fingers.

Sitting at my desk, I switched the office lines over to voicemail and called Ashley's number from my cell phone. She answered on the second ring.

I said, "Sorry to bother you, but I'm calling for Mrs. Kenneth Terry Jr."

"Speaking."

"Mrs. Terry, this is Dante O'Donnell with Sunny Junket Vacation Rentals. Your husband arranged for his parents to rent one of our properties in Rancho Mirage."

"Yes, of course." With a wry laugh, she added, "Unless I'm mistaken, you showed up at the pool party on Sunday."

"Guilty—that was me—along with our security guard, Jazz Friendly."

"I remember her, too. We had a chance to talk."

"Right," I said, "Jazz told me about that. Now, I assume you're aware of what happened at the house yesterday—to Noreen Penley Wade."

"Well, yes. It's awful. And Skip says he thinks he's a *suspect*." Ashley giggled. "Can you imagine? I told him he was being overly dramatic. He's good at that."

"I'll bet he is. But you see, Mrs. Terry—"

She interrupted: "Ashley's fine."

"Thank you, Ashley. Thing is, Skip's parents are concerned about the direction of the investigation—it's shaping up as a murder case—and they've retained Jazz Friendly to conduct a private investigation of her own, in Skip's interest."

Ashley paused before saying quietly, "Oh, my."

"Jazz wants to begin by collecting interviews of everyone who was at the party. I do a bit of side work for her, and, well, you ended up on my list. Is there a convenient time for us to meet?"

"Um, just checking my calendar, Dante. Tomorrow's no good at all. Friday's open. Where did you have in mind?"

"I'm in Palm Springs, but I can come to Rancho Mirage—I believe you live there."

"Tell you what. I have a dinner meeting in Palm Springs on Friday—board work—but it always wraps up by eight thirty. If that's not too late, I could meet you afterward."

"Sure." I suggested Huggamug Coffeehouse and gave her directions as well as my cell number.

"Got it," she said. "See you Friday night."

When we hung up, I had to close my eyes and sit quietly for a moment. My pulse was racing. I could feel it pounding in my neck, making me light-headed.

What had I done? She seemed nice enough. Sweet, even. I'd already participated in her husband's disregard for their marriage, and now I had set her up for a sham interview, the sole purpose of which was to determine if suspicion of murder could be lifted from her husband—by shifting it to her.

I hadn't asked Jazz what she planned to pay me for these services, but the amount didn't matter. I'd sold a part of myself in a transaction that didn't make me proud.

■

Later that afternoon, Ben was still away from the office, but Gianna had returned, freeing me from any phone duties, so I was idle at my desk, staring at my computer screen. Resigned to my commitment to meet with Ashley, I began drafting notes and questions for the interview. After filling a couple of pages, I sat back to read them, making a few edits. Devious, I thought—but not bad for an amateur. I was getting into it.

Spotting Jazz's card on the desk, I added a note to the back regarding Friday's meeting time with Ashley. Then I flipped to the front side.

It reminded me of the crappy blowups that Jazz had made, which served as her office's signage to the world. As a firm believer that to criticize is to volunteer, I was sure I could do better and decided to give it a try. After setting up a horizontal letter-size format on the computer, I went to work copying the information from the card, and within a few minutes I had composed three replacement signs—for the lobby door, the stairwell, and the office entrance. I printed them on heavy buff-colored paper and ran them through the laminator we had at Sunny Junket. It was a quick job, but the results were a vast improvement over the originals.

■

Thursday, I looked forward to running the signs over to Jazz during my lunch break, but the day turned busy.

The entire morning and most of the afternoon had me driving back and forth around the valley, and it was nearly four o'clock when I returned to Sunny Junket's office. As I walked through the door, Gianna made a show of checking her watch. "Glad you could make it."

"And a pleasant good-afternoon to you as well."

"Find any bodies today? Or did a naughty pool boy need spanking?"

Without comment, I removed my sunglasses and walked back to my desk. When I switched on my computer, I spotted an email from Jazz, which was unusual, as she seemed to prefer phoning. Opening it, I found that she had sent me an enlarged screen grab from the video of the presumed hit man who had drowned Noreen—a naughty pool boy, indeed. Jazz wrote, "Arcie says this was digitally enhanced. Still looks like crap. Call me."

When she answered my call, she said, "Where were *you* all day?"

"Working."

"Banging another client?" She broke into a belly laugh.

"Now, don't *you* start. I've been taking care of business. And you?"

"Same. Managed to run down five or six of the folks who were at the pool party—basic phone interviews. They were all cooperative, happy to help, but nobody knew a damn thing. So I'll just keep working my way through the list."

I told Jazz, "I called Skip's wife."

"And?"

"I'm meeting her tomorrow night."

"Now, *that*," said Jazz, "should be interesting."

■

Around six, I finished up at my desk and drove home to my apartment. It would be nearly three hours till dark, but at that end of town, the sun had already slipped behind the wall of the San Jacinto Mountains, which defined the western edge of the city. Although the sky was still bright as day, my entire neighborhood now lolled in the cooling blue shadow of massive granite peaks.

Mitzi the rat terrier yapped as I stepped from the street and through the gate to the terrace surrounding the pool. It seemed no one ever used the pool, but during a balmy evening following a hot day, various tenants of the six apartments often relaxed on their patio chairs before or after supper.

"Hello, Mrs. Templeton," I said. She greeted me in return as Mitzi raced to circle and sniff my ankles. The dog then darted back to Mrs. Templeton and hopped up to her lap, panting.

Some of the front doors were open, but I noticed that Isandro's, on the far side of the pool, was closed. I wasn't sure what time his hospital shift began. For that matter, I didn't even know if he was working that night. His schedule, like mine, varied from week to week.

Two doors down from my apartment, Zola Lorinsky lounged on the tastefully upholstered cushions of a wrought-iron settee. She was reading a leftover section of that morning's paper while nursing a tall cocktail in a frosted chimney glass garnished with a cherry—it looked like a Tom Collins. As I approached, she let the newspaper droop, raising a hand to twiddle her fingers at me.

I smiled. "How have you been, Zola?" I had been thinking about her.

"Splendid, thank you, Dante." She patted the empty portion of the cushion, and I sat next to her.

An older woman, well into her seventies, maybe eighty, Zola was feistier than most at forty. She was now retired from a long career as an in-demand society decorator, though she "kept up her chops," as she phrased it, by continuing to dabble with a few of her best clients. She exuded style and flair, even in the reduced circumstances of our little apartment complex, where she reigned as something of a grandaunt to all the other tenants. That evening, she wore a gauzy silk kaftan over palazzo pants with wispy little gold-strapped sandals, barely there, showing off a fresh pedicure—her ruby-red toenails matched her fingernails.

She reminded me, "If I were thirty years younger, you'd be in trouble."

I reminded her, "And I'd be highly flattered, but you wouldn't get to first base."

She let out a loud croak of a laugh. "Just watch me try." I recalled that she had already buried two husbands. Or was it three? She wore a cluster of diamond rings on a single finger—like a kebab of her past conquests.

I wondered: Those husbands of yesteryear, had they been gay socialites, looking for cover with a brash and soignée woman, an armpiece of distinction, but fooling no one? Had they sought the approbation of the refined upper crust while getting down with the rough and ready? Had they been men like Skip Terry?

Zola put her hand on my arm and leaned close enough to kiss me, asking with a purr, "Have you heard?" She twitched her brows. "About our neighbor?"

She was not only the honorary grandaunt of our complex. Because she was retired, home all day, and plenty nosy, she was also our most trusted source of gossip. I asked, "Which neighbor?"

Her eyes slid in the direction of the closed door on the other side of the pool. "Isandro."

"No," I said, alarmed. "What about him?"

With a shushing sound, she assured me, "Nothing's wrong. In fact, it's quite lovely. There seems to be a *man* in his life."

"Oh?" I'd seen him bring a guy home the day before—a trick's a trick—but was there more to this?

Zola continued, "He's a bit older than Isandro. *Very* nice-looking, in a Latin sort of way. Isandro dragged him home yesterday at dawn, locked him in, and they've barely come up for *air.* He's still here—except not right now. They must've run out of food. Seems they only step out for meals."

I didn't say anything. I wasn't even sure what to think.

Zola reached for her cocktail and drank. Then she rattled the ice. "Want one?"

"Tom Collins?"

She nodded. "You have the eye of a true professional."

Having tended bar, I didn't drink much anymore, but it did look refreshing. "Sure," I said.

"Then mix it yourself, dah-ling. I left everything out." She wagged a hand toward her open front door.

I stood. "Can I get you another?"

"I *shouldn't*." She handed me the glass. "Why else would I leave everything out?"

I stepped inside and moved to the kitchen. The layout of her apartment was similar to mine, but bigger, with two bedrooms. It was also *far* better appointed, with furnishings and fabrics and art that might be described as Hollywood Regency—too consciously lavish for my tastes. As an expression of Zola's personal style, though, the decorating was spot-on.

I had been inside the apartment once before and now paused, while mixing the drinks, to glance into the second bedroom, confirming that it was still set up as a decorator's workroom—with a sewing machine.

When I returned to the patio and delivered Zola's drink, she reached to clink the glass to mine, saying, "Cheers, love." We drank.

Then I sat next to her again and turned to face her. "May I pick your brain for some advice, Zola?"

"Advice for the lovelorn?"

"No." I grinned. "Decorating advice."

With a broad smile, she asked, "What's on your mind?"

I told her about Jazz Friendly. I told her that I was doing some side work in Jazz's new private-eye service. I told her about the office. And *then*: I took out my phone and showed her a picture of the window with the shower curtains.

Zola's eyes bugged. She gasped as she flopped a hand to her breast, choking for air. "I'm … I'm dumbstruck."

"Trust me," I said, "pictures don't do it justice—it's beyond horrid."

Catching her breath, Zola took the phone from me and zoomed the photo for a closer look at the top of the window. "The hardware is decent—simple exposed iron rod and rings. The *problem* is those hideous curtains."

"Exactly."

"How's the room itself—good bones?"

"It's fine—nice proportions, off-white walls, beige carpet. But the window is the focal point. It could be wonderful, but right now, it's a mess."

She asked, "Did you measure?" I could practically hear the gears turning.

"Of course. Can I email everything to you?"

She gave me her address.

"Look, Zola," I said, "this is a terrible imposition. I respect your talents and would hate to take advantage of our friendship. Any help you can offer, I expect to pay for it. Just keep in mind, I don't have much, and—"

She touched her index finger to my lips. "Let me give this some thought. And yes," she said wryly, "you'll pay for it."

I gulped.

■

Friday morning, I slept later than usual, having sat up with Zola, drinking till dark. She had fussed with snacks while I mixed each round of refills, but I had no semblance of a meal that night. After I stumbled home to bed, the liquor knocked me out.

When I finally woke up to Mitzi's yapping, it was after seven, and I rushed to get ready for work. No problem. But I had missed the hour of Isandro's usual return from his hospital shift, which left me wondering what I might have seen. Was the new boyfriend still in the picture? What did he do while Isandro was working? For that matter, just who *was* the guy? If he was crashing at the apartment, he probably wasn't a local. Where was he from?

By evening, after work, these questions were the furthest thing from my mind as I prepared to meet Ashley Highsmith Terry for our interview at Huggamug. Around a quarter after eight, I left my apartment and drove downtown.

In the dimming twilight, I walked from the car to the coffeehouse. I had thought to bring a notepad and pen, which struck me as a more congenial option than typing on my phone during our conversation. When I stepped inside to scout out a good table, the place was quiet—a long lull until later, when the bar crowd would start piling in to sober up before driving home.

I ordered green tea, iced, then took it to a corner table near the window. While jotting a few notes, I glanced outside to see the streetlights go on just as Ashley opened the door and stepped inside. She spotted me at once, and I stood as she approached the table with a smile.

"Seems we're both early," she said.

"Better early than late. Thanks for coming, Ashley. What can I get you?"

Noting my green tea, she said, "That'll be great."

I signaled to the barista that we needed another. When Ashley and I were seated, I said, "Please, take this one. Haven't touched it yet."

She grinned—"Thank you"—as I slid the plastic go-cup to her side of the table.

Sitting there, taking her first sip, she struck me as not "mousy" at all. In her pictures and at the pool party, she had appeared furtive and nervous, but not tonight. As expected, she was beautifully dressed, having worn a smart silk suit, dusty lavender, probably couture, for her board dinner. As far as I knew, she didn't have a job, but she fit the image of a hardworking club woman—intelligent and poised—dedicated to giving back to a world that had been very good to her. And she was pretty. Though I was inclined to think otherwise, I had to admit that she made an attractive match for Skip Terry.

"Dante," she said, "you certainly know how to pique a person's interest. Since your call on Wednesday, I've thought of little else. This investigation you're involved with—what's going *on*?"

Hoping to get us on the same footing, I asked in return, "Have you discussed this with Skip?"

She shrugged. "Some. Skip seems to keep a lot to himself."

I'll just bet he does, I thought.

Ashley added, "But after what happened yesterday, we *had* to discuss it. A sheriff's detective, a woman, came to the house."

"Arcie Madera?" I asked. "She came to your place at Wasi'chu Hills?"

"Yes—Madera—that was the name. She had a warrant. She and another officer took Skip's phone and laptop, and then they went to his travel office and took the computer. Skip had a fit, of course. They said he'd get everything back—*after* they copied everything inside. Can you imagine?"

I could well imagine that Skip had a fit. Whether he'd been involved in Noreen's drowning or not, his devices surely contained plenty that was not intended for sharing.

The barista brought over the other serving of green tea. When she left, I asked Ashley, "Did Madera—or Skip—tell you what they were looking for?"

"Madera didn't explain a thing. But Skip told me they were trying to prove *he'd* killed Noreen. That's just *nuts*."

"It is," I agreed. "I'm certain Skip didn't kill Noreen." I was clueless, however, regarding the identity of whoever had paid the hit man—a wrinkle I was not inclined to share with Ashley.

Instead, I spent some thirty minutes with her, weeding through queries relating to the supposed purpose of our meeting—gathering her recollections of the pool party, asking her about the background of various guests who were unknown to me, urging her to share any theories she might have about the drowning. As I expected, none of this produced useful insights.

Ashley leaned forward to tell me, "I'm worried sick about Skip. He's always said there were rumors that Noreen had crime connections."

"Even if that's true," I said, "Noreen is no longer a threat to Skip. She's gone." Outside the front window, the night sky had blackened. The traffic on Palm Canyon Drive had vanished, as if transported to some other astral plane—if only for the interval between stoplights.

Ashley said, "But rumors can work both ways. If *Skip* is now the subject of rumors—that he killed Noreen—some 'bad actors' may be out for blood."

My God. Ashley was right about that. A rush of headlights from a fresh wave of traffic streaked the window.

With the slightest sigh, she added, "It seems Skip has always attracted rumors. I can't *count* how many friends have had the gall to ask me why I married him."

I'd been wondering how to nudge Ashley toward the intended topic of our conversation, and she had now opened that door for me. "Talk about nervy," I said. "I hope you've developed a snappy comeback for those so-called friends."

She gave me a weary look. "If they're wondering if it's a marriage of convenience, I can't answer for Skip. But for me, the answer is simple: no, it's not a sham. He's my husband, and I love him."

I nodded. Fair enough.

"We met at Cornell." She smiled at the memory.

"What did you study?"

"Philosophy. Skip majored in business. He's the practical one—me, not at all." She affected a finishing-school accent to explain, "Mummy told me, 'You're a Highsmith, pumpkin. Find a good husband, and you're set for life.'"

I laughed. "So how'd you find him? Or was *Skip* looking?"

"He wasn't. For that matter, neither was I, in spite of my mother's advice. Truth is, Skip and I were set up. Those things rarely work. But we got a kick out of each other. One thing led to another, and here we are."

Affecting her mother's lockjaw accent, I asked, "And who set you up, my dear—a sorority sister?"

"*Hardly.* It was my uncle Iggy."

I responded with a vacant stare.

"Aha," she said, "you've heard of him: Ignatius Highsmith."

"No ..." Or had I? The name did sound familiar.

"We're not exactly, shall we say, *proud* of him. He's my father's younger brother, a Providence blue blood like the rest of us. But his business relations went a little hinky for a while, and he got caught up in the local Mafia. Not *too* far up, of course— he's not Italian. But he was, shall we say, *involved.* Long story short, he served some time and came out clean. But I *must* tell you"—she breathed an airy laugh while leaning confidentially over the table—"Uncle Iggy is now persona non grata at *all* holi- day gatherings."

Confused, I asked, "Why would Iggy try to set you up with Skip?"

"Simple. Iggy was a good college friend—in fact, a fraternity brother—of Skip's father. Back when *they* were both at Cornell."

Odd, I thought. "So how did he get you together?"

"Iggy showed up on campus one weekend and wanted to take Skip and me out to dinner—because of his own connection with Skip's dad. Sure, why not? So he drove us up to this swanky place in Syracuse, lots of flocked red wallpaper. Paid in cash, snapping hundreds from a thick roll of bills. Skip and I were surprised—we had a great time. And that's how it started."

"How long did you wait to get married?"

"About two years. There was no rush—we were still in col- lege, and the college experience is all about exploration and growth. I already had a close circle of friends at Cornell; Skip did, too. Why cut that short?"

I nodded, poker-faced, certain that Skip had been in no hurry to be tied down.

"And besides," said Ashley, "some of Skip's friends didn't quite approve of 'us.'"

Once again, Ashley had provided an opening to a delicate line of questioning. I asked, "You mean, they didn't approve of the two of you—as a couple? Why not?"

She rolled her eyes. "Skip has always had *lots* of gay friends."

"No surprise," I said. "He's a handsome man—and I say that with a measure of authority."

"I'm *sure*," she said with a soft laugh.

"How do you know they didn't approve?"

"Skip *told* me. He blew it off. In fact, he seemed proud of it. He said they didn't want me to 'take him out of circulation.'"

I asked, "Was he *in* circulation?"

She shrugged. "I guess. It was *college*."

"But marriage changed him?" Having sworn my own vows (fingers crossed) to Dr. Anthony Gascogne, I knew how easily those vows were broken—and so did Skip.

Ashley sat as if frozen, staring at me with an expression that made me wonder if she might reach across the table to slap me. Instead, she said, "I've heard many rumors that Skip never lost interest in men. I'm not stupid, Dante. But I choose to ignore those rumors. If they were true, someone's legs could get broken—and I don't mean Skip's."

I must have looked terrified.

She burst into laughter. "Just *kidding*."

"Glad to hear that."

"I don't care if Skip is gay, straight, or anywhere in between—I love him as is."

I smiled. Good for her. But I was still confused. I recalled the conversation with Skip's parents in Jazz's office only two days earlier. Kenneth Sr. spoke of being gobsmacked when Skip brought Ashley home for Christmas and introduced her as his fiancée.

"Ashley," I said, "when Skip's parents finally heard the news about you and their son, how did Skip's father react? Was he bothered that Iggy played matchmaker?"

"Of course not," said Ashley, looking every bit as confused as I was. "The whole thing was *his* idea. Kenneth put Iggy up to it."

CHAPTER NINE

Jazz had thought that Ashley might lose it when confronted with the prospect of Skip's infidelities, but that theory fell flat. Although Ashley was aware of Skip's past yen for men—and the possibility that it persisted—she joked about it when I was ballsy enough to pose some uncomfortable questions.

I didn't know what to make of Ashley's reaction. Was she inordinately open-minded? Was she too trusting—secure in believing that the love of a good woman would ultimately conquer her husband's predilections? Or did she simply not care? Whatever the reason for her nonchalance, it convinced me that Noreen Penley Wade's drowning had *not* been motivated by any scheming on Ashley's part to frame her faithless husband for the murder—the revenge of a jilted and humiliated mousy little wife. That whole notion was now easily dismissed.

Not so easily dismissed, however, was Ashley's revelation concerning the background of how—and why—she and Skip had met in college. Their first date had been set up by her uncle Iggy at the urging of his old pal, Skip's father. I couldn't fathom why Kenneth Sr. might have done this, but I did know that he had told a contradictory story to Jazz and me in front of his wife. What's more, I now knew that Kenneth himself had at least a feasible mob connection through Iggy. Which brought to mind that same conversation in Jazz's office, when Kenneth mentioned—clumsily, I thought—that he had been in LA at the time of Noreen's drowning. It had struck me as a textbook example of protesting too much, as no one had even hinted that he might have something to hide.

So my meeting with Ashley at Huggamug had left me with plenty to think about. While working the following day, Saturday, at the Sunny Junket office, I shared these thoughts with Jazz by phone. She was no less intrigued by Ashley's revelation than I had been. She asked, "Are you working tomorrow?"

I told her, "Not sure—Ben is diddling with our schedules right now. Why?"

"I set up a meeting with Blade Wade, the victim's husband, at his studio."

"Where is it?"

"Right here in Palm Springs. He spends most of his time here, even though Noreen worked in LA. Interested?"

"Let me find out about that schedule."

When I appeared in Ben's doorway, he waved me in, seemingly pleased by the interruption. Had he tired of the weekly puzzle of scheduling the staff? Or was he just happy to see me?

"What's up, Dante?" he said. "Any progress with that drowning?"

"A little." Seating myself in front of his desk, I said, "Ben, there's a meeting or two coming up, and I hate sneaking around on office time—it's not fair to the company. If there's some flexibility with the hours, could I have tomorrow off? And maybe Monday?"

Ben turned to his computer, scrolled through the drafted schedule, then perused our future bookings. He said, "You've got some vacation time left, don't you?"

"Probably." I laughed. "Haven't been away for a while."

Ben checked my records. "Golly, yes." With a chuckle, he asked, "Saving up time for a world cruise?"

"Uh, not exactly." It crossed my mind, however, that six months at sea with the Skipper wouldn't be too shoddy.

"Look," said Ben, "next week is really light for us. If you're okay with using vacation days in the dead of summer, just take the week off. Sunday through Sunday—that's eight straight days for the price of five. And you'll have plenty left if you want to get away later."

He didn't need to twist my arm. "Thanks a million, Ben. I'll do it."

■

I didn't go out that night, even though it was the start of a week's vacation, because I had done far too much drinking with Zola on Thursday. After leaving the office on Saturday, I stayed home that evening—no booze, then early to bed.

Amazing how a sober night's sleep can leave you raring to go the next morning. I awoke at dawn on Sunday, got up, and started the coffee. Although I had no commitments till early afternoon, when Jazz would pick me up for our meeting with Blade Wade, I was ready to begin the day.

Maybe I would throw on a shirt and run down to the corner to pick up an *LA Times*. Or maybe not. Vacations are like that. Maybe I'd just stay put.

An hour later, I had finished my third cup of coffee. Sitting on the sofa with my front door open, I was ditzing on my phone when it rang in my hand. I didn't recognize the number. "Hello?"

"Too early?" a man asked.

Yes, I thought. It was seven thirty. "Who *is* this?"

"Kenneth Terry Jr., at your service. But I wasn't sure you'd be … up."

"*Skip*," I said, "what a surprise. Did you get your phone back?"

"Nope, not yet. But they didn't find *this* one. Make note of the number, by the way."

"Count on it."

"It was a total *circus*, with Madera and some other cop," Skip said as he began to recount Thursday's turn of events, referring to it as a "raid."

While he was speaking, I heard a door open and close on the terrace, followed by voices. I leaned from where I sat and watched through my doorway as Isandro walked with his visitor along the far side of the pool, heading from his apartment toward the gate to the street. Isandro's outfit was dressier than usual, as if he might be going to church that Sunday morning—but I knew him well enough to scrap that notion. His companion was well dressed, too, and I decided they must have made plans for a nice breakfast somewhere.

Though curious to know more about this development, I also had Skip on the line, and while he continued gabbing, I wondered where he was. At that early hour, was he in bed with his wife? That seemed doubtful, as he was so talkative. Was he at home? Did he and Ashley have separate bedrooms?

Since my conversation with Ashley, I had come to feel a measure of sympathy for her odd arrangement with Skip, but she had bought into it as much as Skip had, and I now felt less guilty about my attraction to him.

The attraction was apparently mutual. After a lull in his chatty monologue, Skip cleared his throat, then lowered his voice to ask slowly, "What are you wearing?"

I laughed. "Now, that's original. What are *you* wearing?"

"Not much." His voice was barely a croak.

"Uh...just a sec," I said while stepping over to the door. I nudged it closed, returned to the sofa, and sprawled on it.

"Now, then," I whispered into the Skipper's ear, "where were we?"

■

That afternoon, around one thirty, I was waiting in the apartment for Jazz to pick me up. My phone rang. She told me, "We're here."

"Be right out, just as soon as—" I stopped myself and backed up: "We?"

"Uh-huh."

"Who's with you?"

"C'mon out. I'll introduce you."

Intrigued—and slightly apprehensive—I grabbed my keys and wallet, left the apartment, and headed out to the front gate.

The couple of times Jazz had picked me up before, she had waited behind the wheel and barely given me time to jump in and close the door before she punched the pedal and lurched away from the curb. Today, though, the SUV was parked with its engine turned off. Jazz stood on the sidewalk wearing a broad smile and her Sunday best (I thought, without cynicism, that perhaps she had been to church), and she was holding the hand of a little girl, who also smiled as I approached.

The child had a caramel-colored complexion reflecting her biracial parentage, with wondering brown eyes and her mother's black hair, worn in a lavish burst of curly braids that flopped over one shoulder, held aside by a big tortoiseshell jaw clip. She wore immaculate white canvas tennies with a summery little dress of blue denim, its skirt section sporting a playful pattern of pink and white bicycles. With her free arm, she held a floppy stuffed toy, a black cat with white splotches.

I crouched at her eye level, saying, "Aren't *you* just adorable?"

Jazz's knee nudged her daughter. "Introduce yourself, honey."

The girl slipped her hand from her mother's and offered it to me for a shake. "I'm Emma. I'm four."

I clasped her hand with both of mine. "Hello there, Emma. I'm Dante. I can't even *remember* when I was four."

She giggled. "Hello, Dante."

"Jazz," I said, standing, "you must be so proud." I placed a hand on Emma's shoulder.

Jazz gave me a grateful nod. I knew, of course, that there had been trouble at home—serious trouble—and Jazz had lost custody of Emma to her ex-husband. She explained, "I have visitation rights this weekend, and I wasn't about to return her till I have to, at six. So Mommy's taking Emma along to work today."

I leaned to Jazz's ear, asking low, "To a *murder* investigation?"

She smirked. "Far as Christopher's concerned, we're just running errands." With a clap of her hands, Jazz said, "Okay, Emma, hop back in your seat." She opened the rear door of the SUV and lifted her daughter inside.

Jazz stood with me at the curb, watching as the girl strapped herself into the child seat. When satisfied, Jazz closed the door and turned to eye me with a knowing grin. "My, my," she said, "someone's looking pretty smug today. Get lucky last night?"

"No." I shrugged. "Stayed home all evening."

"Yeah, like ducks. You've got that glow, Dante." She chortled.

Although she had the timing wrong—as well as the telephonic nature of the hookup with Skip—I had to marvel at her perceptiveness. No question, I was feeling some afterglow, bigtime. But I had no idea it showed.

■

During the drive, Emma busied herself with a few toys from the backpack that leaned next to her seat. She improvised quiet conversation between the stuffed cat and a Barbie doll in a ballerina dress. The four-legged cat seemed highly impressed that the two-legged doll could dance on her toes.

Up in the front seat, Jazz glanced over at me from behind the wheel. "Arcie Madera called—asked if we could meet and talk sometime tomorrow. I suggested my office at ten. She agreed. How about you?" Jazz already knew I was clear for the whole week.

"Sure. Any idea what she wants?"

"Didn't say, but her tone was sorta glum."

A few minutes later, as we approached the eastern edge of Palm Springs, Jazz steered the SUV into the right lane of Highway 111 and turned onto a side street that ran through a cluster of high-end car dealers, then narrowed as it led back toward the mountains. We arrived in an area I'd heard of but had never seen.

The neighborhood had a bohemian, arty feel, with a laid-back conglomeration of studios, galleries, consignment shops, whatever. Though the purpose of the area was commercial—there was a good-size parking lot—some of the artists also lived there, in their studios or in ramshackle lofts that nudged up the mountainside behind the street-level storefronts.

Jazz parked in the lot. I got out and waited while she untangled Emma from the safety seat. Standing in the full sun, I scanned the long row of buildings, which resembled a strip mall. Jazz locked the SUV and stepped over to me with Emma, who brought her stuffed cat. Jazz told me, "Blade said his entrance is just a door, letter H, between a couple of shops."

Approaching the buildings from the parking lot, we quickly found door H, which had darkly tinted glass. We stepped inside. The hot, tiny vestibule contained a second, solid door. Above the buzzer was a sign on stretched canvas, painted in bold brush-strokes: WADE STUDIO. *Ring and Wait.*

Jazz lifted Emma to press the buzzer. We waited and baked.

When the door finally opened with a rush of chilled air, Blade Wade said, "Hi there, folks. Sorry to take so long—it's a trek from the studio. C'mon in."

With no further discussion, he led us back through a winding hallway, then up a long flight of stairs. Emerging into a huge open space, he turned to tell us, "Welcome. And who is *this* little darlin'?"

I watched while Blade and Emma introduced themselves. Back when I first laid eyes on Blade, at the pool party, I thought he looked like a thug or a quarterback. He had that build. Couple that with his Blackness, and I'm ashamed to admit that I found him fearsome. But Skip had clued me that he was in fact a man of the arts, and following Jazz's first conversation with Blade, she'd proclaimed him "cool." Now he hunkered down on his massive thighs to chat with four-year-old Emma, whose laughter affirmed that their enchantment was mutual.

He stood to tell Jazz, "You've got a real charmer there."

She nodded. "Thank you. And once again, Blade, I'm sorry for your loss."

He nodded. "It's a mess. But what can you do? Life goes on." Which struck me as a tad too philosophical, under the circumstances.

I stepped into the conversation. "Pleased to meet you, Blade. I'm Dante O'Donnell." I extended my hand, which disappeared within his as he shook it.

"Hi there, Dante." He smiled. "I remember you from last Sunday."

It was hard to believe that so much had happened in the seven days since Kenneth and Claudia Terry's bust of a pool party.

Blade asked us, "Care to see the place?"

"Well, *yeah*," I answered at once.

The whole setup was nothing short of remarkable. We toured his studio, where easels displayed several of his works in progress—huge, dynamic paintings, most at least eight feet high and predominantly red. The studio opened into an equally spacious living room, where a high ribbon of windows framed the interplay of light and shadows on a craggy expanse of the nearby mountainside. Blade pointed up to a loft space. "From the bedroom," he said, "you can see the windmills in the San Gorgonio Pass."

Emma, with those wide and wondering eyes, was quietly fascinated by these unusual surroundings. For that matter, so was I.

Despite my earlier impression from the street, the combined studio and living space wasn't ramshackle at all. It was stunning—a melding of industrial chic with designer furnishings, significant art, and a sleek, drop-dead kitchen—the sort of place that ends up in magazines. In fact, it looked familiar, and I assumed I'd seen it published somewhere.

Jazz asked her daughter, "What do you think, honey?"

Emma turned to Blade with a toothy smile. "Can you learn me to paint?"

Jazz corrected: "*Teach* me, sweetie. But no, he can't. We're not here to make him work."

Blade said, "I think it's a good idea. We're here to talk, right? Grown-up stuff? Let's keep Emma amused." And he led us back into his studio, where he rummaged through a stack of stretched canvases, primed white.

"Here it is," he said, pulling out a small one, about two feet square. He set it on a vacant easel and adjusted the height down to Emma's reach. He asked her, "Why don't we make a picture of your cat?"

She nodded.

"What's her name?"

"Oliver."

Blade laughed. "Okay. And what does Oliver like to eat?"

"Fish," said Emma. She added, "Goldfish."

"Perfect. May I have Oliver for a moment?"

Emma petted the cat first, then handed him over.

Blade curled the cat around the top of the easel, trying several poses. "There," he said. "Oliver looks like he's about to pounce, doesn't he?"

"He does!"

"Great. Now, I don't think I'll ask you to actually *paint* the picture today. That's awful messy, and you're wearing a pretty dress. So …"

When Blade pulled out a big shoebox loaded with a jumble of crayons, many of them mere stubs, Emma looked crestfallen.

Upbeat, Blade said, "Once you've *finished*, I'm going to show you some magic, and then—presto—you'll have a painting after all."

This seemingly struck Emma as a reasonable compromise. She nodded gravely.

Blade gave a quick lesson in how to hold a crayon—not like a dagger, as a child might, but more like a fencing foil, allowing elegant, precise swipes. He got the composition started for her, deftly sketching a few light outlines.

"Here's the edge of the cliff," he said, "where Oliver waits to pounce. Here are the edges of the stream, where he spots the goldfish. Sky, trees, that's all up to you. And Oliver? Maybe he imagines himself as this big, mighty *jungle* cat—and you can show that, too, if you want."

Emma looked mesmerized, itching to begin.

"Have everything you need?" he asked. As Emma sorted through the box of crayons, Blade watched over her shoulder, telling her, "Goldfish aren't really gold-colored. Just use orange."

She nodded, then paused. "I don't see a white one. Oliver has white spots."

Blade explained, "The canvas is white. Where you don't want colors, don't draw anything."

She inhaled the gentle gasp of an enlightened four-year-old.

We retreated as she went to work.

■

Blade told Jazz, "You're right. A biracial marriage can be exciting and loving—good for a lifetime. And just *look* at your beautiful child. But there can be challenges."

I was relaxing with them around a low table at the far end of the living room, where we could keep an eye on Emma in the studio. Some thirty minutes into our conversation, Blade had opened a chilled bottle of good pinot grigio and poured two glasses—for himself and for me. Jazz had water.

She said to Blade, "When I married Christopher, absolutely, it was exciting and loving. But you can bet your sweet ass there were challenges."

With a soft, knowing laugh, Blade asked, "Two different worlds?"

Jazz hesitated. "For us, not so much. That wasn't the problem. To be honest, I think the problem was *me*."

I expected her to talk about the booze and anger issues she had been trying to manage. But what she said surprised me:

"I think, down deep, I married Christopher for the wrong reasons. Everything about him had that glow of white privilege—I mean, even that *name*. Christopher Friendly? C'mon. And know what? I wanted a piece of that."

Blade tossed his hands. "Why not?"

"Amen," said Jazz. "And I wanted it for the babies we'd make—*my* babies. Now that it's over, at least I made one." Her weak, wistful smile drooped. "But *he* took her. Fuckin' bastard."

Blade asked, "Are you *sure* you don't want some wine?"

I tried signaling him with a shake of my head.

"Nope," she said. "But thanks."

Blade sat back. "Noreen and me—we gave it a good try, but we sorta gave up. With her job in LA, she was hardly ever *here*, not even for weekends anymore. So we were just marking time. I didn't think it would last forever, but I never thought it would end like this."

I asked, "No kids, I assume?"

"No. I wanted them, but Noreen wouldn't consider it. Her *career*, you know—blah, blah, blah."

Jazz seemed to rise out of her funk. She slid her notebook from the cocktail table and opened it in her lap. "Noreen's job at the museum—you had some issues with that. You mentioned at the pool party that she wouldn't help promote *your* career."

Blade nodded. "I wasn't asking much. She had connections all over LA—it would've been easy to put in a good word for me, but no, she just wouldn't do it. It's not as if I wanted her to give me a retrospective at M3A."

I asked, "Why not?"

He shook his head. "Not the right fit at all. M3A's collection is highly specialized—and historical. It's a weird focus, as far as I'm concerned: anti-academic art, mostly nineteenth century. They've got a *few* good pieces, one by Rossetti. What's not to love about the Pre-Raphaelites?"

I shrugged. "Exactly." I had no idea what he was talking about.

"But other than that," he said, "the collection is pretty lame. So is the building. You should check it out."

Jazz turned to me. "Maybe we should."

I said to Blade, "You're obviously doing well, with or without Noreen's help. I mean—" I gestured to our surroundings, which bore no resemblance to the garret of a starving artist.

"Two reasons for that," he said. "First, my wife is—I mean 'was'—*very* well paid. I have no idea what she was doing for M3A that they found so valuable, but hey, she never talked much about it, at least to me. Second, my career took off with no help from Noreen because of my raw talent." He broke into laughter. "And I'm lucky to have a great rep."

Jazz asked, "Reputation?"

"No. Representative. Agent. Her name is Sabrina Harris, and she's been promoting me for several years now. Getting all the right exposure, plus, she's *always* showing my work. She's co-owner of the Harris-Heimlich Gallery."

"Where's it located?" Jazz was taking notes.

"Down in Palm Desert, in the gallery district along El Paseo."

"Well, la-di-da."

"Mommy?" said Emma, toddling toward us from the studio. "I have to potty."

With a sputter of a laugh, Jazz said to Blade, "Sorry."

"No problem at all—powder room's down the hall."

Jazz told us, "Be right back," as she got up to take Emma's hand.

"Know what?" said Blade. "That powder room is really cramped. Just take her up to the loft. Big master bath. Our housekeeper was here yesterday—every Saturday—so it ought to be presentable."

Jazz said, "C'mon, honey," and led Emma toward the stairs.

Blade added, "Show her the windmills. It's quite a view."

"I'll do that."

And I watched as they climbed the stairs to the open loft.

■

When they returned a few minutes later, Jazz said, "That's quite a view, all right—clear across the valley."

Emma darted over to us, raising a pinkie. "The windmills were about *this* big."

Blade asked her, "How's that portrait of Oliver coming along?"

"It's finished! And you said you'd show me some magic."

"That I did." Blade set aside his empty wineglass, got up, and led all of us into his studio. Stopping in front of the crayon drawing, he said, "Well, I'll be—"

Jazz and I were at a momentary loss for words as well.

Emma's drawing was beyond cute, beyond childish, combining keen observation—Oliver actually looked like Oliver—with the imaginative flair of abstraction. Her robust and inventive coloring was applied with a sure hand that relied on none of the scribble-overs of a frustrated beginner. And while the composition made a strong visual statement, it also conveyed ideas: the cat's jungle fantasy and the fearless taunting of the fish.

"Um," said Blade, "this doesn't need much improvement, Emma."

"But I want some magic."

"Okay." Blade gathered two old coffee mugs, a can of turpentine, and an artist's brush with a flat head of soft bristles. After setting everything on a taboret next to Emma's easel, he poured an inch or two of turpentine into both of the cups. Emma scrunched her nose.

Blade said, "I know, sweetie. Turpentine smells funny, but it dissolves wax. And crayons are made of wax." He dipped the brush into one of the cups. "So if you apply the turp to part of your picture—presto—the drawing becomes a painting." He did it.

Emma squealed with delight.

Blade told her, "Before you work on an area with different colors, swish the brush in the other cup to rinse it, then dip it again in the clean cup, and go for it. The wetter the brush, the lighter and runnier the results. And you can always go back and work more crayon into the wet canvas."

Standing back, we watched, amazed, as Emma eagerly took the brush and made her own magic.

"Know what?" said Blade. "That's pretty damn good."

"Good?" said Jazz. "Holy cow. It's effing unbelievable."

CHAPTER TEN

Genteel, watered-down euphemisms had never been high on the list of colorful terms used by Jazz to punch up her street talk. Holy cow? Effing unbelievable?

But I noticed a pattern that day. When little Emma was within earshot, Jazz never said a word that might confuse a young child—or offend a maiden aunt. At one level, this might simply be construed as responsible parenting. But at a deeper level, it also told me that Jazz hadn't been born and raised with a street mouth. She had learned it—later—and found it useful. She adopted it and made it part of her own identity. And yet, as I had observed that day, Jazz seemed unwilling to "corrupt" her own daughter with a lesson that she herself had found empowering. Was Emma too young to learn this? Would Jazz wait for others to teach the lesson and rob her daughter's innocence? Or did Jazz hope it would never happen?

After the meeting at Blade Wade's studio, Jazz was driving me back to my apartment, with Emma enthroned in her safety seat behind us. Propped up next to her was the crayon-and-turpentine painting of Oliver the stuffed cat. Blade had urged Emma to sign it; she already knew how to print her name and did so. Blade, in his own hand, then added the date, telling Jazz, "You *really* want to keep this."

In the back of the SUV, Emma now wore a pair of pink plastic headphones and quietly sang a counting song to the cat. She was up to forty-something.

Next to me, at the wheel, Jazz suggested, "Tuesday, maybe?"

We were planning a visit to the museum where Noreen Penley Wade had worked, M3A-LA. The next day, Monday, was no good because we had a meeting with Detective Madera. "Sure," I said to Jazz, "Tuesday's fine. You'll drive?"

The SUV swerved as her head turned from the roadway to face me. "Wouldn't feel safe in your shitbox—not on the 10, for Christ's sake." She steered back into our lane.

A minute or two passed in silence, other than Emma's singing. With eyes on the road, Jazz said, "Know what?"

I said nothing.

She continued: "When I took Emma upstairs to potty, I did some snooping."

I laughed. "Now, *why* doesn't this surprise me?"

"Remember? Before we went up there, Blade told me the bathroom ought to be 'presentable' because the housekeeper was there yesterday. So I checked it out. The little wastebasket didn't have much in it—cuz it was just emptied. Down at the bottom, hardly any trash at all. A Kleenex or two. A few inches of dental floss. And a used condom."

I did *not* need to know this.

"Meaning," said Jazz, "Blade was doin' the dirty deed last night—in the bed he used to share with his wife, who hasn't been dead a week."

I reminded Jazz, "A man has needs. And he told us Noreen stopped spending the weekends with him."

Jazz countered, "He also told us Noreen wouldn't help promote his career, but his agent is bustin' her butt to make it happen. Makes you wonder what *other* services this Sabrina chick has been providing."

Finding this theory far-fetched—not to mention catty—I said to Jazz, "Even if it's true, so what? They're adults. They can do what they want."

"In a suspicious death," she lectured, "a death now known to be a homicide, the *first* potential suspect that needs to be cleared—or accused—is the spouse or significant other. Sure, Blade seems like a great guy, and I flat-out *loved* his 'magic turpentine' with Emma, but he's not off the hook yet."

"I think you're making too much of this," I said, "but in a way, I'm relieved. Sounds like the investigation is losing interest in Skip."

Jazz assured me, "Skip is *far* from off the hook. I'm guessing that's what Arcie Madera wants to talk about tomorrow."

That shut me up—*not* what I wanted to hear.

Another minute or two ticked by. Then Jazz glanced over at me, grinning. "Know what else? After I found Blade's condom, I sniffed his bed."

Oh. My. God. Bewildered, I hesitated to ask, "Why?"

"The maid was there yesterday, okay? So the linens would be changed. Obviously, the bed would've been used last night, and I figured that Blade wouldn't send me up to the loft if he'd left a mess. When I got up there with Emma, sure enough, the bed was put together—not *perfect*, like a maid would do it—but it was fine, 'presentable.'"

Deadpan, I told her, "I'm so glad it met minimum housekeeping standards."

"Meanwhile," said Jazz, "I checked the bathroom for the usual toiletries. Blade had lots of stuff, and so did Noreen—crap accumulates over the years, and Blade hasn't bothered to get rid of her things yet. I didn't find any aftershave or cologne for Blade, but I did find an old bottle of Noreen's Chanel. So I decided to sniff the bedding and see if anyone had left behind a telltale fragrance last night. Bingo. One of the pillowcases *reeked* of perfume—and trust me, it wasn't Chanel."

Hmmm. Jazz's methods were beginning to sound less nutty. I asked, "Any idea what brand of perfume it was?"

With a derisive snort, she said, "Rose Organdy. Christopher always gave me that shit, wanted me to wear it, so I know it well. *Hated* it—made me smell like a goddamn eighty-year-old whore. And it gave me fuckin' hives."

So much for the holy cows.

Behind us, Emma took a noisy breath after her counting song ended at one hundred. Then she started over.

■

Monday morning, I got up at dawn again. Although I was on vacation, with no plans until my ten o'clock meeting with Jazz and Detective Madera, I was not inclined to break my sleep habits. Why waste the cooler hours of the day? Just as important, I enjoyed the early hush before the neighborhood's invasion of landscaping crews with their howling leaf blowers.

As usual, I started the coffee, opened my front door, and strolled out to the pool. Alone on the terrace, except for the birds, I watched the gate to the street, wondering if Isandro would soon return from his nursing job. Then I shifted my gaze to his apartment door, wondering if he and the boyfriend were going at it. Then the gate again. Then the door. Gate. Door.

The beep of the coffeemaker snapped me out of it. Feeling foolish—and peeved at myself for taking such a territorial interest in Isandro's comings and goings—I abandoned my sentry duty and returned to the apartment, closing the door behind me. But not completely.

While standing at the kitchen counter, taking the first sip from a steaming mug, I was startled by a gentle rap at the door and swallowed the coffee too quickly, burning my throat. Stepping over to the door—surely it was Isandro—I wondered if he would be alone.

"Good morning, Dante. Hope I'm not intruding."

"Zola," I said, "what a pleasant surprise. Come in."

As she stepped inside, I ducked into the bedroom to throw a shirt on over my shorts. She was saying, "I saw you on the patio, so I knew you were up and about."

"No problem at all," I said, returning to the living room. "Coffee?"

"I already have a nice buzz, but hell, why not? Bring it on."

I laughed while pouring the second mug. "And what brings *you* out at the crack of dawn?" I couldn't help noticing the small bundle of folded fabric she carried with one arm. It appeared to be a sturdy, neutral textile, like raw linen.

"I have something to show you. Need your thoughts on this."

"Please, get comfortable," I said while settling on the sofa with her. After she set the bundle aside, I handed her the coffee, and we both took a moment to drink a sip or two. Then she set her mug on the cocktail table.

"I've been thinking about your curtain project and reviewing the pictures you sent me. This isn't a huge job, and let's face it, *anything* would be an improvement. But why make do with 'good enough' when we have the opportunity to dazzle."

I nodded. "I couldn't agree more, Zola. But I'm on a *very* tight budget."

She waggled her hand, a shushing motion. "And then I had an idea. If I say so myself, it's rather brilliant." She grinned.

Referencing the bundle of fabric, I asked, "Whatcha got there?"

She didn't reach to display it but explained, "A number of years ago—I won't say how many—I was working on a job for clients down in Indian Wells. They were building this *monster* of a house at Vanguard Ridge and brought me in to coordinate everything, including window treatments. The wife said she was 'sick of stuffy decorating'—she was married to a former ambassador—and wanted something more 'fun,' as she put it. When I asked her to describe 'fun,' she said, 'I want to feel like I'm having lunch at the Polo Lounge.'" Pausing her story, Zola asked me, "Been there?"

The memories brought a smile. "It's been a long time since I've lunched in Beverly Hills. Seems like a different life. But yeah,

I've been there—whenever we celebrated a new film project, back when those dreams still held some promise. And it was fun."

Zola leaned to peck my cheek. Then she stood, unfurled the sample—about the size of a bath towel—and turned it around to show me the pattern. "Recognize this?"

Holy cow.

"Of course," I said. "Giant banana leaves, like the hotel wallpaper. As I recall, it wasn't used in the dining room itself, but it seemed to be everywhere else."

She told me, "This is the same pattern as the wallpaper, but for this fabric, the colors have been stripped away, leaving a monochrome beige pattern against the lighter neutral background. It's subtle, yes? And drop-dead *fabulous*, no?"

"Totally fabulous," I agreed, "and Jazz would be thrilled. But the expense."

Zola shushed me again. "Here's the deal—and it's one you can't refuse. The job in Indian Wells had a heap of windows requiring a ton of this fabric, but I overestimated the order. We had nearly a full bolt left over. I apologized and offered to buy back the remainder at cost, but the ambassador's wife wouldn't hear of it. 'Don't be silly,' she said. 'Just *take* it. You're sure to find *some* use for it.' So I tucked it away." Zola crossed her arms. "And I've been waiting for that special project ever since."

I paused before saying anything. Then I grinned. "Did you honestly think I might not *love* the banana print?"

She asked in return, "One never knows, does one? Do you need to run it past your friend Jazz?"

"She saw me measuring, but we haven't discussed it. Even though she has a take-charge personality, she seems to trust me—at least when it comes to curtains."

"Excellent." Zola folded up the sample. "I still need to figure out the lining, but that's a minor item. This will be … 'fun.'"

As she bustled to the door and swung it wide, I said, "By the way—any sightings of Isandro's new friend lately?"

She rolled her eyes, saying nothing.

I was tempted to ask, What does *that* mean?

But Zola was already on her way, striding across the patio like a wizard with a bag of tricks, as if lost in a silken miasma of taffeta and tiebacks...braids and trims...pleats and fringe.

■

Sometime after nine thirty, I strolled into the Sunny Junket offices.

Gianna looked up from her crossword, asking, "Where's your uniform, Dante?"

I explained archly, "It so happens I have the week off."

She countered, "It so happens I've heard—so why are you here? I'd be home with my feet up, eating Froot Loops."

"But that's what you do *here*, girlfriend."

"Same to you, girlfriend." She gave me the finger nudge of her harlequin glasses.

I went to my desk and retrieved the three laminated signs I had made to replace the ones at Jazz's office. I was going to arrive there early and install them before Detective Madera showed up—a pleasant little surprise for Jazz that would also make a more professional impression on Madera. (News of the planned curtains, a bigger surprise, could wait.)

I recalled that the existing signs were held in place with plain old cellophane tape, but I couldn't depend on Jazz's inventory of basic office supplies, so I grabbed a small roll of tape from my desk, tucked it into my pocket, and left Sunny Junket with the signs.

A block down the street, I turned to walk along the side of Huggamug's building, arriving at the lobby door to Jazz's office at a quarter till ten. Inside, I bounded up the stairs to the entrance to her outer office—and found the door locked. No lights were switched on inside. I knocked on the glass that displayed the ratty, photocopied sign. No answer. And she had told me she would be there by nine.

Where *was* she? What if Arcie Madera arrived a few minutes early and Jazz was a no-show for their meeting? What was *I* supposed to do—make excuses?

The first thing I did was replace the signs on the lobby door and in the stairwell. Then I sat on the stairs and phoned Jazz.

I heard the ring of her phone just as she appeared at the outside door and stepped into the lobby, looking disheveled and barely awake.

I stood, gaping, at a loss for words.

She raised a hand. "Don't ask." Stomping past me, she plodded up the stairs and unlocked her door.

I followed her in as she switched on some lights and headed directly back to her corner office, flumped into her desk chair, and booted up her computer.

Looking in from the doorway, I said, "I made some new signs—it's a start."

She glanced up from the screen with bloodshot eyes and looked at the sign in my hands. "Nice," she said without a hint of enthusiasm.

I checked my watch, then darted out to the front office and replaced the remaining sign. Returning to her desk, I asked, "Coffee?"

"Yes," she croaked.

Within five minutes—having bribed the barista downstairs, telling her, "Three large black, anything, it's an emergency"—I returned to Jazz's desk and commanded, "Bottoms up, damn it."

And at two minutes past ten, I heard the door to the reception room open, followed by Arcie Madera's voice, calling, "Sorry I'm late."

I went out to greet her, closing Jazz's door behind me. "Good morning, Detective. Jazz is winding up a video conference—won't be a minute. Coffee?"

"No, thanks." She offered a pleasant smile while glancing about, checking out her surroundings. At the sight of the shower curtains, her smile drooped.

I said, "The previous renter left those—can you imagine? Next on the to-do list."

She nodded. "It's a challenge, getting started. But the paying jobs have to come first, right? How's business?"

"Never better," I assured her, beaming—and grateful that acting school had reaped a few benefits beyond my piddling screen appearances, mostly walk-ons.

The door behind me opened.

"*Arcie*," said Jazz, whisking out from her office, "so sorry to keep you waiting. The conference room is back here." And she led us to the folding banquet table, still surrounded by lawn chairs— but at least the dead fiddle-leaf fig was gone. While settling in, Jazz offered, "Coffee?"

Arcie declined again.

Jazz removed the lid from another Huggamug paper cup and gulped from it like a camel on empty. Otherwise, to my astonishment, she looked just fine. Her eyes were brighter, she'd finger-combed her hair, and her lips were touched up, leaving a bright red imprint on the cup. She and Arcie small-talked for a minute while jogging a few folders on the table. I watched and listened.

"So," Jazz said at last, "why did you want to meet? Any news?"

Arcie was stone-faced. "Yes. Unfortunately, it's not what I'd characterize as a useful crime-solving development. It's more like ... *pressure*."

Jazz glanced at me while asking Arcie, "The DA?"

"Who else? Peter Nadig, as always, has his eye on the next election. He wants successful prosecutions. And he seems to think making noise about the death penalty buys him votes— maybe he's right. Right or wrong, though, he can't prosecute a case until it's solved. Trust me, Nadig may dream of courtroom victories, but the thing that keeps him up at night is an open, unsolved murder case." Then Arcie turned to look at me.

Staring, as if studying me, she said, "That's it."

Warily, I asked, "What?"

"When I met you last week, Dante, at the scene of the drowning, I had no trouble connecting your name to the Clarence Kwon case—that bizarre 'refrigerator murder.' You and Jazz wrapped it up on the spot. The county thanks you. I thank you. And Peter Nadig thanks you."

What else could I say? "You're welcome."

"But I kept thinking there was something else. And I just figured it out: Dr. Anthony Gascogne."

I nodded. "He was my ex-husband. A year and a half ago, I found him at his home with his skull smashed in. Jazz was among the first responders."

Jazz picked it up: "I arrested Dante, but it turned out he had a clean alibi, and that was the beginning of the end of my career with the Palm Springs PD."

"I know," said Arcie. "These stories make the rounds. But my point is this: Both of you already *know* the frustrations of an unsolved murder case. You've felt the gnawing lack of justice, that sense of an unrighted wrong."

Jazz tossed her hands. "It's dismal. It's hell."

I nodded my agreement.

Arcie said, "I have many disagreements with Peter Nadig, but I totally get his obsession with unsolved murders. For him, sure, there's the element of political bonus points. But for *all* of us who've felt any sort of calling to law enforcement, a cold-case murder is the most glaring failure we're challenged to resolve."

She paused while opening a folder. "Which brings us back to Noreen Penley Wade. From everything I've learned, she was no sweetheart."

Jazz and I grunted our assent, having seen Noreen in action.

"But," said Arcie, "she deserves to have her killer exposed."

And with that, the three of us compared notes, having interviewed many different persons of interest, as well as some of the same witnesses—and suspects. But after spending considerable time in the weeds of the investigation, exploring several enticing threads, both Jazz and Arcie agreed that first instincts are often best. As far as they were concerned, the most likely suspect was still Skip Terry.

"For example," said Arcie, "he never did come up with that grocery receipt—which would prove where he was at the time of the murder."

Jazz suggested, "Maybe there's security footage from the store."

"Hope so," said Arcie. "We're on it."

This worried me—greatly. I already knew that Skip had not shopped for groceries on the day of the murder. Complicating matters, I had not spoken up at the very moment when I could have provided clarity. And I was fully aware that my impulse to protect Skip was rooted in sexual attraction—"thinking with my dick," as Jazz had phrased it. Worst of all, this entire conversation had been framed in the context of the DA's taste for the death penalty. These were not happy thoughts.

So I was relieved when Jazz finally sat back and said to Detective Madera, "Do you mind if I ask if you're married, Arcie?"

Odd, I thought. I found it unlikely that Jazz had an interest in switching teams.

With a soft laugh, Arcie said, "Of course I don't mind. Yes, I'm married—happily, for ten years now, to an architect named Cooper Brant."

I recognized the name. In a valley known for its significant architecture, he was a standout.

Jazz asked, "Kids?"

Arcie shook her head. "We married sorta late."

A moment of silence hung over the table. Jazz seemed to be struggling with her thoughts. She brushed something from the corner of her eye.

Because she had asked Arcie if she had kids, I wondered if Jazz meant to steer the conversation to her own daughter, Emma, seeking the counsel of a like-minded woman. But Jazz said nothing. In the dead stillness of the room, I could smell the coffee on her breath. Having tended bar, I wondered if Arcie, too, had detected the lingering note of bourbon.

If she did, she gave no hint of it. Instead, Arcie gathered her folders, asking us, "What's next on your agenda?"

After a quick review of our immediate plans—Jazz and I were driving to M3A-LA the next day—Arcie stood, telling Jazz, "Remember, the DA is getting antsy. This week could be pivotal. If you think you can clear your client, I wish you luck, but time is running out."

Jazz thanked Arcie for the heads-up. Then we walked with her to the front office and said goodbye.

Closing the door after Arcie stepped out, Jazz noticed the new sign, as if seeing it for the first time. "That looks great," she said to me. "Thank you."

I stood there with my arms crossed and nodded.

"Thanks for the coffee, too," she said. "I needed it. Obviously."

I nodded.

She moved a step in my direction and stopped. "Yesterday was so wonderful—with Emma and the painting and the laughs. And then later, when I drove her back to her father at six, it all *hit* me. I knew again how much I'd lost. It still *hurts*. Last night was awful."

I had no idea what to say.

"So I had a slip. I get it—I'm a bad person and a lousy mother. But no lectures, okay? I'm working on it. Trust me."

I wanted to believe her, but I wasn't sure I could. Trying to offer something constructive, I said, "You're *not* a lousy mother.

If you were, you wouldn't be so torn up about losing custody. If the cards were stacked against you during the divorce, maybe it's time to find a better lawyer and fight back."

"I already *had* a good lawyer—a terrific lawyer. He handled my affairs for years. It was Christopher."

"Your ex? Oh, Christ."

"And I *know* what he charges his clients. No way can I hire someone with fees like that. But Christopher? He has a whole damn law firm working for him—and he'll *never* give up the fight for Emma."

CHAPTER ELEVEN

Next morning, I hesitated—in fact, I held my breath—as I climbed into Jazz's SUV, which idled at the curb in front of my apartment. If there was bourbon to be sniffed, it would be unmistakable within the confines of the cabin. The thought of a two-hour ride from Palm Springs to Los Angeles in heavy freeway traffic was harrowing enough. Throw into that mix a driver who might have had another "slip" with her booze problem overnight, and the prospects were downright frightening.

"Morning, Dante," said Jazz.

At last I inhaled—and we were good. I smelled only coffee and mint on her breath, plus a dab of something pleasant, an innocuous perfume or cologne that I presumed to be something other than Rose Organdy.

I replied, "Howdy, Jazz," chipper as can be. "Sleep well?"

She chortled. "Hell of a lot better than the night before."

It was eight o'clock when Jazz pulled away from the curb, which would get us into the city well after the morning rush. She drove us north out of Palm Springs past the windmill fields, and before long, we were merging onto Interstate 10. We wouldn't need to exit until arriving in LA, just a couple of miles from our destination along Museum Row.

Leaving the windmills behind us, we settled in for the long haul, which was anything but scenic and never relaxing. I'd made this jaunt countless times over the years, and even at best, it was always a bitch of a drive, so I was grateful that Jazz had volunteered. She had programmed M3A-LA's address into the

SUV's navigation, but we wouldn't really need it until the last few blocks. The farther we got from Palm Springs, the more a computerized woman's voice kept haranguing us with advisories and alerts.

Jazz killed the sound, telling the radio, "Shut yo' mouth, honey. Don't matter when we get there."

I said to Jazz, "I assume, then, you haven't told them we're coming."

She laughed airily. "Surprise ... surprise ..."

∎

I had spent much of my adult life in LA—more than twenty years—since fleeing from Indiana until the move to Palm Springs with Dr. Anthony Gascogne, ophthalmologist. Jazz had grown up in LA, so both of us could claim it as home turf. Although I'd been reluctant to leave with Anthony, I now had to wonder what took me so long.

The urban buzz and whir, which had once energized me, now made me anxious. As the skyline loomed closer in the windshield, I could feel my pulse rising. Sitting there, strapped in, I wiped my clammy palms on the legs of my pants. Had my values and interests really changed that much? Or was I simply getting older? Probably both.

Jazz switched on her blinker to exit the 10. Moments later, the ramp deposited us on the surface streets of familiar territory, but it seemed like a different world. I lowered my window and extended my arm, feeling the breeze on my hand. The air was thirty degrees cooler than it had been in the desert. It was also damp. That's June gloom.

The navigation guided us onto Wilshire Boulevard and took us past the sprawling site of the Los Angeles County Museum of Art, being rebuilt from the ground up. A few blocks later, at a side street, the navigation told us to turn left. Jazz glanced over at me, shrugged her shoulders, and turned. Within moments, the dashboard chimed—we had arrived at our destination.

Jazz slowed to a crawl in the busy traffic as we both swiveled our heads, searching for some semblance of a museum. "There," I said, pointing to a sign with sleek, minimalist lettering: M3A-LA. It was located on the ground floor of a high-rise office building.

Jazz mumbled, "Guess we better find a place to park." Her tone confirmed that she, too, had expected something more substantial than a leased storefront. I wondered how they had wrangled an address on Wilshire, almost a block away.

We found a parking lot around the next corner and walked back. The plaza in front of the office building—it had no name, just a number—was peppered with a few kiosks promoting the museum, exhorting would-be visitors to EXPLORE THE FREE-SPIRITED WORLD OF ANTI-ACADEMIC ART.

The door to the museum was separate from the building's lobby entrance. Stepping inside, we were greeted by an elderly volunteer who ran Jazz's credit card for two admissions. He handed us each a slim pamphlet and tapped one of the rooms on the floor plan, confiding to us, "The Rossetti's in Gallery B."

Jazz asked him, "Is that the big draw?"

He beamed. "Yes, ma'am."

I squinted at the pamphlet but could barely read it, as my eyes were still adjusting from the full daylight on the street to the near darkness and black walls of the dramatically lit interior.

Jazz and I ventured in. If there were other visitors that morning, I couldn't see or hear them. The hushed, carpeted gallery had the eeriness of a crypt. We stepped from painting to painting, each of them spotlighted, most from the late nineteenth century. The various artists shared similar themes—legendary and biblical—with a highly realistic style that reminded me of magazine illustration when I was young.

Jazz whispered to me, "Let's check out Gallery B."

It was a smaller room, with a few smaller works on the side walls, but the focus was front and center on the Rossetti—a portrait of a glamorous woman with flowing hair, a brocade robe, and a jeweled goblet—measuring about three feet square.

As I stood there with Jazz, peering at details and checking the printed notes, a door in the black wall behind us opened briefly, admitting a bright shaft of light from an office. "I'll be right back," said a woman's voice as the door closed again.

We paid no attention. I said to Jazz, "Blade was right: What's not to love about the Pre-Raphaelites?"

Jazz chuckled. "Whatever."

Directly behind us, as if speaking into our ears, the woman from the office said, "It's magnificent, isn't it?"

We turned. In the glow from the painting, I recognized her as Riley Uba, who had been Noreen Penley Wade's assistant—until Noreen drowned. She was dressed in the same hip, urban style as when I first saw her at the pool party. A sleeveless blouse exposed her full arm of tattooed manga characters. Earlier, there had been something about her manner that struck me as ambitious. Now, unless I was mistaken, she was in charge.

Jazz grinned. "I don't know much about art, but I'll take your word for it—magnificent."

Riley asked us, "First visit?"

"Yes," I said, "but we've run into you before."

"Oh?"

"The party in Rancho Mirage. When things got out of hand, Jazz and I showed up from the rental company."

Riley thumped her forehead—genuine surprise or bad acting? "Sure, I remember both of you now." After we made a proper round of introductions, Riley said, "So don't tell me: we made such a favorable impression about M3A, you just *had* to come out for a look."

"Something like that," said Jazz. "You see, I'm a private investigator. Kenneth Terry, who's renting the house, hired me to help figure out what happened to Noreen on the Tuesday after the party—a week ago today. And that's why Dante and I are here. Collecting background."

"Of course," said Riley, nodding. Her tone had turned serious. "Kenneth and his wife have been such loyal benefactors to the museum. How can I be of help?"

Jazz said, "On the day of the murder—and we've now determined that it *was* a murder—did Noreen plan to be working here at the museum? Or did her return to the desert on Tuesday seem sudden?"

Voices of new arrivals in Gallery A grew louder as they moved toward us. Riley said, "Maybe we should discuss this in back."

As she ushered us through the secret door in the black wall, my eyes were again forced to adjust—this time to the dazzle of floor-to-ceiling windows and white walls.

While following Riley to her office, I recognized a man walking toward us in the hallway. He was the museum's nervous chief financial officer, Howard Quince. Riley paused to introduce us to him, explaining, "Kenneth Terry asked for their help investigating Noreen's mishap."

"Aha," said Quince, nodding, "excellent. Um, excuse me, but I forgot something I need to check on." He turned on his heel and retreated down the hall, opening a door, then closing it behind him. Jazz and I stole a glance at each other.

Riley led us to another door, labeled EXECUTIVE DIRECTOR. A second placard, removed from its slot, had presumably displayed the name of the deceased. "Pardon the mess," said Riley as we stepped inside.

The office was spacious and comfortable, with a twelve-foot ceiling, a wall of glass, and good contemporary furnishings. In addition to the desk, there was a conversation area with a sofa, armchairs, and tables. On the expanse of wall above the sofa was a huge painting, *not* from the nineteenth century. Although by no stretch an art expert, I thought it might be a Jackson Pollock, and a quick look at the signature confirmed my hunch. What was *that* worth?

Riley's comment about "the mess," however, was apt. Packing boxes were stacked here and there; others gaped open from the floor, containing files and the sort of rubble that collects in desk drawers. Computer cables snaked around the corner of the desk, attached to older equipment that looked, in a word, junky. Riley explained, "Police were here, looking for clues, I guess. They took Noreen's computer—and plenty more."

Jazz turned to me. "Riverside must've gotten some assistance from LAPD."

Riley added, "I try to think of it as enforced housekeeping."

I asked, "Did Noreen have a secretary?"

"Sure—me. An 'executive assistant' isn't quite as glamorous as it sounds. Now, then. Care to sit down?"

As we settled around the coffee table, piled with art magazines, Riley said, "Out in the gallery, you were asking about Noreen's plans on the day she died. I'll tell you the same thing I told the police: To the best of my knowledge, Noreen returned from the pool party in the desert on Sunday night because she was here at the office Monday morning. When she left the office Monday evening, she confirmed the meetings on her calendar for Tuesday. She showed up the next morning at nine, as usual. But then, around nine thirty, she told me to cancel her meetings and try to move them to Wednesday. She said there was something she needed to take care of. Didn't say where or why. And she left."

Jazz checked her notes. "That timing makes sense. Noreen arrived at the house in Rancho Mirage at noon."

I asked Riley, "When Noreen told you she suddenly had to leave and reschedule, did she seem annoyed? Agitated?"

"You know," said Riley, "it's funny. No one's asked me about that. Truth is, she didn't seem upset at all. In fact, I'd describe her mood as upbeat—and for Noreen, *that's* saying something."

We were interrupted by a gentle rap at the door.

"Yes?" said Riley.

Howard Quince opened the door a foot or so. "Sorry. Could I have a word with you, Riley?"

She got up and stepped out to the hall, leaving the door open a few inches. Speaking low, Quince told her, "I just talked to Kenneth, and he confirmed that—"

I watched as Riley's hand reached for the knob and gently closed the door.

■

When she returned from the hall, we spent at least half an hour discussing theories for Noreen's sudden drive to the desert, but they were mere speculation, with no promising insights. At a lull in our conversation, Riley said, "Can I offer you a backstage tour?"

Jazz checked her watch. "I suppose we have time."

I caught her eye and winked. During that morning's drive, Jazz had wondered aloud how we might finagle a look behind the scenes at M3A.

Riley led us down the main corridor, past Howard Quince's office—his name was on the door, but he was not at his desk. Farther along, a large conference room, used for board meetings, had a pleasant view of the plaza. As we moved toward the back of the building, we first saw a shipping area with a loading dock, then a raw-looking workshop used for exhibit construction, but neither area was staffed, and our footfalls echoed as we passed through.

"The curator's office is just ahead," said Riley. "Let's see if Cameron is in."

I recalled my prior sighting of Cameron Vicario as he was leaving the ill-fated party at the Ellinger House. He had kept to himself at the gathering, but I noticed him because of his smart black outfit and his thick black hair—containing sexy streaks of silver. Clean-shaven and wearing round-framed glasses, he had a bookish air. I guessed he was in his forties. I also thought he might be gay.

The door to the curator's office was wide open, and Riley led us inside.

Cameron looked up from a massive workbench where he tinkered with a restoration project—the painting was spread out with the care and precision befitting life-or-death surgery, replete with lights, tools, and instruments. Cameron appeared surprised by the interruption, but not the least perturbed. In fact, he broke into a warm smile as he switched off the work lights and removed his latex gloves. "Welcome," he said. "Who are your guests, Riley?"

Riley introduced us, explaining, "Jazz and Dante showed up at the pool party in the desert when it got out of control."

"*That's* it," said Cameron, stepping around from the workbench and extending his hand. The handshake with Jazz was quick; with me, prolonged. He said, "I'm surprised you didn't call out the cops."

Jazz told him, "I *was* a cop. But I was working security that day."

"And what brings you here today?"

I said, "Just a couple of tourists, taking in some art."

He laughed. "I'll bet."

"Cameron," said Riley, "back in my office, Jazz and Dante were wondering why Noreen made the snap decision to drive back to Rancho Mirage last Tuesday."

Jazz summarized for all of us: "Within three hours of leaving the museum, Noreen drowned, fully clothed, in a swimming pool in the desert. That's not a coincidence or an accident. She was probably lured there to be killed. So *someone* told her *something* to get her to drop what she was doing and take a long drive. Riley says Noreen didn't seem threatened by any of this—she was upbeat about it."

"But when she left," Riley said to Cameron, "she gave me no explanation. Did *you* hear anything?"

Cameron shrugged. "I didn't see her at all that day. Which suited me fine—I wasn't about to go *looking* for her."

I asked, "Why not?" Jazz was already scribbling notes.

Cameron considered the question for a moment. "Allow me to phrase this diplomatically: we had some professional differences."

Riley said, "Noreen wasn't especially responsive to Cameron's recommendations regarding acquisitions and exhibits."

"To be more precise," said Cameron, undiplomatically, "she did whatever the hell she damn pleased. Granted, she was the boss. Those decisions were ultimately hers to make. And she had the eye, the knowledge, the degree. *But.* She had no sense of focus on M3A's mission. Most of the works she shipped in and out of here—it was crap, worthless crap, with no significance whatever to the anti-academic movement."

Jazz said, "There's passion in your words, Mr. Vicario. If I'm hearing you right, your professional differences with Noreen weren't just a pissing match over 'who decides.' It ran deeper than that, correct?"

"Correct. It was a matter of sound judgment. It was a matter of dedication to the museum's core purpose. I'm not talking about minor artistic quibbles or splitting hairs. No. Truth be told, Noreen Penley Wade had far more ego than taste or discernment."

Riley grinned. "I worked with Noreen, day in and day out. She respected my abilities, and in return, I was always deferential to her. My job depended on it. But Cameron is right—she was difficult and demanding. And while I never said anything, I agree that her meddling in curatorial matters was, to put it mildly, odd."

Cameron moved to Riley and put an arm around her shoulders, saying softly, "I can't sugarcoat it—I'm glad Noreen's gone.

The circumstances are dreadful, but the result's the same. She's no longer a threat to the future of this institution. Thank God you're ready to step in, Riley. More than anyone else, you've held this place together. The whole staff is behind you. As for me? I can't *wait* to see where you'll lead us." He gave her cheek a tender peck.

Riley backed off a step and turned to Cameron with a quizzical look. At first, I thought she was reacting to the kiss, but that wasn't it at all. "I'm really touched by your words, Cameron—that's so sweet of you—but I won't be leading M3A."

Cameron looked befuddled. So did Jazz. I asked, "Why not?"

Riley looked at all of us as if we were dense. "Because I'm not *qualified*. Sure, I have an art history degree—big deal—and I love my work. But I don't know the first thing about running a *business*, which is exactly what the executive director does."

Cameron insisted, "You can *learn* that—on the job. In fact, you're already doing it."

She shook her head. "What I'm doing is cleanup. I'm putting things in order for the next director. I'll help with the search, if the board asks me to. If the new boss values institutional memory and wants me to stay on, great, I'd be honored to provide continuity. But I'm not counting on it." She shrugged. "When my work is done here, I'll find something else."

Cameron looked crushed. "Oh, *sweetie*—say it isn't so."

"Sorry." She pecked his cheek.

I said to Cameron, "Think of it as an opportunity. A new broom sweeps clean."

He made a choking sound, as if he might cry.

"Now, now," said Riley. "Beneath all the turmoil at M3A, we're really just one happy family."

Cameron moped back to his workbench and put on his gloves.

Riley turned to Jazz and me, flipping her hands. "And that's about it—our backstage tour doesn't amount to much. Anything else I can show you before you head out?"

Jazz checked her watch—it was just past noon. She said to me, "As long as we're here, do you want to take a look at the rest of the exhibits?"

"You bet."

In a confused tone, Riley said, "When I first spoke to you this morning, you were viewing the Rossetti."

Jazz and I glanced at each other. I said to Riley, "Right."

With a sheepish laugh, she told me, "Well, I'm afraid that's *it*. Gallery A and Gallery B—you've seen it all."

"Ah," I said, "stupid me—should've paid more attention to the pamphlet." I wondered: That's *it*? There couldn't have been more than thirty paintings displayed in the entire museum.

Riley said, "Then let me show you back to the galleries."

We said our goodbyes to Cameron, who apologized for his emotional state, snapped his gloves, and returned his attention to the painting he was restoring.

Riley led us out through the workshop and shipping area, then led us down the corridor toward her office. As we passed the door to the conference room, Howard Quince, the CFO, said, "Ah, *there* you are, Riley—I was looking for you."

Jazz and I followed her into the room, where the elliptical granite table was surrounded by a dozen posh executive chairs upholstered with putty-colored leather. Quince had a pile of papers scattered in front of his seat at the head of the table. Seated alongside was a man I recognized as Jim Landon, the bland banker at the pool party whose voice of reason had helped calm the vicious flare-up involving Noreen Penley Wade, Skip Terry, and Skip's father, Kenneth.

Quince and Landon stood. Landon said to Riley, "Miss Uba—delighted to see you. I understand you're doing a bang-up job in Noreen's absence. What a tragedy."

"Doing my best, Mr. Landon. Thank you."

I noted they were not on a first-name basis.

Riley introduced Jazz and me to Landon, who remembered us from the party. He also mentioned that his old chum Kenneth Terry had told him about hiring Jazz "to help get the Skipper out of a sticky wicket."

I couldn't help thinking how different Jim Landon looked today. Back at the Ellinger House, he had worn pastel shorts, part of a dress code that placed him firmly among the circle of Kenneth Terry's leisure-class friends. What's more, he had been in the company of his glamour-puss wife and their nearly naked nymphette daughter. But now, in their absence and wearing a gray suit, he looked like any other downtown businessman, late fifties, awaiting retirement and the golf course at his club in the desert.

Howard Quince was telling Riley, "… and Jim has some *great* ideas for jump-starting a new capital campaign. The museum's post-Noreen era—God rest her soul—presents us with an opportunity to reframe M3A's mission."

Landon picked up the narrative. "My work with the foundation has taught me a valuable lesson: never think small. So this is the *perfect* time to consider a substantial expansion of the museum's physical footprint. M3A needs a stand-alone building of its own, which would be a plum commission for a top-notch architect. Maybe Gehry could work us in—he's local. Call me a dreamer, but that's my job. The foundation, of course, would need to *substantially* beef up its endowment, and I—"

"Excuse me," said Riley, cutting him short. She turned to Jazz and me. "Sorry, but I should sit in on this. Unless there's something else I can do for you, could you find your own way out? In the hallway, it's the only door on the left. It leads to the galleries."

"Of course," we said. "No problem at all." "Thanks for your help." "Good luck with the big plans."

As we were stepping out to the hall from the conference room, Howard Quince told us, "We have a place in the desert. My wife's out there now. Hope we'll run into you sometime."

"Fabulous," I said. *Not a chance,* I thought.

We quickly found the only door on the left. Opening it, I led Jazz into the blackness of Gallery B.

She leaned to ask, "Are you feeling politely dismissed?"

I quelled a laugh and said nothing. We were being watched by Rossetti's woman with the bejeweled goblet. She seemed to be toasting our departure with a sneer.

■

Out on the plaza, in the midst of the noon rush, we paused near one of the kiosks. I asked Jazz, "Hungry?"

"Starved. And it's a long drive back."

It occurred to me that the Polo Lounge was about fifteen minutes away. I didn't know if Jazz had ever been there, but it might be fun to show her the wallpaper. We looked just fine. They'd let us in. And I had plastic.

But I didn't suggest it.

That place was from another time. In a different world.

CHAPTER TWELVE

After grabbing a burger somewhere, we were back in the SUV, back on the 10, heading east. When we had cleared the tangle of downtown LA, Jazz set the cruise control and steered us toward the desert.

As the monotony of the drive ahead settled in, Jazz glanced over to ask me, "Well, what'd you think?"

"About what?"

"A week ago, at the scene of the drowning, we were talking with Arcie Madera about possible suspects, and you mentioned Riley Uba."

I nodded. "I was under the impression she wanted her boss's job. It was just a vibe, and I thought we should explore it."

"But now?"

"We explored it, and I was wrong. Riley has zero interest in taking over the top job. So she had no motive to convince Noreen to return to the Ellinger House last Tuesday. Someone else set it up."

"Right," said Jazz, eyes on the road. "In fact, everyone we talked to seemed *thrilled* with Riley's work there. Especially"— Jazz paused for effect—"the curator."

"Cameron Vicario," I said. I hadn't taken notes while meeting with him, but when he told us, point-blank, that he was glad Noreen was gone—calling her a threat to the future of the museum—I noticed that Jazz's pen was plenty busy.

Jazz now said, "But I don't think he's the type. Sure, lots of passion, lots of emotion, but c'mon. Can you honestly see that guy arranging for a hit man to drown his boss?"

"Honestly," I answered, "no, not at all. But keep him on the list."

The list also included museum CFO Howard Quince and the bland banker, Jim Landon, whose role with "the foundation" was not clear to us. I said to Jazz, "It seems both of their wives spend most of their time in the desert. They might be good for some follow-up."

Jazz nodded. "They're on the list."

Some twenty miles east of Los Angeles, as the SUV climbed a steep, hilly stretch of highway, the sprawling green grounds of a Forest Lawn cemetery rose from the right side of the road. The peaceful setting stood in stark contrast to the eight-lane gladiator war and the gnashing of truck gears along the interstate. Jazz drummed the steering wheel as if lost in thought. The tapping of her fingers blended with the drone of the engine as she said, "It was weird, right? It wasn't just me?"

I turned to her with a grin. "Could you be more specific?"

"That museum. Hoity-toity address on Wilshire Boulevard. Top-dollar executives. Powerhouse board of directors, not to mention 'the foundation,' plus big plans for a capital campaign and expansion. So we haul our asses out there to take a look. Walk through the door, and what've you got? A rented storefront with two little exhibit rooms. Maybe two dozen pictures, total. I mean, why bother? It all seemed so *puny.*"

I reminded her, "Blade Wade said as much."

"Yeah, he did."

"It was beyond puny," I said. "It was fishy."

The vehicle lost speed as Jazz nodded in thought, then turned to look me in the eye. "All hat," she said, "and no cattle."

■

Wednesday morning, I awoke from a repeating loop of dreams that were pleasingly erotic but devoid of any climax. The "other man" who had teased me through the wee hours was some sort of nocturnal stand-in for Skip Terry—just my type, but not available. Jazz had accused me of thinking with my dick; now, apparently, I was also doomed to dream with it.

No stranger to frustration, I kicked away the covers at dawn and padded into the kitchen to start the coffee. Caffeine would clear the horny inklings of the night, which could be dealt with some other time in the company of some other dreamy (but more cooperative) partner, waking or otherwise.

The prior day's visit to LA must have jiggered my body's thermostat, as the night in the desert seemed hotter than usual. While waiting for the morning's first cup of coffee, I left the air conditioner running and didn't bother opening the front door to check the breeze—or the to-and-fro of my neighbors. Mitzi the rat terrier hadn't stirred yet, so I was content to launch the day in the cool confinement of my apartment.

When it was time to pour a second mug of coffee, I had tired of squinting at my phone and decided to run out for a paper. I threw on a shirt and checked my hair in the bathroom mirror. Then I tucked my wallet into my shorts and stepped toward the front door. Just as I reached for the knob—a gentle rapping without.

"'Tis some visitor," I muttered, grinning to myself, as if a dreamy stand-in for Skip Terry had arrived to relieve my horny inklings of the night. I knew otherwise, of course—it had to be Zola Lorinsky, reporting on her progress with the banana-print curtains. Maybe she had something to run past me. A choice of pleats, perhaps. French, pinch, or Euro?

Again the gentle rapping. When I opened the door, there stood Isandro.

"Morning, Dante," he said quietly. He wore his gym shorts and flip-flops. His hair was wet and tousled. "Got a minute?"

I knew what that meant. "Well, *yeah*. Come on in." Closing the door after him, I offered, "Coffee?"

"Great." He seemed nervous.

While pouring a mug for each of us, I said, "It's been a while. *What* have you been up to?"

"Not sure if you noticed, but I had a guest for a few days."

"Really?" With a wink, I added, "Was it fun?"

He looked confused. "Well, *sure*. Márcio's my older brother. We had lots of catching up to do."

"Do tell?" I handed Isandro the coffee, and we both stood there, having a sip.

He explained, "Márcio works in Chicago, and our parents are in LA. He's using some vacation time to visit them, but he wanted to stop here on the way. It was nice to see him again." Isandro stared at me for a moment with a wry smile. "But it didn't leave much time for ... *you* know ... for play."

I extended my palm. "Enough coffee for now?"

He nodded, setting the mug in my hand. It was practically full.

As I turned and placed both mugs on the counter, he stepped up behind and pulled me close. I felt the heat through his silky shorts as he whispered over my shoulder, "And what have *you* been up to?" He knew nothing of Skip or the drowning or my side gig with Jazz.

"Long story. That can wait." And I led him to my mussed bed. Two minutes flat, and Mitzi was yapping her head off.

■

Jazz needed to review some county records that afternoon in Riverside, about an hour away. I volunteered to drive to nearby Palm Desert and check out the Harris-Heimlich Gallery, which was run by Blade Wade's agent, Sabrina Harris.

"Good idea," said Jazz on the phone. "Don't make an appointment. Just go and hope she's there. Pretend you're interested in Blade's paintings. Try to get her talking about him."

Around one thirty, I drove down valley on 111, passing through Rancho Mirage and entering Palm Desert, where I turned right onto El Paseo, a stylish stretch of boulevard that bypassed the highway for a mile or two before reconnecting. The tony shopping area, which served as the city's downtown, housed an array of luxury-brand shops as well as restaurants and galleries—lots of galleries. The thoroughfare was divided by lush medians where large-scale sculptures mingled with the palms and flowers. Locals often referred to the area as "the Rodeo Drive of the desert."

The comparison had some merit, but it was not entirely accurate. Rodeo Drive, in Beverly Hills, thrived year-round, while many of the shops along El Paseo struggled to survive each summer. By mid-June, while driving along in my Camry, I saw plenty of dark windows displaying AVAILABLE signs.

The higher-end galleries seemed to make it through the hot months, some of them slipping into partial dormancy, keeping their doors open but reducing their hours. I had checked online and knew that Harris-Heimlich would be open that afternoon.

The gallery was located near the far end of El Paseo, where it looped back to the highway. Spotting their sign, I slowed down as I drove by the front windows. There were open parking spaces at the curb, but I doubted if the staff would take me seriously as a potential client if they saw me getting out of my car, so I turned at the corner, parked behind the building, and walked back to the street. In spite of the weather, I wore all black with long pants. Very arty.

Entering, I saw at once that the vast space, as well as the scope of its collected works, was far more substantial than that of M3A-LA. Granted, this was contemporary art—for sale—not a public exhibit of historic masterpieces. Still, this gallery struck me as having life and purpose, whereas my experience at M3A had left me feeling underwhelmed and suspicious.

Music drifted softly through the space—a pleasant, jazzy mash-up of a baroque-sounding piece played by a string quartet. An attractive young man, looking earnest and freshly degreed, approached me with a smile and a name tag reading LIAM. "May I help you, sir? Or are we just taking a look?"

Had I not been sated by Isandro that morning, I would have asked in return, Are you single, Liam? Do you like men? Instead, I replied, "I might be in the market for a little something—or perhaps even a big something—for a new house I'm finishing. Are you Mr. Heimlich?"

I was sure he wasn't. He was far too young.

"As a matter of fact, I am." He laughed. "I'm Mr. Heimlich's nephew. He isn't in today. But the other owner is back in the office. Would you care to meet her?"

"Thank you, Liam. Yes, I would."

"And your name, please?"

"Dante. Dante O'Donnell."

"Nice," he said under his breath, looking me over. Then he turned and strode out of view.

I began browsing and quickly confirmed that the gallery's target clientele was not tourists looking for souvenirs. I saw nothing under a thousand dollars, with many of the works priced in the tens of thousands. All of it—paintings, sculpture, and a special section of glass art—was strikingly modern, mostly abstract.

"Mr. O'Donnell?" said a woman's voice.

I turned as she stepped near. Dressed in a gray silk pantsuit and pecking the concrete floor with four-inch heels, she was thin, blond, pretty, and professional. Extending her hand, she shook mine. "Sabrina Harris. What can I do for you today? You're spiffing up a new home?"

I noticed that Liam had followed her back and now stood at a distance, watching.

"That's right," I told her.

"Have you been to the gallery before?"

"No, first time. But I've driven by many times and was waiting for an excuse to come in"—not true, of course. I added, "Now, with the new house, let's just say I've got a bare wall that's crying for attention."

"Well," she said, flipping her hands, "you've come to the right place for a painting. Are you mainly interested in finding something decorative? Or would you rather go with something—shall we way—more significant?"

"Significant," I said without batting an eye. "Definitely."

She smiled. "It's such a hot afternoon. May I offer you a glass of bubbly?"

"You may. And I'll accept."

Sabrina turned and caught Liam's eye, holding up two fingers. He disappeared.

As we strolled through the front gallery, she talked about various artists and the investment potential of their work. But I assured her, "I'm not here to find something to sell. I'm here to find something I love."

She nodded and smiled. Touching my arm, she said, "Your words warm my heart, Dante. You'd be surprised how many clients are merely shopping for status—and a return on investment."

I shook my head woefully. "Pity."

"Now, since you have a particular wall in mind, what would be the ideal scale for the art? The longer dimension, approximately."

I closed my eyes and used my hands to frame a rectangle in front of me. "About eight feet," I said, opening my eyes.

She grinned. Her eyes widened—like a cat sizing up a plump mouse.

Liam returned with two frosty champagne flutes. He handed one to Sabrina without comment. Handing me the other, he looked me in the eye and said softly, "Skoal."

As he left, Sabrina and I tried a sip. I may not know much about art, but I've served—and tasted—a good deal of sparkling wine. This was no prosecco, no cava. It was a good, solid, bone-dry French champagne.

We strolled and tippled, exploring another gallery, but Sabrina was disappointed that nothing seemed to catch my interest. She suggested, "If you could give me a better idea of what you *like*, maybe I could steer you in the right direction."

I shrugged. "I like red."

"Oh!" She called out, "Liam? Bring the bottle, please." And she led me toward the back of the building, where we entered a cavernous, shadowy exhibit space that might have been converted from a loading dock.

Switching on the lights, she said, "Dante O'Donnell, permit me to introduce you to the work of Blade Wade."

"Now, *that*," I said, "that's more like it."

■

Liam brought the Perrier-Jouët, filled our glasses, and left the bottle as Sabrina walked me through the space, extolling the work and the talents of Blade Wade, "whom I happen to represent." She added, "Blade's career is about to skyrocket. I know you're not looking for art as an investment, Dante, but trust me—your heirs will thank you."

"That's a plus, I guess." I chuckled, having never thought about heirs.

"So. See anything you like?"

"Plenty," I said honestly, in spite of the subterfuge behind my visit. "The style, the scale, the *redness*—love them all. Difficult choice."

"Understood." She led me to an upholstered bench in the middle of the room, where we could sit and view everything at once while I considered the best pick for my imaginary bare wall.

With an impending sale shaping up, Sabrina became visibly more relaxed. The hard sell was over; all that remained was to wait and to reel me in. Sitting at my side, she refilled my glass. "Did I mention that Blade Wade is local?"

"No, you didn't."

She nodded. "Lives right here in the desert. Works at his studio in Palm Springs."

Feigning deep thought, I said, "The name does seem familiar, actually."

"I'm not surprised. He may *live* here, but his work has caught the eye of cognoscenti everywhere—and I mean worldwide."

"Maybe. But I think I've read his name in some other context. Something... bad. Or am I mixed up?"

"Unfortunately, Dante, you're not mixed up. Blade's wife died last week in a horrible accident. A drowning. It's being investigated." Sabrina took a sip of champagne, then added, "It was strange. And tragic."

"Dear God," I said. "How dreadful. My condolences to Mr. Wade. Such a sudden loss—I hope it won't be a setback for his work."

"We've talked, of course. He's fine, under the circumstances. He's just grateful to have his art to fall back on. Remaining creatively engaged can help us get through the worst of times, don't you think?"

Watching her speak, I saw no concern in her face, despite the grave and sympathetic tone of her words. I said, "Sometimes, misfortune brings new possibilities."

"*Yes*," Sabrina agreed at once, breaking into a smile. "If anything, Blade seems to be reenergized by this. Did I mention his career is about to skyrocket?"

"You did."

I judged her to be forty or so, about ten years younger than Blade. Clearly, her devotion to him went well beyond that of an agent's commitment to a client's professional advancement. Her eyes seemed to sparkle as she again lifted the bottle to my glass.

"No, thanks," I said. "I need to drive."

"Ah. Then you've decided?" Her hand slowly glided past the dozens of paintings surrounding us, as if to ask me, Which one?

"May I take a few pictures?"

"Of *course*."

"I'd like to 'try them out' at home, so to speak. And I'll need to get exact measurements."

Sabrina stood. "You go ahead and snap your photos while I get an inventory sheet—it has the measures and prices."

I stood and took pictures with my phone. Within a minute, she returned with the list and handed it to me. Her business card was attached. I patted a pocket, saying, "Sorry, I don't seem to have a card with me, but I'll get back to you soon."

"Splendid." She leaned near, circling numbers on the list that corresponded to the works that had interested me. I noticed a strong whiff of her perfume.

"If you don't mind my asking, Sabrina, what's that fragrance you're wearing?"

With a surprised smile, she asked, "You like it?"

"Very much—and I think my sister might, too." There was no sister.

"It's called Rose Organdy. It's a little old-fashioned, but I've always worn it."

■

Sabrina walked me out to the front gallery, shook my hand, and said she was eager to hear back from me.

When she retreated to her office, I crossed the main exhibit space toward the front door, but I paused while passing a small side gallery, previously unnoticed, tucked between two larger exhibits. The spaced lettering over the open portal spelled out the name REX KHALAJI.

I stepped into the room, where the walls displayed many photographs—forty or fifty—with thick white mats and simple black frames. Lettering centered on the far wall identified the photos as ARCHIVAL PRINTS FROM FILM. A lengthy block of text explained that the exhibit consisted of "examples of the famed photographer's pre-digital portraits from the twentieth century."

I quietly made the rounds, recognizing many of the images, which I had seen as published reproductions, lacking the intense detail that emerged from these darkroom prints. Models and celebrities—men and women, some of them legendary, others long faded—peered out from the walls, in the company of couturiers, designers, and artists, their faces unknown to me.

One of the walls displayed portraits of people not from the celebrity world. These images were less dramatic, less posed, and more candid, more like snapshots—though very *good* ones. Khalaji had stalked people on the street, travelers at airports, gardeners at work, surfers, waitresses, punks, and cops—all of them captured by an artist's eye. Each seemed to tell a story. Each seemed to share a secret, a razor-thin slice of a private life, glimpsed through the click of a shutter.

Then I froze. I drew a sharp breath and held it while drinking in the sight of the next picture. A beautiful young man—truly an Adonis—sprang from the water, lifting himself, dripping, from the edge of a swimming pool. He grinned at the camera, inviting the viewer—the voyeur—to invent a fantasy.

"Incredible, isn't it?"

I turned to see Liam watching me from the entry to the tiny gallery, which now felt like a peep show.

"Yes," I agreed, "incredible."

As I returned my attention to the picture, I heard Liam step up behind me. I sensed him looking over my shoulder.

"I think I must've stared at *that* one for hours," he said. "A little young, but Jesus. Now I see him in my dreams."

"So do I, Liam."

My eyes were stuck on the photo. I had no doubt—it was Skip Terry as an adolescent.

CHAPTER THIRTEEN

Out in the parking lot behind the gallery, I used my phone app to start the car. While it cooled down, I walked to the shade of a sculpture garden that displayed a few oversize pieces. Then I sat on a bench near a fountain, where I placed a call to Jazz.

"Hey," she said. "What's up?"

"Just visited the Harris-Heimlich Gallery. Talked to Sabrina. You were right—she wears Rose Organdy."

"Uh-huh."

"And she's definitely got the hots for Blade. Says he's doing 'fine' with his wife's death—because he has his art to fall back on. She called the drowning an accident."

"Uh-huh. How'd you get her to open up about it?"

"She thinks I'm going to buy one of Blade's paintings."

Jazz laughed loud. "How *sweet* of you."

"Thirty-five grand. She even popped a good bottle of champagne."

"Can't say I blame her."

"So," I said, "where are you?"

"Driving back from Riverside. Checked a few files. Didn't learn much."

I said, "The reason I called: Do you happen to have contact info for Rex Khalaji?"

She reminded me, "I'm *driving*—on the 10."

"But do you have it?"

"Probably. If not on my phone, then back at the office on Kenneth Terry's party list. Why?"

"Sabrina's gallery has an exhibit of Khalaji's photography. One of the pictures jumped out at me—an adorable young man."

"Christ. You are *so* predictable."

I elaborated: "It was a picture of Skip Terry in a swimming pool—at least twenty years ago."

"Interesting. But we already know that Khalaji goes way back with the family. Skip's parents told us their son became Khalaji's 'foster nephew.'"

"True," I said, "but trust me—in this picture the photographer's connection to his subject rose to a different level. The brazen look on Skip's teenaged face was flat-out seductive."

"So what? Guys that age are always horny."

Jazz had raised a valid point. "Even so," I said, "I think we should pay Khalaji a visit. He was at the pool party. He's obviously fond of Skip. And he knows a lot of family history. He might have some insights."

Jazz seemed to mull my suggestion for a moment before telling me, "Okay. I'll call him later and try to set something up for tomorrow."

■

By the next morning, Thursday, I hadn't heard back from Jazz, so I figured she had not yet nailed down a meeting with Khalaji. Didn't matter—my day was wide open. And it began, as usual, at dawn, when I stepped outside my front door hoping to find that the daybreak had been cooled by the night.

Perfect. I went inside again, leaving the door open a few inches. I switched off the air, switched on the coffee, and put on a shirt over my workout shorts—the hot spell had broken, at least for a few hours.

And then, as yesterday, there came a gentle rapping at the door. At that hour, there were only two likely callers—Isandro or Zola. Since Isandro had come scratching for attention the previous morning (and had never done so on two days running), it was now Zola's turn to brighten the dawn.

"Dante, dah-ling," she said as I swung the door wide, "I saw your lights. If it's not too early, may I show you something?"

I smiled. "Sure."

She raised an index finger, made a come-hither gesture, and led me over to her apartment, where the door stood open. She babbled, "Excuse my appearance, love, but I was up late, working."

"You look fabulous, as always."

"And *you're* a shameless liar—but thank you."

She took me into her spare bedroom, the workroom, where she had rigged a broom handle across the top of two open closet doors. Hanging from the makeshift rod on antiqued metal rings was a finished section of the banana-leaf drapery, which fell to the floor in generous rolling folds, barely grazing the carpet. "What do you think?"

I wrapped her in a hug. "I am *so* blown away."

She laughed softly. "It's not worth *crying* over, love."

Oops. I'd gotten soppy. "Honest, Zola. Never in my wildest dreams—"

"Now, now." Holding me at arm's length, she asked, "Permission to proceed?"

I gave her a quizzical look.

She spelled it out: "Is it okay for me to finish the other half?"

"Of *course*." With a laugh, I added, "How could it *not* be okay?"

"Honey"—she rolled her eyes—"some evening, over drinks, I'll recite for you a litany of my clients from hell."

"I'll take you up on that. And the drinks are on me."

"Deal. Now, then: you can get back to your coffee, and I'll get back to work. I should wrap this up in a couple of days."

When she tired of my effusive thanks, she shooed me out to the patio and closed her door.

Just as I was about to step inside my own apartment, I noticed headlights through the street gate, then heard the thud of a car door. I waited, and as expected, Isandro entered the courtyard, returning from his hospital shift.

"Hey," he said, a quiet exclamation not likely to rouse the neighbors. Even in the half-light, I saw that he had broken into a smile.

He walked over to me and, extending his arms, offered a casual hug. With a handsome grin, he told me, "Thanks."

"For what?"

"Yesterday morning. It was *very* much needed." As a token of his appreciation, he kissed my lips, and we lingered, exploring each other's teeth, sharing a little moan of satisfaction. Then, with a polite peck, he backed off. "But today? Afraid I'm shot."

"No explanation needed. You've been working—while I'm on vacation."

"Oh, yeah? Doing anything special?"

I shrugged. "Just tryin' to catch a killer."

He sputtered a laugh. "Sorry I asked."

"Go get some rest."

He leaned in for another kiss, a quick one—plus a friendly grope—then he stepped away, heading for his apartment. But he paused and turned to stage-whisper through the hush of the early morning, "Good luck with that manhunt."

I gave him a thumbs-up.

•

Sometime after nine, Jazz phoned. "Hey, Dante."

"Hey there, yourself. Did you get through to Khalaji?"

"I did. I was afraid he might be all *attitude*, but no. Very gracious—anything to help 'the Skipper' and his parents. He's happy to meet with us after lunch, his place at one thirty. But there's a little wrinkle."

"Oh?"

"Just after I got off the phone with him, not three minutes ago, Christopher called."

"Your ex."

"Right. Emma doesn't have preschool during the summer. She has day care with a sitter at home—Christopher's home. And the sitter phoned in sick this morning. Christopher asked if I could take Emma for the day."

"What do you want to do?"

"She's growing up *without* me, Dante. You know how that breaks me up. Of *course* I'll take her."

"I totally get it."

"So here's the deal. I can bring Emma with us to the meeting—or you can go alone. What do you think?"

"I'm fine either way."

"Good. I'd like to be there. Khalaji sounded ... *interesting* on the phone. Hope he won't mind the little party crasher."

I reminded Jazz, "He wanted kids but never had any. I bet he'll be charmed by Emma. Where does he live?"

"Rancho Mirage. I'll pick you up by one fifteen."

"Got it," I said. "Now go pick up Emma."

"Way ahead of you, Dante. I'm just pulling into Christopher's driveway."

■

A few minutes past one, Jazz phoned and asked me to be waiting at the curb.

When she arrived in the SUV, I hopped inside and barely had the door closed before she sped away. Getting myself buckled in, I turned to Emma behind me—secure in her safety seat—and said, "How nice to see you again, Miss Friendly."

She waved the paw of her stuffed cat. "Oliver's glad to see you, too, Dante."

I reached behind, shook the cat's paw, and then squeezed the girl's hand.

While Emma busied herself in lively conversation with the cat, Jazz said to me, "That painting she made at Blade's studio? She took it home to her dad on Sunday, and he sent it out to be framed. When I picked her up today, Christopher was at home—waiting for me so he could go to work—and he told me he was 'astonished.'" She chuckled.

"What's so funny?"

She explained, "Christopher Friendly, Stanford grad, Order of the Coif, attorney at law—he wasn't surprised, wasn't amazed. No, Christopher was 'astonished.'"

I laughed. "Astonished in a *good* way, I hope."

"*Hell*, yeah. Said he had no idea that Emma 'harbored artistic inclinations.' Said it didn't come from *him*—and he's right, cuz he can never figure out what tie to wear with his damn socks, so it's just easier for him not to try, and that's why he always dresses so fuckin' *blah*—know what I mean?"

"Uh, maybe." I had no idea where she was going with this.

"So. Yes. Christopher liked Emma's painting. A lot. Said it was 'simply fabulous.'" Jazz glanced over to ask me, "Think he's gay?"

"Probably not."

"And the bottom line—get this—is that he actually *thanked* me. He thanked me for nurturing Emma's talents."

"Glad it worked out that way."

Jazz shrugged; the SUV swerved. "Truth is, any nurturing, that was Blade Wade's doing. But I didn't mention that."

With the slightest shake of my head, I told her, "I wouldn't either. Christopher might ask, 'Who's Blade Wade?' And then you'd need to explain how you'd taken Emma along on a murder investigation."

Jazz rumbled with a low laugh. "And here we go again."

■

In Rancho Mirage, Jazz slowed at the entrance to Desert Towers and pulled up to the guardhouse. The complex, unlike most other country clubs in the area, consisted of a cluster of seven-story condo buildings, surrounded by a golf course. Other clubs resembled villages of separate dwellings; this one looked more like a resort hotel. I had visited friends at Desert Towers over the years, and while the condos lacked the charm of individual homes on winding streets, they boasted some unmatched views from the upper floors.

Jazz told the guard, "Mr. Khalaji is expecting us."

"Yes, ma'am. Building A, unit 701, the penthouse."

When the gate swung open, we drove onto the grounds. At a fork in the entryway, one road led to the golf club, the other to the residences.

Emma got a kick out of the elevator—kids in the desert don't see many—so from her perspective, our adventure was off to a good start. On the seventh floor, other than a stairwell exit, there were doors to only two penthouses, at opposite ends of the long hallway. We rang Khalaji's bell and waited in the processed air of the muffled corridor. The building creaked and popped.

"Coming, coming," said a man's voice within, accompanied by the sound of his shoes on hardwood flooring. When the door swung open—double doors, in fact, lacquered black, with big brass Hollywood-style knobs centered on each—there stood Rex Khalaji, dressed in cream-colored linen and beaming a huge, toothy smile. "Who's *this* little sweetheart?" he said, hunkering down to extend his arms to Emma, who toddled into his hug.

Jazz apologized for the unexpected guest and began to explain, but Khalaji cut her short. "Nonsense, nonsense—please, come right in." He stood again, with a bit of effort, and welcomed us into the entry hall, where we introduced ourselves. He assured us, "I remember you both from the pool party." With a little laugh, he added, "Wasn't *that* quite the commotion?"

As he led us into the living room, the view of the surrounding mountain valley unfurled before us, even more spectacular than I recalled, having never seen it from the top floor. Jazz and I babbled, wowed by the posh setting—the vista, the career memorabilia, the photos everywhere—but Emma was focused squarely on a discovery of her own. "Kitty!" she said with a squeal.

The cat watched the child with brave curiosity, perched on the wide rolled arm of a nine-foot sofa. Khalaji took Emma's hand and led her over for a closer look. "I see you have a kitty, too, Emma. What's his name?"

"Oliver."

"Well, that's perfectly charming. Now, Emma—and Oliver—I'd like you to meet Ragamuffin, but I just call him Muffin for short."

Emma instantly fell into a conversation with Muffin, who purred. Oliver watched obliquely, hanging by one leg at Emma's side.

"Tell you what," said Khalaji. "I have just the spot for the three of you to get better acquainted." He picked up Muffin and led Emma and Oliver into a den that opened from the far end of the living room. He plumped some pillows for his guests, pulled some picture books from a shelf, and switched on a TV, finding cartoons, played low.

Returning to us, he said, "That ought to amuse them while we delve into more adult matters."

Jazz said, "That's sweet of you, Mr. Khalaji. Thank you."

"Please, Jazz—call me Rex. You too, Dante." He winked at me. "Shall we sit down?"

We settled around an antique leather-topped game table near the windows. Khalaji took away a backgammon set to make room for Jazz to write notes.

She flipped back through several pages, then looked up. "Rex, I understand you've known the Terry family for many years."

He nodded and smiled, as if savoring the memories. "Since before Skip was born, long ago in LA. I heard you've already spoken to Kenneth and Claudia. Then you probably know I was married back then."

"Yes," said Jazz, "and I was sorry to hear of your wife's untimely passing."

He sighed. "It's the rhythm of life—joy and grief. I'm seventy now. On balance, life has been good to me. And Skip is such a treasure."

I asked, "Do you get back to LA much? Mingle with the celebrity crowd?"

He laughed. "Not like I used to. Those were the golden days, to be sure. And now, these are the golden *years*, as they say. A while back, Skip told me, 'Life in the desert can be paradise.' And I've learned to appreciate the wisdom of a young man's words."

I noticed that Khalaji had chosen to frame the conversation, three times already, in terms of Skip. Jazz caught my eye—she'd noticed it also.

"Rex," I said, "just yesterday, I went into the Harris-Heimlich Gallery on El Paseo. Finding your exhibit there was such a pleasant surprise." For Jazz's benefit, I added, "I was…astonished." She rolled her eyes.

Khalaji said, "Kind of you to mention it, Dante. It's all *older* work, of course. But the prints from film seem to have a special, lasting appeal. The exhibit is more or less permanent now. The prints don't sell much, but the gallery finds the collection good for foot traffic. It was Sabrina's idea. Do you know her?"

"I met her yesterday. Jazz and I heard she represents Blade Wade—Noreen's husband—so I wanted to go in and check out his work."

Khalaji asked, "It's wonderful, isn't it?"

"Astonishing," said Jazz.

Ignoring her, I said to Khalaji, "Sabrina seems thrilled to be working with Blade—says his career is ready for blastoff."

"That's one way of putting it." With a chuckle, Khalaji added, "In case you haven't heard: their relationship is a tad more involved than *that*."

"Oh?" said Jazz.

"My *dear*," he told her, "it's common knowledge, at least within certain circles, that Sabrina is Wade's longtime mistress. But *now*, of course, with Noreen out of the way, Sabrina can stop sneaking around."

"Imagine that," I said.

Khalaji paused. "Perhaps I should back up. As you know, Kenneth Terry is one of my oldest friends. Through his board work with Noreen at M3A, he came to know of her husband. Blade was looking for a new agent at the time. Kenneth mentioned this to me because of my art-world connections, wondering if there was anyone I could recommend. I've known Sabrina forever, and because she's done some repping, I suggested she might consider Blade. She checked him out, and needless to say, things started to develop."

Khalaji sat back in his chair and blew a breathy sigh. "So in a way," he continued, "their little romance is *my* fault—or at least my doing. Sabrina has cried on my shoulder about being 'the other woman' since the start. Well, boo-hoo. And now? Oh, brother. As far as she's concerned, it's open season. I've advised her to wait at *least* until after the funeral. Frankly, I find it embarrassing. But Skip thinks it's funny—and won't let me forget it."

Again, Khalaji had spun the conversation back to Skip. "Rex," I said, "I meant to ask you about one of your photos at Harris-Heimlich. It's a young man in a swimming pool. I thought he looked familiar, and then I realized it might be Skip—quite a few years ago."

"Really?" he said. His tone was dismissive. "I forgot about that one."

"When was it taken?"

He shrugged. "Twenty years ago? He was about sixteen."

Our discussion ambled on for another quarter hour. At a lull, Khalaji suggested, "Lemonade? Nothing better on a hot afternoon. Well—*gin*, maybe—but it's far too early for that."

I said, "We'd hate to impose, Rex."

"No bother at all. There's a pitcher all made up, waiting in the fridge. I'll bet Emma would enjoy some, too—she's been so *busy* with the two felines."

"Uh," said Jazz, "Emma would just spill it."

"Not to worry. We'll keep an eye on her. Worst-case scenario? I have a marvelous woman who comes in twice a week. She's a wiz with faux pas." Khalaji got up from the table.

Jazz also rose. "I'll check on Emma."

I offered, "Can I help you, Rex?"

"Of *course*, Dante. This way." And he led me back to the kitchen.

■

Even the kitchen had a drop-dead view. Not the typical apartment-style galley, it was a big, serious kitchen meant for entertaining, with barstools at the center island and a table for breakfast or lunch overlooking the golf course, the mountains, and the arching blue sky that rose from the craggy horizon.

While Khalaji puttered with glassware and ice, arranging a tray, I browsed the framed photos that filled a wall near the table. Khalaji bustled about, then stepped over to a door and opened it. Inside was darkness—I assumed it was a pantry or storeroom. Standing in the doorway, he switched on the interior lights. "Dante," he said, "you might like to see this."

When I followed him inside, I saw no canned goods, Tupperware, or the expected shelving stacked with party supplies. Rather, the room was outfitted as a cozy gallery space, with dark gray walls, track lighting, and thick wool carpeting that produced a ringing silence as Khalaji closed the door behind us.

"As you can see," he said, "this is a special space, devoted to a special subject."

All four walls displayed framed photographs of Skip Terry— old and new, large and small, many in color, others black-and-white. Although the photos depicted Skip at every stage of life (one of them must have been shot in the maternity ward), their arrangement was not chronological. Instead, the walls were composed for dramatic impact, covering a variety of themes: birthdays, cars, dress-up, sports, travel, and most conspicuously, swimming pools, which occupied the main wall, across from the door.

Naturally, the pool shots were the most alluring, and I immediately stepped over for a closer look. I found a duplicate of the Harris-Heimlich photo of Skip at sixteen, but the one that froze my attention was much larger, front and center, in full color— and considerably more recent.

Skip lounged on a baby-blue pool raft, not unlike the one at the Ellinger House. His arms were splayed like wings, with his head resting in both palms. My eyes drank in the sight of him, with his sandy hair and stubbly beard, wearing the same classic Ray-Bans he had worn ten days earlier—on the morning when he seduced me in the pool.

I knew for a fact that Skip and I had been alone at his parents' rental house that day, so I did not react to the photo with sudden, wild suspicions that Khalaji had been lurking there, stalking with his camera. The similarity of the photo to my actual encounter with Skip, though remarkable, was nothing sinister, merely a coincidence. It did not creep me out.

What did creep me out, though, was the very existence of Khalaji's secret gallery, his photographic shrine to Skip Terry, his obvious obsession with a man he seemingly fetishized.

Khalaji said, "Call me an old fool, but that boy has been a constant source of beauty in my life."

I reminded him, "That boy is thirty-six."

He laughed. "Still a pup. The Skipper." Then his tone turned thoughtful. "Skip's father is worried, Dante. He tells me the sheriff's department took Skip's phone and computer. It seems impossible, but they actually suspect Skip of killing Noreen. Crazy, isn't it?"

"Crazy," I agreed. "That's why Skip's parents hired Jazz—to dig deeper and faster than the cops."

Khalaji nodded. "Keep digging. If I can be of any help, just let me know." As he reached to open the door, he added, "I'd do *anything* to protect Skip."

A nice sentiment, I thought, but it also muddied the investigative waters. It sounded like a newfound motive for someone to dispense with the woman who had openly threatened Skip.

■

Khalaji and I returned to the living room. I carried the pitcher of lemonade; he brought the tray of glasses and whatnot. Little Emma had ditched the books and cartoons in the den and now stood at the windows with her mother, who pointed out landmarks that the four-year-old had previously seen only from ground level. Muffin sprawled with rag doll Oliver on the sofa.

While Khalaji fussed with the refreshments at the game table, Emma joined him, bringing him up to date on her conversation with the two cats. I was examining yet another wall of photographs—it was impossible to take them all in—when I spotted something. With a finger wag, I summoned Jazz, who came over for a look. Hanging there, framed and matted, was one of the *Vogue*-style photos Khalaji had shot of Noreen Penley Wade with Riley Uba at the pool party.

"Rex," I said, tapping the picture, "this turned out *great*."

He looked over his shoulder and smiled. "Didn't it, though?" Then he picked up two tall glasses of lemonade and brought them over to Jazz and me. "Sometimes, it's as if the fates themselves clicked the shutter. If I say so myself, there's genuine serendipity in that image."

Handing us the drinks, he added, "That's probably the last picture ever taken of Noreen—before she died."

CHAPTER FOURTEEN

The next morning, Friday, I had no visitors at dawn. Zola Lorinsky must have still been busy with the curtain project—or maybe she had decided to give it a rest the prior evening, spending the time instead with her old pal Tom Collins. As for Isandro, his schedule was so irregular, the chance of his appearance on any given morning was always a crapshoot—though when he did come calling, the odds of a payoff were promising. That day, however, my early hours were spent alone.

Shortly after nine, Jazz phoned me to strategize. She was planning to pump Arcie Madera for an update on Skip's confiscated electronics, but the likelihood of Arcie divulging anything was sketchy at best.

Meanwhile, reviewing our Tuesday trip to M3A-LA, we decided there were two threads of the investigation worthy of follow-up. Investment banker Jim Landon and museum CFO Howard Quince, whose jobs were based in Los Angeles, both had wives who spent most of their time at second homes in the desert. The wives might be useful as background sources regarding any M3A politics and infighting. Plus, they were locally accessible. Jazz gave me each woman's phone number and asked me to handle the interviews, concluding, "You'll probably have better luck with both of them than I would, so turn on the charm."

I could do that.

Also on my to-call list that morning was Sabrina Harris, who awaited my decision regarding which of Blade Wade's pricey paintings would brighten up a bare wall in my new home. Ah, the irony as I sat there in my cramped apartment, shirtless and sweating, trying to tamp down the next air-conditioning bill. I waited till ten, picked up Sabrina's card, and placed the call.

While the gallery phone rang, I reasoned that Rex Khalaji would not have had the opportunity—or inclination—to report to Sabrina that I had visited him as part of the murder investigation. Doing so would surely raise her suspicion that I had misrepresented myself at the gallery. She would find out eventually, but I wanted to buy some time.

"Good morning. Harris-Heimlich Gallery. This is Liam. May I help you?"

"Hello, Liam. This is Dante O'Donnell."

"*Hello*, Mr. O'Donnell. All's well?"

"Yes, thanks. May I speak to Sabrina, please?"

"She won't be in this morning. Care to leave a voicemail?"

"Just tell her I called. I'm still deciding on a painting by Blade Wade. Things got busy."

"She'll be delighted to hear you phoned, Mr. O'Donnell."

"Great. And, Liam—if you prefer, you can call me Dante."

"I'd *love* that." His tone turned playful as he added, "Know what else?"

"Uh…no. What?"

"I'd *love* to meet you for a drink sometime. Or dinner? Hope I'm not out of line."

"Not at all." I was tempted—but I couldn't let him see my car, let alone my apartment. If our evening got serious, I'd be exposed as a highly unlikely art client. "There's a snag, though," I told him. "I'm sort of *involved* with something right now."

"Something?" he asked. "Or someone? He's a lucky guy."

"It's complicated. So maybe we can discuss this again—later."

"*Definitely.*"

■

My next phone conversation didn't require such a delicate dance, but the results were no more conclusive.

When I called Fauvé Landon—the va-voom wife of the bland banker, Jim Landon—the number supplied by Jazz connected me to a real-estate office in Indian Wells, which transferred my call twice before I landed with Fauvé's sales assistant, Vivian. Her voice dripped with upscale ennui as she informed me, "Fauvé is a very busy woman—she has several showings scheduled today. If you'd care to explain the reason you want to meet, I'll have her try to get back to you."

There was only so much I was willing to tell Vivian, but I said that Kenneth Terry Sr. had referred me to Fauvé, "regarding an unfortunate incident at his rental house in Rancho Mirage."

"Oh, my, yes, I heard about it," said Vivian without a breath of emotion. "Let me see what I can do."

I asked, "When do you think I might hear back from Fauvé?"

"I'm afraid I have no idea."

And that was that.

Far more productive was my call to Hannah Quince, wife of M3A's chief financial officer, Howard Quince. When I punched in the number, Hannah herself answered. After introducing myself, I explained, "You might remember me from the pool party hosted by Kenneth and Claudia Terry a couple of weeks ago. The rental company sent me over when things got noisy."

"That's putting it mildly, Dante. What can I do for you?"

"I'm sure you've heard about what happened to Noreen Penley Wade—it was two days after the party. I'm working with a private investigator hired by Kenneth, trying to figure out exactly what happened. He supplied his guests' phone numbers. I wonder if you have time for me to meet with you."

She offered at once, "If you think it would be helpful, how about this afternoon?"

■

Sunnylinks Country Club was a pleasant little golf community on the fringes of Cathedral City, just outside Palm Springs. Unpretentious condos, many of them duplexes, surrounded cul-de-sacs that meandered through a shorter, lower-par executive course, designed for older golfers who simply enjoy the game.

When Hannah Quince invited me to join her there at two that afternoon, I felt compelled to double-check: "That's Sunnylinks, in Cat City?" Given her husband's position at M3A-LA, I expected their desert getaway to be located in a development at the tonier end of the spectrum, such as Wasi'chu Hills, home to Skip Terry and his wife in Rancho Mirage.

"That's right," Hannah confirmed, laughing. "Nothing fancy, but we enjoy it—nice people here."

When I pulled into the visitors' lane at the gate, the guard found my name on his list and handed me a map highlighted with a yellow squiggle that traced my route through the winding roads and hundreds of residences.

They all looked pretty much alike, with sand-colored stucco and red tile roofs. When I pulled into the cul-de-sac marked BOGEY CIRCLE, I spotted Hannah outside her gate, waving me in. As I got out of the car, she asked, "Find it okay?"

I flipped my hands. "Here I am."

"C'mon in, Dante." She led me through a tiny courtyard and into the house. The decorating was tastefully modern, and the fairway view from the living room was gorgeous on that hot, bright afternoon, but the rooms were small, almost cramped. She offered, "Iced tea? Maybe something stronger?"

I laughed. "Iced tea would be great."

"Make yourself at home," she said, stepping into the kitchen area off the living room. While rattling around back there, she spoke to me over the breakfast bar. "Talked to Howard. He tells me you and that lady detective—Jazz?—drove out to the museum this week."

"Right. Tuesday."

"What'd you think?"

"About what?"

She returned to the living room with two glasses. "Everything. Here. Have a seat."

I joined her at a round pedestal table, maybe three feet wide, looking out on the links. It reminded me of those all-purpose tables they put in hotel rooms near the window—not exactly right for dining or reading or working—just a generic placeholder of a table. Four golfers trundled by in two carts.

Hannah was still waiting to hear what I thought of the museum. I said, "Honestly? I didn't know what to make of it. It wasn't what I expected."

She shrugged. "Join the club."

The only other time I'd seen Hannah, at the pool party, she'd worn a tweedy wool skirt and jacket, looking distinctly out of place. Today she wore casual summer clothes—tailored shorts with a polo—basic golf attire, which would have fit right in with Kenneth and Claudia's crowd at the Ellinger House. This led me to believe that Hannah and her husband had never been entertained by Skip's parents, despite the museum connection.

What's more, Howard Quince had been nervous and irritable at the party, snapping at his wife when she offered soothing words to him. Later, when Jazz and I encountered him at M3A-LA, he was congenial and professional.

Sitting there now with Hannah Quince, I asked her, "How long has Howard worked at the museum?"

"Just over a year—he still talks about being the newbie. It used to be sort of a joke."

"But now?"

Hannah placed her fingers on my hand. "Please don't repeat this. Fact is, Howard wants out. Says he inherited a mess."

"Because of the cruise fiasco?"

She nodded. "That happened well before he got the job. The guy before him just up and quit."

"What did Howard think of Noreen?"

"Noreen *hired* him. They worked together every day. She wasn't what you'd call a pleasant person—you saw her in action at the party—but Howard could look beyond that. He's a numbers man, analytical. Got a problem? Just plot out the solution, point A to point B. Except he was getting more and more frustrated with Noreen."

My tone was facetious: "He wanted to kill her?"

Hannah laughed. "Said so all the time—but, you know, that's just an expression."

"Of course." I drank some of the tea, then sat back to ask Hannah, "Your husband's growing frustration with Noreen—was there a particular issue, or was he just sick of her abrasive personality?"

"He could handle her bitchy attitude just fine. Whenever he'd tell me a new story about her, he'd wrap it up saying, 'But that's just Noreen being Noreen.' In *his* line of work—being the 'money guy' in someone else's business—he's used to people who don't play nice. It's part of his job."

"So," I asked, "what was the cause of Howard's frustration with Noreen?"

"The cruise."

"Ah."

Hannah explained, "The financial mess was bad enough. But the head-butting involved how to *deal* with it. From Howard's perspective, every setback has its protocols. Like I said, point A to point B: lawyers, insurance, settlements, what have you. Then you chalk off your losses and try to start over."

"Sounds logical to me."

"Logical—exactly, that's Howard. But *Noreen*, he said, became obsessed, like threatening to make the board responsible for the lost funds. Howard told me, 'I can deal with solving problems, but I can't deal with batshit crazy.'"

I said, "At the party, Noreen got into a shouting match with Skip Terry, and there were threats. There were also hints of connections to organized crime. Does any of that make sense to you?"

Hannah leaned back in her chair. "Oh, *Lord*. Howard's heard that talk before, but he figured it was just part of Noreen's act, her mystique—hard as nails. But now, after she died, and the *way* she died, who knows?"

"So," I said, "in a sense, the crisis has passed. To put it bluntly, Noreen is out of the picture. Has that improved the situation for Howard?"

"It's relieved a lot of tension—it seems *no one* at the museum is missing Noreen. And everyone seems to like the way Riley Uba is moving things along. But at the end of the day, none of that solves the underlying mess of the canceled cruise." With a sigh, Hannah added, "Howard won't be there much longer. We've made these 'transitions' before."

Another golf cart drove past, this one in the distance. It was well over a hundred degrees by now. Who would *do* that?

"Cookie?"

I turned to Hannah. "You bake during the summer?"

"The air-conditioning works." Then she laughed. "I bought a *bag*."

"Sure. And the tea's great, by the way."

She stood. "I'll get some more."

As she moved to the kitchen, I said, "When I first arrived, you asked what I thought of my visit to the museum. I told you it wasn't what I expected, and you agreed with me. Before you first saw it, what were *you* expecting?"

"Well," she said, speaking from the other side of the breakfast bar, "a *museum*. You know—pillars, gardens, gift shop, cafeteria, and *lots* of art. But not at M3A."

"It *is* weird," I said. "With so little that's actually *there*, you have to wonder how they ever got up and running. But they seem to have an active board and donors."

"Not to mention big plans." Hannah returned from the kitchen with the pitcher of tea and an open bag of Oreos, which she set in front of me. "Go for it. Want a plate?"

"Nah, this is perfect." I ate one—it took me back to my boyhood—while she refilled my glass. After washing down the cookie, I said, "You're right about the museum's big plans. While Jazz and I were there, Howard was meeting with Jim Landon, the banker—I guess he's involved with the foundation—and they told us about ideas for a new capital campaign. One of the items on the wish list was a stand-alone building, designed by a big-name architect. No harm in dreaming, but I thought it sounded *way* out of reach."

Twisting an Oreo open, Hannah nodded. "That's what Howard says. If you heard him say otherwise at the office, he was probably trying to sound supportive. If they ever do get that campaign off the ground, he won't be around for it." She ate the frosted half of the cookie and set the other half aside.

I told her, "I'm a little confused. Just what *is* 'the foundation'?"

"It's a charitable organization with the sole purpose of raising funds for the museum, which is itself a nonprofit. That's a fairly common setup in the arts world. The museum and the foundation have parallel functions and a shared goal, but the foundation is a separate entity, with its own board and accounting. The foundation raises funds from donors on behalf of the museum, then it turns around and writes a collective gift for the museum's support."

With a laugh, I said, "Sounds a little like money laundering."

She echoed my laugh. "I guess it does, when you think about it. But it's all for a good cause—and strictly aboveboard."

I said, "I like Jim Landon. At the pool party, when things got crazy, he spoke with the voice of reason. In the boardroom at

M3A, he spoke with drive and vision. I was impressed with him. A little bland, maybe, but hey, he's a banker, right? Goes with the territory."

With a hoot, Hannah said, "*Tell* me. I'm *married* to a bean counter."

"So Jim and your husband have a similar mindset. I assume they work closely on museum matters. Are they also close friends?"

"Oh, *no*," said Hannah. "They're 'friendly,' of course. But we've never socialized with Jim or his family. Did you get a look at that wife? Not to mention their *daughter*."

I had to admit, "They were hard not to notice."

"And besides, Howard doesn't work closely with Jim, if at all. The foundation, remember, is a separate entity, and Jim maintains that independence. Howard minds the museum; Jim minds the foundation. And never the twain shall meet."

I asked, "But the foundation isn't Jim's *job*, correct?"

"Correct. I guess you'd say the foundation is Jim's client. He's an investment banker at Palm Mesa Trust in LA. As I understand it, he handles the museum's endowment and oversees the foundation's accounting. He reports to the foundation's board."

I said, "And your husband reports to the separate *museum* board."

"Sort of. Howard reports to the executive director, who in turn serves at the pleasure of the board." Wryly, Hannah reminded me, "But the executive director is currently indisposed."

We gabbed on in this vein for another twenty minutes, finishing most of the tea and all of the cookies (the bag was only half-full when we started). I hadn't seen another golf cart in quite a while. At a lull in our conversation, Hannah grinned, asking me, "Have I bored you stiff?"

"Not at all. You've been really helpful." We stood.

She walked me to the door, then out to the tiny courtyard, where a dried-up hummingbird feeder swayed beneath an eave in the hot breeze. Checking my watch, I asked Hannah, "Taking off soon?"

With a quizzical look, she asked, "Taking off... for where?"

"It's Friday. This time of year, I thought you'd probably drive over to LA and join Howard for the weekend."

Hannah explained, "Howard doesn't live in some 'main house' in LA. He has a tiny studio there and returns *here* on weekends. He'll drive back tonight, after the rush."

Embarrassed, I said, "Sensible to avoid the traffic."

"So this condo, Dante—this is *not* a getaway." Everything drooped in the intense afternoon sun, even a snaky specimen of some dusty-green succulent. "This," said Hannah, "is our little slice of paradise. This is home."

CHAPTER FIFTEEN

By the next morning, Saturday, I still hadn't heard back from real-estate maven Fauvé Landon—banker Jim's wife. After my conversation with Hannah Quince, who had proved to be a solid, willing source for gossip as well as facts, I was more eager than ever to meet with Fauvé and try to flesh out some of the new details I'd learned.

I waited till noon and then phoned Fauvé's office in Indian Wells. This time, I avoided the runaround, knowing to ask directly for Vivian.

She explained lifelessly, "I spoke with Fauvé shortly after you called yesterday, Mr. O'Donnell. If she hasn't gotten back to you, she hasn't had time."

"It's important," I said. "It's urgent."

"Fauvé has her own priorities, Mr. O'Donnell. She has several open houses this weekend."

"Please. Could you try again? I'll be waiting for her call."

"Very well," said Vivian, who then instantly hung up.

I had no faith that she—or Fauvé—would follow through, but I kept my phone at hand while scavenging for lunch in my refrigerator. A few eggs were left, and reasonably fresh, so I decided to improvise an omelet with odds and ends—lunch meat, Parmesan, frozen peas, whatever. I had just oiled the pan when my phone rang. The caller ID was LANDON C.

I answered at once. "Hello, Mrs. Landon. Thanks so much for getting back to me."

"It's *Miss* Landon," the voice informed me. "Hello, Dante."

Boing. I realized it wasn't Fauvé, but the sultry daughter. "Is this ... Cherisse?"

"Uh-huh."

"Sorry for the mix-up. I was calling your mother."

"Yeah, I know. She called me about that. Seems you want to meet with her. But she told me, 'I just *cahn't* be bothered.' Then she asked if I could 'handle' you. Well, *duh*? So here I am. How may I handle you, Dante?"

Holy Christ, help me. "Look, Cherisse. It's good of you to offer, but I need to ask your mother some background questions about the drowning." I backed up: "Do you have *any* idea what I'm talking about?"

"Yeah. Sorta."

"So," I said, "could you ask your mother to return my call? Please?"

"She's *not* available—got it? It's me, or you're out of luck."

"Well ... since you put it so nicely. Where might we meet?"

"My place. I'm at a club in Rancho Mirage. Have you been to Wasi'chu Hills?"

"Of course," I lied.

"I'm in one of the cottages, just a starter place." She gave me the address.

I asked, "Time?"

"Oh, gosh. Let's say ... eight."

"Really? It's Saturday. Don't you have plans?"

With a low laugh, she told me, "They just changed."

The omelet could wait. As soon as we rang off, I pulled up the Wasi'chu Hills website on my phone. I already knew the basic history of the place, and I was aware that over the years it had drawn celebrities and titans of industry as its members, who built sprawling custom houses there. But I had not heard of "the cottages."

Turns out, they were a development built by the club itself, with smaller freestanding homes that shared design themes similar to those of the architecturally pedigreed clubhouse. The modestly described "cottages" were each about three thousand square feet and, when introduced, were considered a bargain for entrée to the club. They now rarely changed hands, but when they did, they fetched millions.

When I did a map search for Cherisse Landon's address, I had no trouble spotting it on the satellite view, between the main gate and the clubhouse. Out of curiosity, I also entered Skip Terry's address and found that house as well. It was considerably bigger—on the far side of the golf course—but within the same outer walls that surrounded the entire grounds of the legendary club.

■

That afternoon, while laying out an umpteenth variation of the clothes I planned to wear that night, I was interrupted by a knock at my apartment door.

"Dante, sweets," said Zola Lorinsky, "guess what."

Distracted, I asked, "What?"

"The *curtains*. If you'd care to come get them, they're all yours—with my compliments. May your friend's new spy business enjoy great success."

"Zola, I can't let you do that. I'll figure out some way to—"

"Shush," she commanded. Then she led me over to her apartment.

I thought she might have the curtains rigged up for my approval again, but no, they were already folded and packed—in two boxes—ready for me to load into my car. She apologized, "I can't lift them, or I'd help."

"Don't be crazy—you've done more than enough already." When I tried lifting them, I discovered that I would need to make two trips to the car. Within a few minutes, they were stowed in my trunk.

Returning to Zola's apartment, I thanked her again, hugged her again, and promised to show her pictures after the curtains were installed.

"If they need any final adjustments," she said, "just let me know."

Then, back in my own apartment, I phoned Jazz. When I asked if I could get into her office the next morning, Sunday, she didn't ask why.

She simply asked, "How about ten o'clock?"

"Fine," I said, "but don't you want to know what I'm up to?"

"Nope. I've got an idea, though. I mean, gimme credit—I'm a licensed private eye." Her low laughter rumbled over the phone.

■

Halfway into June, it was less than a week until the longest day of the year. As I drove into Rancho Mirage a few minutes before eight, the sun was just setting, but there was still an hour's worth of light in the sky.

The gatekeeper at Wasi'chu Hills didn't blanch at the sight of my battered car—the place was *that* classy. He merely asked if I needed directions to Miss Landon's cottage.

"I know the way, thank you."

And he pressed his magic button.

Entering the hallowed grounds, I'd have sworn I heard harps. The contrast with Sunnylinks, visited the day before, could not have been more pronounced. I had always heard that Wasi'chu Hills was in a league all its own, and now, if only briefly, if only as a guest, I was part of it. The plantings and fountains, the date palms and paving stones, the attention to detail, the sheer luxury of space—everything said, *Welcome home. You have arrived.*

Cherisse's cottage shared the surrounding aura of fastidious but understated elegance. As I parked at the curb and got out of the car, I nodded to an older couple strolling along the walkway on the opposite site of the street. Smartly dressed, they smiled in return, heading in the direction of the clubhouse. Dinner at eight—how very genteel. Through the rustle and murmur of birds in the trees, I heard her say to him, "Probably the help."

When I rang the cottage doorbell, I heard the peck of high heels on a tile floor. Through the translucent windows of the double doors, I saw a shadowy figure approach. The heavy chrome-plated hardware clicked, and one of the doors swung open.

"Dante—you came."

"Am I late?"

"No, right on time. But I was afraid you'd stand me up."

"I'm a man of my word, Cherisse."

"And you're every bit as hot as I remember." She licked her lips.

Ignoring that, I entered. "Wow. Swell place. Not bad—just out of college."

She shrugged. "A girl's gotta live *somewhere*." As she led me into the main room, I studied her as well as the surroundings. She wore a lacy white blouse and a barely-there black leather miniskirt that matched her heels. Music played softly, and—*uh-oh*—candles flickered throughout the room, adding a warm glow to the twilight that filled a wall of glass looking out to the base of the mountains.

She asked, "Have you eaten?"

"Yes."

"I'll bet you have room for dessert."

I didn't like the sound of this—or her naughty tone. But I was relieved to learn that her reference to "dessert" was literal when she stepped over to the dining table, telling me, "Voilà."

The oblong table was at least ten feet of polished rosewood, with chairs for eight. Candles burned at one end, where Cherisse had arranged a few things at two of the seats—one at the head of

the table, the other alongside. Pulling back the daddy chair for
me, she offered, "Join me?"

I sat. She seated herself in the adjacent side chair and
scooched it in. Her knee grazed mine.

"Cookie?"

Directly in front of me on a gold-rimmed bread plate was a
large, thick, nubbly cookie bursting with macadamia nuts, enor-
mous whole cashews, and chopped slivers of dark chocolate. A
sprinkling of shredded coconut was held in place by a drizzle
of caramel. "I brought this back from dinner," said Cherisse.
"The club makes these—their specialty. Everybody fuckin' *loves*
them."

Even the sight of it was a far cry from yesterday's Oreos in a
torn cellophane bag. I broke off a chunk and ate it, confirming
that the cookie, like Wasi'chu Hills, was in a league all its own. I
broke off another chunk, asking Cherisse, "Want some?"

She shook her head. "Had two already." Instead, she was
spooning a bit of gooey fruit glop from a thin-stemmed crystal
balloon goblet.

Another serving of it waited within inches of my cookie
plate. I swiped a spoon through it and tasted—crumbled pound
cake, custard, raspberries, whipped cream, all of it spiked with
a pronounced boozy accent. "Fabulous," I said. "Another club
specialty?"

"Nah." Cherisse clattered the glass with her spoon. "Mom
makes this."

I laughed. "Really? Fauvé Landon actually *cooks*?"

"Not much," Cherisse assured me. "Hey. Thirsty?"

Now that she mentioned it, the cloying sweetness of both
desserts was overwhelming. I said, "Water would be great."

"Right back." She got up and stepped into the kitchen. I heard
the clinking of glasses and ice.

I nibbled, alternating between the cookie and the berries.

When she returned, she set two glasses of ice on the table, then sloshed some water from a bottle of Evian.

While she poured, I said, "Your mother's a woman of many talents. A wiz in the kitchen, plus—just *look* at this place—Fauvé must've scrambled to land you here. I mean, first thing out of college, I was still looking for a *job*. And you?"

"Still thinking about that." Cherisse put down the bottle but remained standing. "And the cottage? Mom had nothing to do with it." While Cherisse spoke, she was ... good God ... she was unbuttoning her blouse. "Dad lined up the cottage and got it for me." She tossed the blouse on the table and plumped her breasts. "Dad always jokes that Fauvé's real-estate gig is just an expensive hobby. She loves the limelight. He says he 'subsidizes' it. Different strokes, I guess." Cherisse stroked one breast, now within inches of my face.

"Kiddo," I said, "you are barking up the *wrong* tree."

"*Woof-woof!*"

"For starters, I am *far* too old for you."

"Au contraire. You're just right."

"And in case you haven't figured it out, I'm gay."

"I just adore a challenge." She nudged my head with one of her big purple nipples.

"Back *off*," I said, standing. "And forget it."

She stared at me in frozen silence. Her jaw clenched. Then she reached for the lacy blouse on the table and tore a sleeve, ripped a pocket. "I'll have my way—or I'll accuse you of assault. *Rape*, Mr. O'Donnell."

Calmly, I told her, "Go to hell." Then I turned, crossed the room, and walked out.

As I pulled the cottage door closed behind me, I heard her scream at me—not words of invective, but a primal, painful yell.

Something shattered on the tile floor.

■

Out at the curb, in the car, I sat weighing my options—and chiding myself for having been so smitten with the mystique of Wasi'chu Hills. Was it worth fussing all afternoon over my *outfit*? Had I always been so shallow? And where did it get me? I had no idea whether Cherisse would follow through on her attempted-rape threat—she was screwy enough—or would she just brush it off as a fizzled date?

Perhaps because Skip Terry lived right there on the grounds of the club, or perhaps because I hadn't seen him in ten days, I had a sudden urge to talk to him.

I started the car, drove away from the cottage, and parked in the lot at the clubhouse, where I pulled out my phone and found the number Skip had given me—the private line not known to Detective Madera. I placed the call.

"Dante!" he said. "Hi there, stranger. It's been too long."

"You have *no* idea," I told him, smiling at the sound of his voice. "Way too long. I'm probably nuts to ask, but is there any chance of seeing you—tonight?"

"Where are you?"

"Long story, but I'm parked at the clubhouse in Wasi'chu Hills. I don't suppose you're home alone."

"I am, in fact, alone—but not at home. Ashley and I don't spend *every* night together, if you catch my drift. I have a little place of my own on the side. Not far from there. Wanna come over?"

"*Yes*," I told him, laughing at my own good fortune, "I certainly do."

He gave me the address, and I made note of the keypad code for the gate.

"On my way," I told him.

The street address he gave me, I realized as I pulled up to the gate, was a side entrance to Desert Towers, the seven-story complex where photographer Rex Khalaji lived. Glancing at my phone for the gate code, I also checked Skip's apartment number, 601, which placed him directly below Khalaji.

When I got off the elevator, I noticed that the hallway had doors to five or six apartments, as opposed to the two double-doored units on the top floor. I pressed the button outside Skip's door.

He opened it, grinning. "Sorry—it's no penthouse. I heard you paid a visit upstairs on Thursday."

I stepped inside. As he closed the door behind me, we fell into each other's arms. I said, "Let me just hold you for a minute."

"Hold on as long as you like. I'm in no hurry."

■

Skip shrieked. "She did *what*?"

"You heard me—right there at the table—hooters, hair, teeth. Total nightmare."

"You poor thing. I'm *so* glad you called. Hope I made it better."

"Much." I burrowed under the covers with him, resting my cheek on the fuzz of his chest.

He declared, à la Freud, "In my professional opinion, although the encounter must have been traumatizing, it left no permanent damage."

The sky beyond the windows of his bedroom had slid from golden to indigo to black. Planets winked at us above the jagged silhouette of the mountains. The room was dark—not even the glow of a clock—perfect for some pillow talk.

"So tell me," I said. "It can't be pure coincidence that Rex Khalaji lives ten feet above you."

"Uh, no. Not a coincidence at all. When Rex took the penthouse about six years ago, he snapped up this unit too, thinking he might break through and have a duplex in the sky. Later, he was having second thoughts, so I offered to rent it from him. I wanted a hideaway—and now I need it more than ever, since I still have a phone and computer here. Plus, it's my private turf, a place to play. I haven't been 'chaperoning' many cruises lately."

"I've heard about some of those cruises ..."

"I'll bet you have." He turned quiet for a moment, then said, "Tell me about yourself."

I traced a finger around his lips. "I'll tell you anything you want. But I have no idea where to start."

"Well, I heard you used to be married—to a *man*—and then things went sour, and you tended bar, then got a job at the rental company. And now, it seems, you're doing backup for a private eye."

"Now, *where* did you hear all that? Sure, you've met Jazz Friendly. But the rest, the earlier stuff—who's your mole? That's a term we use in the spy biz, by the way."

The bed shook as Skip laughed in the darkness. He said coyly, "Things get around."

I laughed. "It *is* funny, or at least strange. Noreen's drowning was actually the second murder I discovered with Jazz. The first was a few months ago, in February, at a rental house in Little Tuscany. That victim, like Noreen, was involved in the LA art scene—he was a print dealer. Odd coincidence."

"Maybe it wasn't," said Skip. "Pure coincidence is rare."

"There's more. A year before that, when my ex-husband died—he was murdered—I discovered that body, too. Maybe you read about it."

"I did."

"It was horrible. Then, later, when I discovered the body of the print dealer, the circumstances were *so* similar, it felt like a bad dream, like déjà vu, another gory coincidence."

Skip repeated, "Pure coincidence is rare. So maybe it wasn't."

"My husband," I said, "he was an ophthalmologist—"

"Dr. Gascogne," said Skip.

I paused. "Correct. My husband was Dr. Anthony Gascogne. And the print dealer was Edison—"

Skip finished the name: "Edison Quesada Reál. I knew him." Skip leaned over and switched on a bedside lamp. Then he sat up in bed, facing me. "I also knew Edison's husband, Clarence Kwon—and *your* ex, Dr. Gascogne."

"Whoa," I said, sitting up to face Skip. "How did—"

"They were all on a cruise I organized—a gay cruise, about two years ago."

I recalled that Anthony had recently returned from a cruise when his office called one fateful morning to say he'd missed his early appointments.

Skip explained, "The cruise was intended mainly for the Palm Springs crowd, but we also promoted it in the LA area. Anthony Gascogne signed on from Palm Springs. Clarence Kwon—he went by Clark—and his husband, Edison, signed on from LA. As the tour organizer, I went along for the ride and came to know everyone I'd booked. Clark slept his way through the crowd of older, well-heeled passengers, and I saw him spending time with Anthony during several of Edison's afternoon naps."

With a groan, I said, "This fits. Clark came on to me, too. He was something."

"Indeed he was," agreed Skip. "Later, Clark confided to me that he hoped to see more of 'the doctor' after the cruise. Now, don't freak, but Clark also told me he saw photos of a hot guy in the doctor's stateroom, and the doctor said the guy was his ex, who had just taken a job with a Palm Springs rental company, Sunny Junket. When Clark mentioned that he occasionally needed a rental in Palm Springs, the doctor told him to ask for Dante."

I was staring blankly at Skip, speechless.

He added, "When I booked the Ellinger House for my parents, I remembered all this, and I asked for Dante." He grinned. "I wanted to meet that guy."

"I'm glad you did." I leaned to kiss Skip, then said, "But something tells me there's more to this."

"There is," said Skip, "or there *was*. Shortly after the cruise, I heard from Clark—he was coming out to Palm Springs for a few days and thought maybe we could get together. I asked if he was renting a house. No, he'd made other arrangements. He also mentioned something that didn't make sense: he was looking for a Bentley convertible."

Dryly, I noted, "He already had the SUV."

"A few days later, I heard about your ex's murder—it was all over the local news—but I hadn't heard a single word of follow-up from Clark, who'd said he wanted to get together. Which left me with an eerie feeling and a gnawing question: Was Clark involved in the doctor's death? It was just a hunch, of course, and I couldn't prove anything, so I let it slide. But then, this past February, everyone heard the news that Clark had murdered *his* husband, Edison—with a toppled refrigerator. Jesus. At least he's now behind bars."

I nodded. Yes, there was intense satisfaction in knowing that Clarence Kwon had been brought to justice, and all the more because I had played a role in bringing him down. Even though he was now locked up, maybe his troubles were just beginning— if in fact he had murdered not once, but twice.

The possibility seemed promising. It also left me perplexed.

Skip asked, "What's wrong?"

"Suppose Clarence Kwon did kill both Edison and my ex. How does *any* of that link to Noreen Penley Wade?"

Skip shrugged. "I doubt if it does." With a laugh, he added, "now, *that* would be a coincidence."

I reminded him of his own words: "Pure coincidence is rare."

"Goofus," he said, mussing my hair. He reached to switch off the bedside lamp before pulling me close and wrestling me under the covers. Grinding against me in the dark, he said into my ear, "You've heard all my secrets. We're family now."

I couldn't help asking, "Then isn't this a bit incestuous?"

"Well"—he reconsidered—"kissing cousins, maybe."

And while we kissed, I recalled his father saying the same words to Jazz, "We're family now—we're in this together," on the morning he hired her to help exonerate his son. The wording had struck me as odd that day. And again tonight.

It sounded like mob talk—*famiglia*—a godfather thing.

CHAPTER SIXTEEN

He asked me to spend the night—the best offer I'd had in a long, *long* time. In spite of any misgivings I might have felt about the mob talk or the sham marriage or the wife's black-sheep uncle Iggy, in spite of all that, Skip Terry was, to my way of thinking, as good as it gets. And if that meant that Jazz was right, that I was thinking with my dick, so be it. Skip wasn't merely offering jollies on the phone or a fling by the pool—or a quickie at dawn between hospital shifts. He asked me to spend the night.

Which would mean ending our Saturday in a woozy embrace, then waking up together on Sunday. Followed by what? Maybe a nice brunch—private or public—wouldn't matter, as it had nothing to do with food, but everything to do with prolonging the hours we shared.

However. That Sunday morning was not to be for lolling. I had curtains to install. So sometime after midnight, closer to one, I kissed his face again, left him naked at his door, went down the elevator, and got back to reality.

■

Jazz had phoned. She left a message confirming that she would be at her office by ten in the morning "for whatever it is you're up to. Can I go ahead and trash those shower curtains?" *Beep.* Then a second message, sent shortly before midnight: "Just heard that Blade Wade is having a planning session tomorrow afternoon at his studio—for Noreen's memorial service. The museum crew will be there, so we should go, too. Hope you'll be free." *Beep.*

By the time I got back to my apartment and came down from the high of my evening with Skip, it was well past two. I went to bed and managed a few hours' sleep, not rising at dawn, as was my habit, but an hour or two later, when Mitzi got fired up on the other side of my bedroom wall.

That Sunday was the last day of my vacation from Sunny Junket. It marked two weeks since a raucous pool party at the Ellinger House had set into motion a chain of events involving anger and intrigue, threats of revenge, moments of lust, and just possibly love—not to mention murder.

At ten that morning, I parked on Palm Canyon Drive a few spots away from the Huggamug building and carried one of the boxes of curtains back to the side entrance. I set the box inside the small lobby, then made return trips to the car—first for the other box, and finally for a tool kit I kept at the apartment, since I doubted that Jazz could provide even a basic screwdriver.

Before lugging everything upstairs, I went up to make sure the door was open. It was. "Hey, Jazz, I'm here."

"Come on in," she called from her back office. "Just updating an account." As far as I knew, Kenneth Terry Sr. was her only client, but he'd been racking up plenty of billable hours.

After a few more trips down and up the stairs, I opened the toolbox on the floor and paused to catch my breath.

"Well, well, well," said Jazz, strolling out from her office, "what have we here?"

I grinned. "I thought you were going to trash the shower curtains."

"Never heard back from you—thought I'd better wait."

"Uh, yeah," I said, "I got sidetracked last night."

"How was he?"

"Just dandy, thank you."

"And *who* was he?"

"Not gonna say—yet. I need to check something out first, but if I find what I think I'll find, you'll thank me."

"That remains to be seen." Despite her skeptical words, I could easily read the interest in her features—the curiosity revealed by the tilt of her head, the arch of her brows. "Need any help with your little project?"

"Let's get rid of the shower curtains. Then I'll take care of the rest."

"Deal."

It took about two minutes to remove the old plastic curtains and stack them near the door. I said, "If you want to haul those down to the alley, I'll get busy."

When she returned, I had set out my supplies and finished remeasuring, but the curtains themselves were still boxed. I asked coyly, "Care to see what I brought you?"

She hesitated, biting her lip. "*No*," she blurted, "surprise me." And she hurried back to her office.

It took me nearly an hour to get it right. I'd put a small travel iron in the toolbox, knowing the folds of the curtains would need steaming after being packed for a day. With some patience and fussing, I soon had them looking showroom perfect. Then I called, "Jazz? All set."

I heard the slide of her chair, the cautious approach of her steps.

She emerged. "Oh, my *God*." She looked aghast.

"What's wrong?"

"Nothing!" Her scrunched face bloomed with a radiant smile. "What a *difference*. Suddenly, this dump belongs in a magazine."

Running a finger down one of the draped folds, I asked, "Like the fabric?"

"I *love* the banana leaves. Where did you *find* these?"

"I didn't 'find' them." Pausing for effect, I told her, "I had them made."

"No *way*."

I told her about Zola Lorinsky, the years-ago project in Indian Wells, the leftover fabric. "And best of all," I said, "Zola wouldn't let me pay her a nickel. A stranger would've paid at least a couple grand."

"I don't believe it," said Jazz.

"Oh," I added, "Zola told me to wish you great success in your 'new spy business.'"

Jazz looked like she might cry. "Well," she said, "I guess I should send Zola some flowers or something."

"I guess you should." I gave Jazz the name and address for delivery.

We arranged a couple of lawn chairs (they were next to go) in the outer office, where we could sit and just look at the transformed window.

"Tell me," I said, "about this meeting today at Blade's studio."

"It's not a meeting. They're calling it a 'retreat'—a planning retreat for Noreen's memorial."

"How'd you hear about it?"

"Blade himself called me—last night, it was late. He said the meeting, the *retreat*, was in the works for a few days. And he just got off the phone with Kenneth Terry, who thought I should be there, too—cuz I'm doin' this job for him. Kenneth said he'd let me know about it. But Blade was like, 'No, man, no—*I'll* call her, *I'll* let her know.' So he gets on the phone with me, and he's tellin' me about it, and he's doin' this superdude thing. And I'm like, say *what*? Is this guy comin' *on* to me?"

■

The meeting, the *retreat*, wasn't until two, and although that day was the end of my vacation, I wanted to check my desk at Sunny Junket, a short walk from Jazz's office. This would save me from being overwhelmed by a ten-day pileup of crap on Monday morning—plus, I wanted to do some snooping.

Approaching Sunny Junket, I saw through the windows that the lights were on in the customer area, but the entire office space behind it was dark.

From the front desk, Gianna looked up at me as I strolled through the door. She glanced at her wrist, then shook her watch, as if to make sure it was still working. "Did I miss a day or something?"

"Probably. Hitting the bottle again?"

She gave me a puke face.

I said, "Don't mind me, girlfriend. Just wanted to check on things before tomorrow's grand entrance." And I whisked past her.

"Knock yourself out." She returned her attention to something on her phone—that, and a guzzler-size concoction from Huggamug, which resembled a milkshake more than coffee. The straw squeaked in the lid as she sucked a mouthful of frothy cream.

My desk, as expected, was a fright, but since I had the entire office area to myself, I was easily able to trash what I could, organize what I would deal with later, and hide the remainder under the piles on other workers' desks. There—that wasn't so bad.

I booted up my computer. WELCOME BACK, DANTE! Yeah, right. There were certain functions of the office system I used all the time, while others I had never touched. I now needed to find something specific, but I had no idea where to look for it, which would require geekier knowledge than my own.

I heard the squeak of the straw again.

"Gianna, sweetness? Could you help me with something?"

With a sigh of a thousand tribulations, she descended from her perch and trudged back to my desk. "What?"

"Silly me—I guess I've been away too long. Can you remind me how to check the records of past reservations?"

Again the sigh. She reached for my mouse, gave it a single click, and up popped a screen I'd never seen before. "There. What are you up to?"

The phone at the front desk rang, nipping her curiosity. As she trotted back to answer it, I got acquainted with the new screen and figured out how to search bookings by date.

I quickly located the current reservation for the Ellinger House and pulled up the online form. The reservation had been made by Kenneth Terry Jr. on behalf of his parents, arriving on Saturday, the first of June.

Because the property he was booking was listed in our Luxury Retreats Portfolio, he was given the option of requesting VIP Check-In Service, which he indicated he wanted. Then, in a field provided for comments, Skip had written, "Have heard good reports about one of your people, named Dante. Would appreciate his service."

This confirmed one of the details he had told me the previous night. I was even more curious, however, to confirm another detail, regarding an earlier rental.

I scrolled back to February and found the reservation made for the house in Little Tuscany during Modernism Week. As expected, it had been booked by Clarence Kwon on behalf of Edison Quesada Reál. As expected, he had opted for our VIP Check-In. Consistent with Skip's revelation, Kwon had written, "Dante, please. Heard he's great."

This confirmed that two important details of Skip's story were true. As for the rest—Skip's theory that Kwon had been involved in the death of my once husband, Anthony—I knew there wouldn't be anything in Sunny Junket's records that might prove it.

But I had an idea.

While pondering this, I was interrupted by the ring of my cell phone.

It was Jazz. "Hey," she said, "I'm in a fix."

"What happened?"

"Nothing bad. But it's inconvenient. Christopher called."

I laughed. "Sick babysitter?"

"No, *listen*. Christopher enrolled Emma in a ballet class, or *pre*-ballet, or some damn thing. Don't get me wrong—that's great—God knows, I never had anything like that when I was a kid. But here's the pisser. He wants to get Emma off to a nice start with the group, so he's throwing a party for the class and the teachers—at his house—today. This afternoon. And Emma just asked him if I was coming, and then he musta realized, duh, of *course* Mommy should come—which frankly surprises me—so he wants to know if I can be there." She paused for a deep, loud breath. "Dante, what should I do?"

"You should follow your heart. If you think I can handle Blade's shindig on my own, you should be with Emma for this."

She took another breath, sounding more relaxed. "Thank you."

"Jazz," I said, "this will sound totally out of the blue. It regards the unsolved murder of Dr. Anthony Gascogne."

"Whoa. What about it?"

"Do you know if the investigation included any records of Anthony's office schedule—specifically, on or near the day he died?"

"That was a year and a half ago, but I'll bet it did. Those records should still be available."

"Any chance you can get a look at them?"

"Maybe. What's the point?"

"Complicated. I'll fill you in later."

■

Around a quarter to two, I arrived in the parking lot of the arty strip mall on the fringes of Palm Springs where Blade Wade had his home and studio. Sunday afternoon was apparently prime time for browsing the various shops and galleries, and I ended up taking a tight parking spot between an SUV and a van.

Leaving the Camry and walking toward the storefronts, I watched a couple approach Blade Wade's smoked-glass door H and step inside. Unless I was mistaken, they were the bland banker, Jim Landon, and his va-voom wife, Fauvé. I was relieved that their horrid daughter, Cherisse, was not with them, but I couldn't help wondering what, if anything, they knew about my encounter with her the previous night.

By the time I entered door H, the Landons were already somewhere beyond the second door, which was unlocked and held open a few inches by a brick on the floor. Blade, expecting multiple guests, had posted a note near the buzzer: COME ON UP.

While climbing the long flight of stairs, I wondered if Sabrina Harris, Blade's agent and mistress, would be there. If so, I'd have some explaining to do.

I heard the quiet babble of the gathering as I neared the top of the stairs. Given the somber purpose that day, I would not have expected a party atmosphere.

And yet, when I arrived in the main space of the combined studio and living room, the mood of the guests, while respectful, was not morose. There was even an undercurrent of gentle laughter that accompanied the wistful bromides about life and mortality and the relentless march of time. Blade's red paintings lent an upbeat pop of color.

Not laughing, however—and looking decidedly stressed— were Skip's parents, who were not accompanied by their son. Kenneth and Claudia rushed over to me as soon as I arrived upstairs. "Dante," said Kenneth, "I'm worried. The Skipper keeps telling me that it'll all work out, but he doesn't seem to grasp that Detective Madera is now focused squarely on *him* as the main suspect."

Claudia said, "And she still refuses to return Skip's phone and computers—says they're still 'digging.' That doesn't sound so good."

No, it didn't. But I tried to reassure the Terrys that Jazz was running down some promising new leads even as we spoke. Although a lame excuse for her absence, it seemed to calm them.

Even more concerned about Jazz's absence was Blade Wade, who came over to ask, "Where is she? She said she'd be here."

"Something came up," I said. "She said to tell you she hopes to see you another time soon." In truth, she had said no such thing.

"Really?" Blade brightened.

I offered a weak smile in response. Scanning the room, I concluded that Blade's paramour, Sabrina, had not been invited.

Rex Khalaji, the photographer, was someone else I thought I might see that day but did not. I reminded myself, however, that his connection to the events of the past two weeks involved only Skip's family, not the museum.

Representing the museum that afternoon, as expected, were Howard Quince, the CFO, and his down-to-earth wife, Hannah; the museum's curator, Cameron Vicario; and Noreen's temporary successor as executive director, her former assistant, Riley Uba, who was fawned upon by everyone present and praised for her efforts to "keep the ship afloat."

Jim and Fauvé Landon—first glimpsed entering door H while I was in the parking lot—now mingled and gabbed with other guests, but they seemed to keep their distance from me. Naturally, I wondered if their pampered princess, Cherisse, had cried rape.

I did not recognize perhaps eight or ten of the remaining guests, but I discreetly snapped a few pictures with my phone, intending to review them later with Jazz.

There was a catering crew, whose offerings of drinks and nibbles proved popular—and lavish. I'd been to weddings involving far less caviar, which today was served a dozen different ways.

Blade clinked his glass with a spoon. The "retreat" had begun.

∎

After a predictable round-robin of tributes to Noreen and condolences to Blade, the group began to focus on the afternoon's purpose—to plan a suitable memorial for the museum's fallen leader.

Timing was a consideration: Wait for definitive findings from the police investigation? Or move quickly?

Type of event: A traditional funeral? Or something more along the lines of a free-form "celebration of life"?

Or no event at all: A statue or plaque instead? A building or gallery bearing her name? An endowed professorship at a prestigious art school?

And what about expense?

"Let me address that," said Blade. The room grew quiet, as this was surely the crux of the discussion that would help decide all the other issues. Who would pay? And how much?

Blade cleared his throat. "Goes without saying, these past two weeks shook my world. Sudden death brings sudden challenges. Noreen and I always had separate finances—she wanted it that way—but the bottom line is, we had a comfortable life together. Very comfortable. When she died, I assumed all of that would change. But since then, I discovered something."

He paused and seemed to struggle not to smile. "God's honest truth," he said, "there was a *lot* of money I never knew she had. I'd like to find out where it came from, sure. But now it's mine, they tell me. And the least I can do for Noreen is to honor her memory—through the museum. So tell me what you want, and you got it."

Everyone stood there for a moment, stunned. Then the room swelled with ripples of conversation. Cameron Vicario, the curator, stepped forward and, standing near Blade, told the gathering, "This unexpected news—to say nothing of Blade's magnanimous offer—is such a reassurance to the entire M3A family. A suitable tribute to Noreen can be studied and decided on, unhindered.

But the museum has a current and pressing need. Let me suggest that the highest tribute we could give Noreen would be to permanently endow the museum's leadership position, its executive director, and to fill that vacancy at once with the one person who not only knows the job, but has earned the trust and affection of the staff, board, and donors. I speak of Riley Uba."

Well, *that* got things revved up. Despite Riley's protests, the others took turns singing her praises, begging and cajoling, uniting to convince her to stay on. At last she tossed her arms. "Sounds like an offer I can't refuse. And I'm highly honored."

Someone said, "Blade? What do you think?"

"I think you should do whatever *you* think best." He turned to Howard Quince, the CFO. "Unless I'm mistaken, Howard, you're currently the man in charge."

"Temporarily," he said, "on a day-to-day basis, yes, I've been running the museum's affairs. But hiring the director is *not* within my authority. I serve at the pleasure of the board."

Kenneth Terry said, "I believe I can speak for the board."

Several others, unknown to me but presumably board members, responded, "Hear, hear." With a quorum present, and with Blade committing to underwrite the position, and with unanimous ayes—they appointed Riley Uba the new executive director of M3A-LA.

▪

To the pop of champagne corks and with the passing of more trays laden with caviar treats, the gathering, despite its solemn purpose, ended on a festive note. I took a few more pictures— everyone was doing it now—and I chuckled while rehearsing, under my breath, how I would report this to Jazz: "You are *not* gonna believe this."

And fifteen minutes later, the catering crew began tidying up, and everyone was thanking Blade, and then we all trundled down the stairs and through the long hall to the tiny vestibule where door H led out to the parking lot. Everyone lingered a bit, congratulating Riley again, who seemed overwhelmed by all the love, saying more than once, "I guess I've got my work cut out for me."

And at last it was time to leave. The parking lot had cleared out some, and the guests walked off in different directions toward their cars, which baked in the afternoon sun. As I approached the sad-looking Camry, my phone rang. It was Jazz.

"You are *not* gonna believe this," I told her while walking back to the shade of the storefronts.

She said, "After spending an afternoon with a bunch of four-year-olds in tutus, I'd believe just about anything. So tell me all about it."

While recounting the surprise developments of Blade's new-found wealth and Riley's new job, I watched the others get into their cars and drive away. Riley had paused for a last hug from someone but now crossed the parking lot, heading for the SUV parked next to the Camry. She stood at the door of her vehicle, digging for something in her purse.

"Hold on a sec," I told Jazz. "I want to cool down the car."

Tapping the starter app on my phone, I felt the shock wave as my car blew up.

"Dante!" squawked Jazz through the phone. "What the fuck just happened?"

I couldn't begin to describe it to her—how the earth shook, how store windows shattered behind me. My car was just...*gone*...reduced to hissing rubble on the asphalt. Next to it, the mangled SUV was flipped on its side. And nowhere in the smoking, hellish mess could I see a trace of anything that might be Riley.

Horrified onlookers were now screaming.

But Riley Uba never had a chance.

PART THREE
WORKS IN RED

CHAPTER SEVENTEEN

Dazed, I saw Jazz tear into the parking lot and run from her SUV as sirens seemed to approach from every direction.

"Are you okay, Dante?"

I was sitting on the curb, numb and crying. At the sound of her voice, I looked up and mumbled, "I'm not sure. Am I bleeding?"

She sat next to me on the curb and put an arm around my shoulders. "I don't *see* any blood." With her free hand, she wiped tears from my face. "Are you in pain?"

I had to think about it. As my head began to clear, I recognized the mental anguish, but I seemed to be physically intact. "No," I told her, "no pain."

"Let's see if you can stand." She stood and extended both hands. "Try getting up."

I took hold and pulled. On the second attempt I made it to my feet. When I felt I could stand on my own, I let go of her.

"Here's your phone," she said, retrieving it from the curb.

"Thanks, Jazz." I shook my head and, feeling more normal, pocketed the phone. I told her, "Someone just tried to kill me. Your call saved my life." Pointing to the wreckage, I added, "But they got Riley Uba instead."

Jazz took it all in, then closed her eyes. "Holy shit."

■

Arcie Madera arrived on the scene, summoned by Jazz. The Palm Springs police were already there, since it was their jurisdiction.

Fire trucks came, but the fire hadn't spread from my bombed car—although its remains still smoldered. Paramedics' vans lined the curb, available for casualties, but other than Riley's grisly fate, the injuries were few and minor, with collateral damage from the blast limited to broken glass and jangled nerves. Barricades were thrown up, keeping at bay the onlookers who gathered, along with a couple of local TV stations. The emergency response to the bombing and its initial forensic investigation would drag late into the night.

But it didn't take nearly that long for a picture to emerge of what had happened that afternoon.

First, Detective Madera conferred with the Palm Springs investigators, explaining a suspected connection between the bombing death and the earlier drowning in Rancho Mirage, a homicide being investigated by the sheriff's department under her direction. The county DA had already staked out a strong interest in the earlier case and would have an eye on this seemingly linked case as well. What's more, the county could offer greater forensic support than was available to the local police, so the two forces agreed to tentative cooperation, despite the territorial prerogatives of jurisdiction.

Which is to say, Arcie managed to wheedle her way into the bombing case. By extension, so did Jazz. As for me, I was already involved—as the bombing's intended victim.

While Arcie, Jazz, and I compared notes in the shade of an awning outside one of the storefronts, a plainclothes detective from the Palm Springs force came over to see us, walking briskly. Jazz called him George, but I thought the name might correctly be Jorge—he was a savvy, fit, and handsome Latino cop. They had apparently worked together on occasion when Jazz was still on the force, and from the tone of their casual exchange, it was clear they got along.

But when George got down to business, he turned to the sheriff's detective. "Arcie," he said, "we found two eyewitnesses who noticed activity in the parking lot earlier—from two different shops—and their stories are identical."

Detective Madera asked, "What can you tell me?"

George said, "Why not go to the source?" And he led us into one of the shops, a small crafts gallery. The owner was trying to tidy the place while a board-up crew covered the broken window. George introduced us, then asked the man to repeat his story.

"It was a busy afternoon," said the gallery owner, "so I pretty much kept behind the counter, making room for the customers—mostly just browsing—while I'm facing straight out the window. About two thirty, I see this tow truck pull into the lot—a Triple-A wrecker—and it circles around awhile, then pulls in directly behind some beat-up old Camry, and I'm thinking to myself: Right, good luck getting *that* heap started." He laughed.

Jazz turned to catch my eye, but she refrained from commenting, apparently aware that I was in no frame of mind for shitbox jokes.

The shop guy resumed his story. "So the driver gets out of the truck—"

"Uniform?" asked Arcie.

"Just coveralls. So he gets out of the truck, lugging this big box of tools, and he moves around to the front of the car, pops the hood, and goes to work. I'm thinking: No fan belt's gonna fix *that* heap. But he spends a few minutes on it—looks like he's in a hurry—then takes off in his truck. Maybe an hour later, the party upstairs lets out, and everyone's starting to leave. Then, *boom*, damn thing blows up. Holy *moly*, what a mess. Hope no one was hurt."

I told him, "A woman was killed."

He went ashen.

"And that heap? That was *my* car—that guy meant to kill me."

"Cripes," said the gallery owner. "Real sorry to hear that."

■

Outside the shop again, George told us, "The other eyewitness—same story."

Jazz said, "So I assume you've checked with Triple-A."

I butted in: "In case anyone's wondering, I did *not* put in a service call."

"Didn't think so," said George. "A Triple-A driver reported his truck stolen in Palm Springs this afternoon, around twenty past two."

"Do tell," said Arcie. "Not sure how much you know about the drowning in Rancho Mirage, but the killer posed as a pool guy, stealing a pickup from a pool service just before he struck."

Deadpan, George mused, "What a coincidence."

True coincidence is rare, I recalled Skip saying.

Jazz told George, "That's one more reason Arcie's convinced that these two cases are linked. Has the Triple-A truck been found yet?"

George nodded. "Just got the report. Abandoned in a parking lot about three blocks from here."

"That's our guy," said Arcie. "Same methods in Rancho Mirage. We got lucky there—we have a security tape of him ditching the pickup. Maybe there's video of the Triple-A wrecker, too."

"Working on that," said George. "Any leads on this guy's identity?"

She echoed his line: "Working on that. But this has all the earmarks of organized crime—come on, a *car* bomb? So the killer's a hit man, obviously."

Jazz said, "But that's not the end of it."

"Not at all," said George. "That leaves a more fundamental question to be answered in both cases."

I finished the thought: "Who hired the hit man?"

George looked at me, nodding. Then he frowned. "Do you need police protection, Dante? Surveillance at home? Someone tried to have you killed, and by now, they've probably heard they missed."

"Huh?" His offer hit me like a gut punch. I had visions of armed guards stationed on the pool deck outside my front door. What would Zola think? What would Isandro think? Even Mitzi—what would *Mitzi* think? There would be no rest.

Jazz clicked her tongue in her mouth. "Might not be a bad idea, Dante."

Arcie told both of us, "You two are in this *way* over your heads. Whoever's behind it doesn't hesitate to kill, so don't say you weren't warned."

"Think about it," said George. "At the least, we can assign beefed-up patrols of your street." Someone called to him from the forensics team working at the blast site. He told us, "Gotta go. But let me know."

Arcie Madera went with him, walking across the parking lot.

Jazz and I were left standing in front of one of the shops. She said, "Let's sit down."

We strolled over to a concrete bench that marked the end of the strip mall and its pavement. Beyond the bench, weedy scrub littered the sand that rose in drifts at the foot of the mountain, which now cast its growing shadow into the parking lot. We sat.

She said, "I haven't been fair to you."

"What do you mean?"

"You're not trained for this. You're not armed. I shouldn't have sent you here alone today."

Her words made sense. "But," I told her, "if we *had* come together, we'd have left together—and we probably would have been blown up together. As it turns out, we both got a lucky break. Plus, we know that someone's feeling threatened. So we must be doing *something* right."

With a quiet hoot, she said, "You are one *smooth* talker."

I shrugged.

"And you're right," she said. "Someone did feel threatened—a *car* bomb. Who knew you'd be here today?"

"Ahead of time? As far as I know, only Blade Wade and Skip's parents. Blade called last night to invite you, and you agreed to come. He could've guessed I'd be with you."

Jazz asked, "What about Skip Terry?"

I shook my head. "He didn't hear it from me. The topic never came up last night."

Jazz grinned. "Aha. Then you *were* with Skip last night."

Letting that slide, I pointed out, "He wasn't even here today."

"Doesn't matter. His parents were the ones who asked Blade to invite us. *They* could've told Skip."

I looked Jazz straight in the eye and told her firmly, "Skip is not involved in this."

She laughed. "You don't *know* that."

"And besides," I said. "Whoever hired the bomber didn't need to know in *advance* that you or I would be here. The tow truck was stolen at two twenty. So *any* of Blade's guests could have seen me upstairs, placed a call, and ordered the hit."

She mulled all this before telling me, "Arcie Madera is strongly leaning toward Skip. So is the DA. And frankly, so am I."

I reminded her, "It's your *job* to not 'go there.'"

"It's my job to help exonerate Skip by proving someone else is guilty—if I can. But if the evidence ends up pointing to Skip, I can't just *ignore* that because his dad is my client. I've sworn an oath to uphold the law. And I will."

I was sure she was mistaken, but I couldn't argue with her ethics. I stood. "Seems time is running out. So we need to get moving."

"Tough day." She stood. "Let's pick it up tomorrow."

I nodded as we both walked to the parking lot.

She clapped my shoulder. "Get some rest." And she headed off toward her SUV.

Then she stopped. Turning back, she asked, "Need a ride?"

CHAPTER EIGHTEEN

Monday morning.

What is it about those two words that can fill even the most sparkly-eyed optimist with a sinking sense of dread? As a corker, that particular Monday morning marked the abrupt end to a "vacation" that had proved not only adventurous, but deadly.

I awoke at dawn, not out of habit or eager to greet the new day, but riddled with anxiety. There would be no time to flirt with my neighbor. In fact, there would be no time for more than one cup of coffee, versus the usual potful. I was dressed and showered and out the door by seven, wanting to get down to the office early—which in itself presented a problem.

Since my car had been destroyed—not just totaled, but blown to charred scraps—I obviously couldn't drive. A cab or rideshare was an option, but I wanted to walk. It wasn't hot at that hour, and I could be downtown in twenty minutes. Plus, the walk might clear my head and allow me to focus on "what's next," whatever that might be.

The day's first surprise, as I left the apartment courtyard through the street gate, was the sight of not one, but two, patrol cars parked at the curb. One of the officers actually gave me a jaunty little salute. The gesture was probably intended to make me feel more secure, but all it accomplished was to heighten my paranoia. I returned the greeting with a weak smile and kept walking.

I planned to check in with Jazz that morning, but I first needed to have a talk with Ben, my kindly boss at Sunny Junket.

I was going to need another day off—soon—to make arrangements for another car, which was essential to my job. I had no idea what the situation would be with my insurance. Are car bombings even covered? Feeling the drip of something acidic in my stomach, I was grateful I'd limited the coffee to one cup.

I walked past Huggamug, which was hopping at that hour, and a minute or so later, after crossing the next street, I entered the Sunny Junket offices.

Gianna glanced down at her watch and then up at me, saying, "You're early. But I won't razz you about it—seems you had quite a day yesterday." She handed me that morning's *Desert Sun* as I walked by without comment.

Tossing it on my desk, I knew what to expect. The bombing was headline news, at the top of page one. There were pictures of the scene, but none, thank God, of me. The story did give my name as owner of the destroyed vehicle, but there was far more space, including a file photo, devoted to Riley Uba, the victim.

Then, when I unfolded the paper to continue reading the story, my eye snagged on another headline, lower on the page, announcing: COUNTY PROSECUTOR PREPARES CHARGES IN RANCHO MIRAGE DROWNING. The story, datelined Riverside, didn't name the accused—but I could guess. And Peter Nadig, the DA, planned to issue an arrest warrant "soon."

Jesus.

My cell phone rang. It was Jazz. "Hey, Dante. Can I give you a lift to work?"

"Already here, but thanks. You've heard the news from Riverside?"

"Yeah. I need to get busy on the horn. But can you get away later? Stuff to talk about. Maybe lunch?"

"Sure, that should work."

"Good. Noon or so, my office. I'll grab something for us downstairs."

And the moment we hung up, I saw Ben arrive. As he waddled toward my desk with a rolled newspaper under his arm, I braced for a hug. He was *that* nice—a Minnesota thing, maybe.

■

A few minutes past noon, I climbed the stairs to Jazz's office. Stepping through the door, I called, "It's just me, Jazz."

She emerged from the conference room. "All set. Back here." But she paused there, at the far end of the front office, staring at the window—or rather, the curtains. "Still can't get over it. And I sent your friend some flowers."

I gave her a thumbs-up. Then I followed her into the conference room.

She'd arranged a selection of Huggamug's lunch offerings at one end of the folding banquet table—and two of the lawn chairs at the other end, with plastic place settings and giant go-cups of iced tea. "I wasn't sure what you'd want."

"This looks great." Reaching for my wallet, I offered, "Let me pitch in."

With a snort of a laugh, she shook her head.

We made up our plates, sat, and tried a few bites, making favorable comments on the chicken salad—but the quiche was so-so. Then we got down to business.

Jazz slapped a notebook onto the table, next to her plate, and opened it to a page chock-full of scribbles and doodles. "Item one. Kenneth and Claudia Terry are in *shock* over the DA's announcement. They want to move fast."

I reminded her, "So do I."

She scratched through something on her list. "Next. Side topic. George. Remember meeting him yesterday?"

"I was a tad rattled—but how could I forget *George*?"

"You whore. He's married. To a woman. So forget it."

"So what's the point?"

"George and I are pals. When I was on the force, I didn't have many friends, but he was a good detective and always supported my efforts to move up. Didn't work out, but like I say, we're still pals. So I asked him about the old files from your ex's murder, and he agreed to let me look at them."

I singsonged, "You're gonna thank me for this."

"We'll see about that." She scratched another item from her list. "Next. Yesterday's bombing. Arcie Madera was successful in getting security video from the parking lot where the hit man ditched the stolen wrecker. She sent me a link. The guy's wearing long pants, so you can't see the fake leg, but he does walk sorta gimpy. What you *can* see, though, are his bare arms—and yup—right arm, *big* honkin' tattoo up and down. Arcie pieced together two stills, side by side, showing the guy leaving the pool truck and the guy leaving the tow truck." Jazz pulled it up on her phone and showed it to me.

"Same guy," I said. "No doubt at all."

"Meaning," said Jazz, "the two killings are definitely linked, so we're on the right track." She slashed at her list. "Next—"

I asked, "May I intrude with an item of my own?"

She stopped to take a breath. "Go for it."

"As a licensed private investigator, are you able to get a summons or subpoena or warrant or whatever?"

"Be more specific."

"I'd like to get some information—some records—from a person who probably won't want to cooperate."

She explained, "That's a subpoena, for documentary evidence. And no, I can't get one. But Arcie could probably get a court to issue one—assuming there's good cause. And then, I could serve it."

"Perfect."

"So tell me," she said. "What's this compelling evidence you want to get hold of?"

I told her.

Her eyes widened with interest. "Consider it done."

"And meanwhile?"

She made notes while she spoke. "I'll call Kenneth and Claudia and tell them to invite everyone back to their rental house tonight—the scene of the drowning. If they ask what reason to give people for another gathering, I'll say it's to reveal some big discoveries we've made about Riley Uba."

I nodded. "The guests will be plenty curious to know what's *really* going on. And if they think a murder or two might be solved, they'll be there—out of fear that *not* showing up would look suspicious."

"Exactly," said Jazz. "I'll tell the Terrys to schedule it late, like nine o'clock, in case anyone needs to drive back from LA. Also, at that hour, there's no need for a meal or entertainment. And *no booze*, I'll tell them—it ain't a party."

"The neighbors will appreciate that."

"I'll pick you up at eight thirty."

■

Jazz pulled up to the curb in front of my apartment right on time, letting her SUV idle behind a squad car still stationed there. I climbed in on the passenger's side and waved to the cop as Jazz slowly pulled away from the curb and signaled her merge into the nonexistent traffic along the wide, quiet street. When the cruiser was out of sight, she gunned it.

Glancing over at me, she said, "It finally clicked."

"What did?"

"Those banana leaves. I was *sure* I saw them someplace else. The Beverly Hills Hotel—where the Polo Lounge is."

"Oh, yeah? You've been there?"

"Once. I mean, the banana leaves are different there—they're green, on the wallpaper—but it's the same pattern as the curtains. Still love it."

"And the restaurant," I asked, "did you like it?"

"Well, *yeah.*" With a happy sigh, she recalled, "It was our first anniversary—Christopher and me. Emma was still a year or so down the road, so Christopher wanted to take me into LA for a long weekend. Second-honeymoon sorta thing. And we went to dinner that Saturday at the Polo Lounge—both of us all duded up. I mean, we were lookin' *good.*"

"Nice," I said.

"Mm-hmm. So we're having dinner, and it's wonderful, and the waiter walks over with a bottle of champagne—good stuff. Says it's compliments of the couple over there. So we look. And there's this man and woman, older, sorta look like someone's *folks*, you know? And they're all smiling, so we raise a glass to them, and they do the same. When we finished dinner—and the champagne—they were still there, sorta watching us sideways. So we stepped over to thank them."

"Did they say why they sent the bottle?"

"Uh-huh. The woman, she's all kinda giggly, and she says, 'The staff thought I was mistaken, but I insisted—I'd know Viola Davis *anywhere.*'"

I howled. "Oh, my God!"

"And the husband, he's all sorta proper, and he says, 'We do hope you enjoyed it, Miss Davis.' So I'm all proper, too, and I tell him, 'It was splendid, thank you.'"

"They must have been thrilled."

"They were—when I signed their dessert menu. Then I posed for selfies with them. As soon as Christopher and I got to the hotel lobby, we started to laugh. But by the time we were ready to leave, the word was out. So the valet helps me into the car and says, 'Good night, Miss Davis.'"

Jazz and I both shared a few waves of chuckles over this, but then her tone turned pensive. "I was Viola Davis for a few minutes. For a few years, I was Christopher Friendly's wife. And before that, I was Jasmine Banks."

I turned in my seat to face her. "That's a beautiful name."

She grimaced. "Think so? I never did. And now I have a daughter—Emma Friendly. So there's no going back."

■

The summer sky was nearly black as we rolled into Rancho Mirage. Five minutes before nine, Jazz turned off the highway and drove along the winding road that led up through the cove, up to the mesa, up to the lofty perch of the Ellinger House.

Two weeks earlier, when Jazz and I drove up here because neighbors had complained about a noisy pool party, there were cars parked at slapdash angles on the surrounding streets, a clear violation of city ordinances—not to mention the racket and the crowd. Tonight, though, the street was empty. The neighborhood, dead quiet.

Jazz drove her SUV through the open gate and into the courtyard, where seven other vehicles were neatly parked. I recognized Skip's Karmann Ghia and his parents' Maybach, but I couldn't pair the others to the expected guests, whose cars weren't known to me. While Jazz and I walked from the courtyard toward the wide-open entry to the house, she leaned to tell me, "Jesus—not a peep from *this* crowd. Guess they learned their lesson."

"And yet," I said, "here we are again. Only this time, it's not about noise. It's murder."

Claudia Terry rushed to us as we stepped inside. "I'm *so* glad you're here, Jazz. We're *praying* you'll be able to figure this out. Kenneth had a long talk with the Skipper, and he finally seems to understand what a mess he's in."

Jazz said, "We'll do our best, Mrs. Terry."

To my ear, that was less than encouraging, so I told Claudia, "Wait and see—I think you'll sleep well tonight."

In gratitude, she flopped a hand to her bosom.

Skip came over with his father, who instantly huddled with Jazz, grumbling with concern. Skip stepped me aside, asking, "Is there any way out of this?"

"Are you guilty?"

"Of course not."

"Then sit tight." Just inside the entry space, where it stepped down to the main room, a three-foot blowup of the *Vogue*-style photo of Noreen and Riley was propped on an easel, swagged with purple velvet. I asked Skip, "Is Rex Khalaji here?"

Skip nodded. "Out by the pool."

Guests drifted between the living room and the terrace, some of them carrying dessert plates. As dictated by Jazz, however, no one had been offered cocktails.

Cameron Vicario, the museum curator, stepped over to the photo and studied it. His cheeks were moist with tears. And he was not alone. I had earlier sensed that no one truly mourned Noreen Penley Wade's death, but now they openly wept for Riley Uba. And since Riley's death was happenstance—I myself was the intended victim—the killer now had the luxury of hiding behind honest tears.

With Skip, I walked across the main room to the glass wall at the rear of the house, fully opened that night to the terrace, the pool, and the shimmering view of the valley below. Skip's wife, Ashley Highsmith Terry, stood near the far end of the pool, talking quietly with Sabrina Harris, the gallery owner and mistress of Blade Wade, who stood a few feet away, conversing with Howard Quince, the chief financial officer at M3A-LA.

Ashley glanced over from her conversation with Sabrina and noticed me standing with Skip. She smiled at me and gave a little wave. Sabrina turned to take a look and, seeing me, appeared confused. She asked Ashley something, and Ashley responded. If Sabrina hadn't already figured it out, she now knew for a fact that I was not in the market for one of Blade's paintings. She turned to me again—and smirked.

Rex Khalaji had left the terrace and now stood inside the living room near the grand piano. He held a plate of the gooey dessert while gabbing with Hannah Quince, wife of the museum CFO, and Fauvé Landon, the real-estate maven whose daughter had thrown herself at me. "Let's say hello," said Skip, leading me over to the piano.

Rex, Hannah, and Fauvé immediately surrounded me, offering bewildered words of regret regarding my car—and the obvious attempt on my life.

"It'll haunt me for a long time," I said. "Disturbing as it was, for me it was just a close call. But for Riley? My God, poor Riley."

They nodded sad agreement. After a moment of respectful silence, Rex leaned to tell me, "Be sure to try some of Fauvé's dessert—it's pure ambrosia."

"Actually," said Fauvé, "it's a raspberry trifle. When I asked Claudia if there was anything I could bring this evening, she didn't hesitate to ask for it."

Rex added, "Fortunately, in spite of tonight's puritanical ban on liquor, the trifle is nicely spiked." He lifted his plate to my nose.

"Aha," I said. "Cointreau."

Fauvé arched her brows. "Very *good*, Mr. O'Donnell—I'm impressed."

I shrugged. "Used to tend bar."

Fauvé's husband, the bland LA banker, Jim Landon, stepped into the conversation. "Uh, Mr. O'Donnell," he said, sounding serious and uncomfortable, "may I have a word with you?"

I excused myself from the others and stepped out to the terrace with him. "What can I do for you, Jim?"

"You're ... Dante, correct?"

When I nodded, he continued, "I had a distressing conversation last night—with my daughter, Cherisse."

Uh-oh.

"And all I can do now is offer my profound apologies. She pulled the same damned stunt two weeks ago with the cable guy." I was tempted to ask, Was the cable guy hot? Instead, I said, "No harm done. But she seems to have some growing up to do." "Ughhh." Jim shook his head. "She is, to say the least, a handful. And I bear some responsibility for that—but honest to God, it's Fauvé's doing. I keep telling her she's *enabling* Cherisse. Our daughter is a woman now, she's twenty-two, but she still acts like a pampered adolescent—Mommy's little treasure—who gets everything she wants. And when she doesn't, there's hell to pay. Which you found out, Dante. So once again, I'm sorry." With the slightest bow of his head, he stepped away.

He had spoken with the voice of reason. I'd heard it before. His old friend, Kenneth Terry, had twice described Jim Landon to me as levelheaded. I now watched as Jim struck up a conversation with Kenneth, who had just finished speaking to Jazz.

Jazz spotted me alone on the terrace, checked her watch, and came over to ask me, "Time to get this rolling?"

And before long, the truth was at hand.

■

Cameron Vicario sat in the middle of a long sofa that anchored the conversation area of the main room, defined by the piano on one side and the fireplace on the other. An ample grouping of armchairs and ottomans fanned out from the sofa, allowing everyone to gather and sit facing one another in a loose circle. Jazz and I stood nearby. Altogether, I counted fourteen of us.

Some picked at another helping of Fauvé's popular dessert. No one drank anything stronger than coffee. And most, eventually, had something to say.

But after a half hour of kind words lamenting the sudden loss of Riley Uba (and not a mention of Noreen, not even from her surviving husband, Blade Wade), it was Cameron who finally asked the group, "Is it just me? Or isn't it pretty clear that Riley's death is somehow connected to Noreen's? What do you think, Jazz?"

By now, everyone in the room had come to understand her role tonight. They watched as Jazz stepped forward.

She said to Cameron, "I think you're right. In fact, I'm sure of it. And something else is clear: Even though Riley's death is linked to Noreen's drowning two weeks ago—right here at this house—Riley wasn't the intended victim yesterday. That would be Dante. Most of you already know him. He's working on this case with me, and he has some thoughts to share with you."

I stepped into an imaginary spotlight—that theatrical training had paid off at last. "We've learned a lot since Noreen's drowning, and *someone* was afraid that this investigation was getting too close to the truth."

"Someone *here* tonight?" asked Skip.

"Maybe. Probably."

A stir of conversation rose from the room, then ebbed. Skip's mother asked, "What makes you think that, Dante?"

I hedged. "It's logical. Let's back up. Some people—including the sheriff's department and the county prosecutor—are convinced that Noreen was drowned by a hired killer, a hit man. They're also convinced that yesterday's car bombing was the work of the same hit man. So in the strictest sense, he's the killer. But he only did it for the pay, so there's someone *else* who had a background motive—and is now guilty of setting up two murders."

"Hit man?" asked Sabrina Harris, Blade's agent. "Isn't that a bit over-the-top for the art world? I mean, it sounds like organized crime."

"Yes, it does," I said. "And to that extent, the prosecutor has it right. I have confidence in their resources to identify the killer and bring him to justice. But they're on the wrong track when it comes to the question of who *hired* the hit man—and why."

Skip told everyone, "They think I did it because of the cruise fiasco and the threats."

Claudia Terry said, "But that's nonsense, dear. What possible connections could *you* have to organized crime?"

Skip said nothing. But his wife and his father exchanged a glance. Had Skip's mother never heard of Uncle Iggy?

I told his mother, "You're right, Claudia. It's nonsense—about Skip. But organized crime? You bet it played a role in this. And sad to say—forgive me, Blade—but Noreen was up to her ears in it."

Blade Wade blew a breathy sigh. "I never wanted to believe it, but it sure adds up. There was a *ton* of money I never knew about. I have no idea where it came from—except it must've been fishy."

Jazz stepped back into the conversation. "Fishy money—unexplained wealth—that's what ties everything together."

I took that line of thinking to the next level. "And the buck stops"—I turned to look Jim Landon in the eye—"right here."

Bland. Levelheaded. The voice of reason. He told me, "You're out of your fucking mind."

"Mr. Landon," said Jazz, street-mouth Jazz. "I'll thank you to mind your language, sir. You're in refined company here."

"Oh, for *Christ's* sake ..."

Fauvé, his wife, must have thought I was joking. With a laugh, she said, "Don't be ridiculous, Dante. How could Jim have connections to the *mob*? He's devoted his entire professional life to serving the Los Angeles arts community."

Jim nodded. "I have *proudly* aided the arts through my position at Palm Mesa Trust—for nearly thirty years."

I asked, "And just what exactly is it that you *do* there, Jim? You're a banker, right?"

"In layman's terms, yes."

"Meaning," I said, "you approve loans, set up trusts, maybe serve on a few boards and foundations. But essentially, you handle *other* people's money. And while I'm sure you earn a healthy salary, that's not the kind of job that makes a man wealthy, right?"

He hesitated. "I'm well paid. I know how to invest and reinvest. I've managed nicely."

"*Very* nicely," I said. "I was sorta shocked to get a look at your daughter's so-called cottage two nights ago—nice graduation present. Wasi'chu Hills? I've lived here for *years* and never once got beyond the front gate. It was an eye-opener."

Jim said nothing.

But Jazz did. "Unexplained wealth. Just like Noreen at the museum. And the two of you worked together." She asked the room, "Have you guys *seen* that place, that museum? I mean, it's *nothin'*. The day Dante and I drove back from there, we were laughing about it—all hat and no cattle—like it must be some sort of money-laundering operation. And you know what?"

I answered the question. "That's precisely what it is."

Jim Landon closed his eyes.

"The staff," I said, "was dismayed by Noreen's lack of focus on the museum's mission—because for her, the purpose of the place had nothing to do with art. But it had everything to do with some byzantine scheme for moving funds—probably cash, probably drug money—through the museum's shipping room. And Jim, banker Jim, was the guy with the connections and the financial know-how."

Jim laughed at me. "You ought to write this down, Dante. It would make quite a fairy tale."

Jazz assured him, "We might not have all the facts—yet—but they should fall together pretty quick."

Jim laughed again. "Do you *honestly* think I ordered a mob 'hit' on Noreen? And then on Dante's car?"

"Honestly?" I said. "That's exactly what I think you did. First, Noreen's drowning: On the Tuesday morning after the party, you told her to drive back to the desert, back to this house, for some invented reason. You knew that Skip's parents weren't here because they'd returned to LA for a few days. And since you yourself had been at the pool party, you knew the gate code to give to Noreen's killer. Posing as a pool cleaner, he let himself in and then waited for Noreen—maybe telling her the renters would be right back, maybe suggesting she could wait on the patio, by the pool, where there was still some shade. And then, the rest was simple."

Jim glared at me.

"Next," I said to him, "the bombing of my car: You saw me at the museum last week with Jazz, and you knew we were investigating Noreen's death. You could easily guess that we found the whole setup at M3A to be suspicious. And then, yesterday, I attended the 'retreat' at Blade's studio. After I parked in the lot, while I was walking toward the strip mall, I saw you and Fauvé just as you stepped inside Blade's door. Meaning, you were there, outside, when I arrived. You saw me. And you saw my car. The rest? All you had to do was make a quick phone call. But then, things went a little hinky, didn't they? You managed to blow up my Camry, but in the process, you killed Riley Uba—minutes after she was selected to lead the museum out of its crisis."

A grumbling arose from the guests, brought together that evening while still mourning the loss of Riley.

Jim insisted, "That's wild speculation, all of it. But even if it were true, why would I do *any* of that? I had no bone to pick with Noreen. We had our quibbles, sure, but I had no motive to *kill* her."

"Yes, you did," said Jazz. "The cruise fiasco."

"What about it? Yes, it put the museum in an awful bind, but we were working our way through it. We had a plan."

I said, "Maybe *you* did, Jim, but Noreen didn't buy into it. She had no interest in 'protocols'—she wanted instant action. She expected the *board* to fork over the shortfall. She made threats. She was just *begging* for lawsuits and countersuits and a deep dive into forensic accounting. Which would expose … everything."

From behind me, Howard Quince said, "As the museum's CFO, I warned her about that. Not that I gave a second thought to the issue of forensic accounting—as far as I knew, there was nothing to 'expose.' But now? Oh, boy."

"*Howard*," said Jim, sounding betrayed, "you don't *believe* this bullshit, do you?"

Jazz again warned him, "Language, Mr. Landon."

I said, "Know what, Jim? There's an easy way to clear some of this up. Just give us a look at your client list—that should end all the speculation."

"Like hell. I can't do that. I *won't* do that. Banking records are confidential."

I shrugged. "A subpoena might override that."

"Go ahead," he said, looking smug. "Try to get one."

Jazz stepped over to him, pulled the paper from inside her jacket, and delivered it to him. "Have a look, smartass."

He didn't even glance at it. His shoulders drooped. After a prolonged, tense silence, he mumbled, "I always felt the safer gamble was to let it go."

I asked him, "Let what go?"

With a sigh of resignation, Jim said, "The lost cruise deposits. Noreen made up her mind to push hard for a quick resolution, but I knew it would only lead to more trouble. Better to wait, let it play out slowly, stuck in a legal limbo long enough to be abandoned—especially if the museum went under, which was always a possibility."

"The scheme," I said. "How did it work?"

"You've already described it pretty well. Noreen and I got involved in laundering hefty sums of drug money. As an investment banker at Palm Mesa, I handled the museum's endowment fund, which is not overseen by Howard, but by a separate foundation. It has its own board of directors, whose functions are largely advisory and honorary—affording me lots of wiggle room."

I asked, "And Noreen's role in this?"

"She used her M3A job as a front for moving cash through customs with crated art, while I converted a portion of the funds to cryptocurrency. That allowed us to skim the cash and hide it in other, legit investments for our own gain. I want to stress, though, that Noreen's role in this—as well as mine—was purely functionary and limited to the movement of funds. We had nothing to do with the actual drug trade."

Jazz got smarmy. "I do hope that distinction gives you some comfort, Mr. Landon. But your white-collar services still place you and Noreen squarely in the arena of organized crime."

He didn't deny it.

I said, "I'm still wondering, Jim. When you decided that Noreen's approach to recovering the cruise money was too dangerous—when you decided you had to get rid of her—how did you convince her, on the day she was to die, to make a sudden return drive to Rancho Mirage?"

Jim looked over to his old friend Kenneth Terry Sr. "Don't hate me, Ken. I knew you and Claudia wouldn't be here that day—you were back in LA—but Noreen didn't know that. So I told her you had called me, saying you wanted to put the whole cruise mess behind you—for Skip's sake. You planned to write a fat check, covering everything, and she was welcome to drive over and pick it up. She was on the road within ten minutes."

Kenneth was visibly angry. So was Blade Wade. For that matter, so were Howard Quince, Cameron Vicario, and even Jim's wife, Fauvé. One by one, they rose from their seats and moved to surround Jim where he sat. Jazz planted her hands on her hips, spreading her jacket open, exposing her shoulder holster.

Jim turned to Jazz and me. "The rest was easy—just phoned it in. And that's the end of the story."

"Not … quite," I said.

Jazz asked me, "Really?"

I said to Jim, "When we get that client list of yours, and we take a close look, I'm wondering if we'll find a certain name."

"Which one?" he asked.

"Edison Quesada Reál."

Jim nodded. "He was a prominent member of the local arts community. I was happy to be of service. Fauvé and I counted him as a friend."

"Was he crooked?"

"A little," said Jim.

"And what about Edison's husband, Clarence Kwon—was *he* crooked?"

"A lot." With a coarse laugh, Jim added, "*That* little prick would do anything for a buck."

Conversation swelled in the room as Jazz pulled out her phone and called sheriff's detective Arcie Madera, parked only a block away. "Come and get it," said Jazz. She listened briefly, then responded, "Uh-huh. Confessed to it all—and we've got a dozen witnesses."

Arcie was already on her way and would arrive momentarily.

While keeping an eye on Jim Landon, Jazz leaned to tell me, "Pretty slick. How'd you figure out the connection to Clarence Kwon?"

"Just a hunch."

I didn't care to admit that the giveaway had been Fauvé Landon's distinctive gooey dessert, spiked with Cointreau—and beloved by *all* her friends.

Fauvé had called her concoction a raspberry trifle.

Rex Khalaji had described it as ambrosia.

But to Edison Quesada Reál, it was simply pink fluff.

CHAPTER NINETEEN

For the first time in two weeks, I was able to enjoy a night of deep, restorative sleep.

When I awoke Tuesday at dawn, I felt ready to roll, but there was no rush. I wasn't expected at the office that day—Ben had given me the day off so I could try to straighten out the mess with my pulverized car. I couldn't start making those calls till eight or nine, so I had some leisure time before wrangling on the phone.

Coffee by the pool. A stroll to the corner to pick up the local paper. There was nothing in print yet about last night's arrest, which had taken place at a private gathering, well after deadline. Walking back to my apartment, I noticed that something was missing that morning—the security detail outside the front gate.

In the courtyard, I took the long way around the pool, passing Isandro's door. I considered knocking, thinking he might have returned from his hospital shift, but no—if he did *not* work last night, he'd be asleep, so I kept moving.

Making my way around the pool, I approached Zola's door, which was open. I heard her puttering inside, singing softly, something about youth, wasted on the young. When I rapped on the doorjamb, she turned to me with a smile. "Look," she said. "Look what your friend Jazz sent me—banana leaves."

The bold arrangement featured tropical flowers, but mostly banana leaves, a clever thank-you for Zola's curtains.

While kissing my neighbor's cheek, I assured her, "Jazz *loved* them."

"I hope I'll get to meet her sometime."

"I hope you will, too, Zola."

■

Back in my own apartment, I had spread out on the breakfast bar all the paperwork I could find that was relevant to my car—title, registration, insurance policy, the agent's letterhead, and last but not least, the police report, which was essentially the Camry's death certificate. With a pen and legal pad at the ready, I was prepared for a runaround.

After pouring one more cup of coffee, I settled on a barstool, dreading the drudgery ahead. I was about to pick up my cell phone and place the first call when it rang. Seeing the readout, I felt a glow spread across my face. It was Skip—calling from his old phone, not the spare he'd kept hidden from the sheriff's department.

"Hey there!" I said.

"Morning, handsome."

"Looks like you got your phone back."

"Computer, too. Laptop. The works. I'm in the clear—thank you, Dante. Free for lunch today?"

"Yes and no." I explained my predicament with replacing the car—and a day off from the office to take care of it.

"Tell you what," he said. "One way or another, you've gotta eat. And since you can't drive, I'll pick you up. Eleven thirty?"

That would give me three hours to hassle with bureaucrats— by then I'd need a break. "Sure," I said. I gave him my address, along with a caveat. "It's *not* Wasi'chu Hills."

He laughed. "Stop that."

I managed to make some progress with the insurance—there would be a modest settlement, but they couldn't say exactly when I'd get it. While this left me with no idea when I'd be able to replace the car, at least I'd made some headway, so I was able to set aside my frustrations by eleven thirty, when I met Skip at the curb.

The Karmann Ghia looked freshly polished. Skip looked his preppy best, wearing a dove-gray polo and his classic Ray-Bans. When I got into the car, he leaned to give me a friendly kiss, then asked, "Okay with the top down?"

"Perfect."

"If it gets too hot, I'll close it up and turn on the air."

"I didn't think these ol' boys even *had* air."

"It was a bit of a trick, but I got it installed—that's life in the desert." While pulling away from the curb, he added, "It'll be cooler where we're going."

I had to ask: "Where are we going?"

"Pioneertown. Ever been there?"

"No, but I've heard about it." Pioneertown was built as a "living" movie set during the heyday of Western films and TV serials, with actors and crews residing there while filming. Located about thirty miles north of Palm Springs in the high-desert region of the San Bernardino range, the small rural community remained home to a mixed crowd of artists, free spirits, and anyone else with a taste for something different—including a music scene that took root and thrived there among the Joshua trees and the massive *Flintstones*-style boulders.

Zipping up through the mountains in Skip's open car felt like rocketing to a different world. When we arrived at a roadhouse, the only restaurant in town, and parked in the gravel lot, there was no one else in sight. In the radiant June sunlight, the cooler air felt chilly. A breeze carried the smell of barns and the distant neigh of a horse.

Inside, we were the only customers. The old adobe building was dark and ramshackle—in a welcoming sort of way. The thick clay walls were inset with whole liquor bottles of various hues, creating a stained-glass effect that dappled the rough timber floor. A smiling gal of twenty-something served as waitress, bartender, and cook. When we asked about favorites, she said, "The pork chop is amazing."

"I've never been amazed by a pork chop," I said. "Let's do it."

Skip had a beer, I settled on wine, and while waiting for lunch, we talked. It was the easy banter of friends enjoying each other's company, but when our conversation hit a lull, there was still a touchier topic that could not be avoided.

"On behalf of Sunny Junket Vacation Rentals," I said with mock formality, "I hope the remainder of your parents' stay at the Ellinger House will be much less eventful."

"I'll drink to that." Skip raised his glass, swallowed a slug, and set it aside. "And I'm sorry this turned into such a nightmare for you."

"Are you kidding? I met *you*. I wouldn't miss that for anything."

He reminded me, "Someone—a friend of my father, in fact—tried to kill you."

"Well, there's *that*," I admitted with a laugh.

"But you're right. It's been really special—you and me. Plus, you saved my ass."

I winked. "Duty called."

We were sitting at a rickety square four-top, not across from each other, but at adjacent sides, allowing us to touch legs, ankle to knee. Skip extended his hand on the table, palm up. I curved my fingers over his.

"I'll miss you," I said.

He gave me a quizzical look. "My parents will be leaving. I'm not going anywhere."

"I know. But... Ashley. So let's just say I'll miss the *fantasy* of you. Of us."

"Ah." He nodded. "Yes, that's a bit of a wrinkle, isn't it? I can't expect you to understand my life with her, Dante, but it's an arrangement that suits us. After so many years, I don't see any changes on that front, and neither does she. People think it's weird—I get it—but for Ashley and me? It works. It meets our needs." He paused, searching my face for reactions. We still held hands.

He continued, "And that's why I travel so much. That's why I have my getaway at Desert Towers. You're welcome there any-time—now and then."

Coyly, I made him wait. I grinned. "If I'm available."

"Goofus," he said, mussing my hair with his free hand. His other hand, holding mine, pulled me close, nearly spilling my wine. Then he gave me a kiss—a serious lip-lock—laced with the bright notes of a craft-brewed lager and the spicy scent of his stubbly beard and the animal warmth of his breath.

"Don't mind me, boys." The waitress left our lunch plates on the far side of the table.

And I found the pork chop—as described—amazing.

■

Leaving the roadhouse, walking to the car with me, Skip dangled his keys. "Wanna drive us back?"

"Well, *yeah*. Happy to." I took the keys. "But why? Are you stewed?"

He laughed. "Uh, no—not on one beer. I'm *giving* you the car."

I stopped in my tracks. "What?"

The gravel crunched as he turned back to me. "I owe you more than a damn *car*, Dante. Plus, you happen to need it, and I don't. I have others."

"That's *nuts*."

"No arguments. It's yours. I'll have someone drop the papers at your office tomorrow. So get in—and drive."

I stepped to the Karmann Ghia, hesitated, then opened the door.

"There, now. You *belong* behind that wheel," Skip said from the passenger seat as I pulled out of the lot and headed back to the highway. Lounging next to me with the wind in his wavy hair, he closed his eyes and reached over to rest his hand on my leg. I gunned it.

And a few minutes later, I was cruising down the mountain toward Palm Springs—with a hot guy in a cute convertible.

CHAPTER TWENTY

Life in the desert slowed to a crawl as June surrendered to July and August. And then, like clockwork, September brought its cooler, later mornings. It wasn't sweater weather yet—still many weeks ahead—but the hot, dry days now felt more therapeutic than deadly. In the minds of full-time desert dwellers, autumn was in the air.

By Labor Day, visitors had begun to return, along with a trickle of early snowbirds who ventured back to their seasonal roosts. With them came the first signs of renewed life for the dormant social scene.

The invitation was unexpected. The event itself—a Friday-night art opening—was nothing unusual, but I was surprised to see that I had somehow remained on the mailing list of the Harris-Heimlich Gallery.

"I got one, too," said Jazz on the phone. "Are you going?"

"Probably. Want company?"

"Sure, but let's meet there, okay? I've got some iffy business late that afternoon at Christopher's office—don't know what time I'll get down to Palm Desert."

"Uh-oh," I said. "Your ex's law office—what's that about?"

"We'll have to wait and see."

■

Friday's opening reception for the exhibit, titled WORKS IN RED, was scheduled from six to nine that evening. The artist was none other than Blade Wade, so I figured he must have freely contributed to the guest list. Why else would Jazz and I be invited?

I arrived on the early side, before six thirty, but could see from the street that the gallery was already crowded. Last time I was there, I felt I needed to hide my car in back of the building—but not tonight. I rolled up to the curb in the Karmann Ghia and handed the keys to the valet, a hunky college guy who nodded and said, "Sweet."

Waiting inside, checking the guest list at the door, was Liam, the attractive young gallery assistant who had asked me for a date—nearly three months earlier. He said, "Great to see you again, Mr. O'Donnell."

"Same here, Liam. Sorry to be out of touch. I haven't forgotten about you."

"No problem, Mr. O'Donnell. I'm sorta 'seeing someone.'" He used air quotes.

With a low laugh, I told him, "So am I." Then I asked, "Who's the lucky guy?"

Liam grinned. He turned his head to glance through the glass door, where the valet had just trotted back to the curb.

I gave Liam a thumbs-up. "He's more your type, anyway. Have fun." Then I wandered into the fray.

The entire main space of the front gallery was now decked out with Blade's growing collection of oversize paintings, mostly red. A catering crew in tuxedo vests offered brimming champagne flutes and trays of whatnot. A jazz trio played something cool and sophisticated beneath the babble. And weaving their way through the room were Blade Wade, the artist himself, and gallery owner Sabrina Harris, his agent—but not together. They were working the crowd from opposite ends of the exhibit.

I caught Blade's eye, and he rushed right over with a broad smile, but it was tainted by a look of concern. "Dante! Welcome!" Before I could respond at all, he added, "Where's Jazz?"

"On her way. Had a meeting or something."

He nodded. "She told me about it—keeping her fingers crossed. Something to do with Emma."

Intrigued, but not wanting to invite gossip, I asked, "And you—how's everything?"

"Fine," said Blade. "You figured out before I did that Noreen had a lot of, shall we say, ill-gotten gains. I'll never see any of that—the feds took it. But on the plus side, the painting gig's better than ever. Just look at this turnout tonight. So I'm ... well, I'm *grateful* to Sabrina."

"Grateful?" I asked. In the context of his not-so-secret love, the word seemed off.

Blade eyed me with a wry smile, then leaned near. "It's over. She's still my rep, and she's still gung ho for my career, but the rest—the relationship—it ran its course. We're friends now. *Just* friends."

I nodded. "Got it." I wondered if this had anything to do with Jazz. Tonight was the second time he'd sounded panicky when I entered a room without her.

And then, as if summoned by my thoughts, she appeared.

Jazz looked radiant, drifting through the crowd. She wore a dark suit, as usual, but it was her facial expression that glowed. Maybe she loved art openings. Or maybe she had good news. When a waiter approached her, offering champagne, she dismissed him with a warm smile and a gentle shake of her head.

She stepped over to me and gave me a little hug—something of a milestone, considering that the first time we met, she arrested me. Then she gave Blade a hug, which also seemed like something new.

He asked her, "How'd it work out?"

"Way better than expected." She grinned.

I asked, "What'd I miss?"

Her tone turned serious. "When Christopher divorced me, he called me an angry drunk—and an unfit mother. I probably was. And that's how he got custody of Emma, which made me even more pissed. It hurt. With the help of friends, though"—she gave my arm a quick squeeze—"I managed to focus on my new job, be my own boss, and get my shit together."

I told her, "I noticed."

"So did Christopher. It started after Emma brought her painting home from Blade's studio—as if *I* could take credit for that."

Blade told her, "Of *course* you can."

She shrugged. "Christopher said he started to realize that Emma *needs* a mother. He also said he 'approved' of the change in my behavior—he can still be so *damn* condescending. But I get it. He stopped smelling booze on my breath." With a laugh, she added, "Can't stand the smell of it myself now."

"Bravo," said Blade. "But what about Emma?"

"As of tomorrow, Christopher and I will share joint custody. Perfectly fair—I want Emma to have a father as much as Christopher wants her to have a mother."

"Fabulous," I said. "Sounds very civil of him."

Jazz looked perplexed. "It was more than civil. Maybe I was reading this wrong, but I got the impression Christopher might be having second thoughts about the divorce."

Now Blade looked perplexed.

"But you know what?" said Jazz. "I'm not interested. Now that I've got Emma back, I sorta like things the way they are."

Blade brightened. "Hey, I've got an idea. Do you have Emma tomorrow night?"

"In fact, I do."

"Bring her over to the studio. She can try another crayon painting. We can all have dinner. *I'll* cook. And, Dante—you come, too."

I turned to Jazz, thinking she might not want me there.

"Well, *yeah*," she said without hesitation. "Join us."

So I needed to be up-front: "I'd really love to, thanks. But I have plans."

"Uh-huh," said Jazz. "Don't tell me—'the Skipper' rang you up."

I smirked. "You think you're so smart."

"Well, look who's here," said Blade.

We followed his glance to the door. I thought maybe Skip had shown up, but it was Detective Arcie Madera, accompanied by a man who must have been her husband. She had told us she was married to an architect.

Blade waved them over.

Arcie made the round of introductions. Her husband, I now recalled, was Cooper Brant. A nice-looking man, he was a few years older than Arcie.

He told Blade, "I've admired your work, Mr. Wade. Delighted to be here tonight."

Blade draped one of his massive arms across the architect's shoulders. Referring to the rest of us, he said, "I have a hunch *these* folks are gonna be talkin' shop. If you'd rather talk art, Cooper, can I show you around?"

Cooper answered by blowing his wife a kiss and then walking off with Blade.

Jazz quickly told Arcie about the developments with Emma, and Arcie offered congratulations on the happy news. Then Arcie said, "I want to share a few updates with you, but I wonder if there's a quieter place where we can talk."

"I know just the spot," I said, remembering the sculpture garden behind the gallery.

■

When we passed through a rear exit, we found ourselves in the caterer's makeshift staging area. Servers shared quick smokes while waiting for trays to be replenished. They parted as we passed through, and I led Jazz and Arcie across the parking lot to the garden. Since all the action was indoors, we had the place to ourselves.

The heroically scaled sculptures, which I had previously seen in full afternoon sunlight, were now bathed in the gentle glow of landscape lighting as dusk began to fade the sky above the valley. As before, in a clearing among the surrounding ficus hedges, a fountain piddled. We sat facing it on a curved stone bench.

Jazz got down to business, asking Arcie, "Is the DA happy?"

With a soft laugh, Arcie said, "Peter Nadig is one *very* happy fella. He thought he could get a quick conviction of Skip Terry, and instead, he got Jim Landon, who proved to be a gold mine. Landon cooperated on a plea deal, exposed the whole drug-money scheme, and led investigators straight to the hit man—and a web of mob connections. That 'simple drowning' in Rancho Mirage has now netted Nadig not one but *four* bad guys behind bars, awaiting trial. And this isn't small-time stuff, remember. It's organized crime and at least two murders—that we know of."

I said, "Two murders: Noreen Penley Wade and Riley Uba. Noreen was part of the problem, but Riley was an innocent victim."

Jazz reminded me, "All victims deserve justice."

"True," I said.

Arcie told me, "It's been almost two years since your former husband was killed, and he's had no justice. But thanks to some clever detective work by Jazz—and you, Dante—we'll soon put to rest the unsolved murder of Dr. Anthony Gascogne. It's not a happy story, but it's closure. And it's justice."

I said, "Anthony's killer was closer than we thought. Clarence Kwon, right?"

Arcie nodded. "Once Jazz was able to get a look at Anthony's office schedule, courtesy of the Palm Springs police, we saw that Kwon had an eye appointment on the morning Anthony died— an appointment he missed."

Jazz said, "During the initial investigation, that information was right there, but it was meaningless. Anthony had lots

of appointments, but there was no known connection to Kwon."
Jazz turned to ask me, "How did you piece that together?"

Without mentioning Skip Terry, I explained, "I heard from
a friend that Kwon and his husband, Edison, as well as my ex,
Anthony, were all on a cruise together. Later, Kwon visited Palm
Springs around the time Anthony was killed. I knew Anthony for
nearly thirty years, and he had an embarrassing habit of pushing
his ophthalmology services on new friends. I kept telling him it
was tacky, but he did it anyway. So that's why I suggested taking
another look at his office schedule."

"Glad you did," said Arcie. "Once we established that connection, the case was open and shut. It was easy to go back and
trace phone and email records, as well as DNA evidence collected from the crime scene. Kwon was already looking at a
death sentence for killing Edison, so when we confronted him
with the new evidence regarding Anthony Gascogne, he crowed
about it—how he was *staying* with Anthony at the time he was
killed. Some nonsense about a Bentley convertible. Kwon tried
to extort Anthony for the car as 'consideration' for his visits and
sexual favors. Anthony laughed at him and threatened to report
everything to Kwon's husband. So... Kwon made sure Anthony
wouldn't talk."

With feigned sympathy, Jazz said, "Too bad the DA couldn't
nail someone who wasn't *already* facing murder charges—a new
notch on his gun, so to speak."

Arcie countered, "The separate charges and added conviction, that's good enough for Nadig. He's planning to *coast*
through the next election with these headline cases. In fact, he
asked me to thank you, Jazz."

Jazz looked befuddled. "Just doing my job. And I had some
help, by the way."

Arcie shrugged. "I'll lay this on the table: Nadig was
impressed, and so was I. The sheriff's department has occasional
openings in the investigations division, and we don't always

promote from within. I was one of the first women to make it. A few others have followed, but I still want to see more women on the force—strong women. Plus, you already have the police training. So think about this, Jazz."

Jazz thought about it, sitting there, but not for long. "Arcie," she said, "that might be the most tempting offer I've ever had. Thank you. But I sorta like working solo. Know what I mean?"

"Of course," said Arcie, rising. With a smile she added, "Just keep it in mind. And now I'd better go find Cooper." She walked off toward the building.

Jazz scooched over to me on the bench.

I turned to face her. "Well, *you've* had quite a night."

"Dante," she said, "when I told Arcie I like working solo, I hope you didn't think I meant *solo* solo. Understood?"

"Still in the market for a little side work?"

"Uh-huh. And that office—the decorating has a *long* way to go."

I nodded. "I'm always around. Just call."

She nodded. "Same here."

■

By the time we returned to the gallery, the crowd had thinned. Many of the guests had probably moved on to dinner somewhere. Arcie was standing with her husband and Blade Wade, gabbing in front of one of the huge red paintings. Jazz and I joined them.

But the party was over, and a few minutes later, I said my good-nights.

While walking toward the front of the exhibit space, I noticed the little side gallery that housed the collection of Rex Khalaji's archival prints from film. Glancing inside, I saw the photographer himself. He must have been on hand to discuss his work with guests from the main event, but I hadn't spotted him through the earlier bustle of the crowd. He was now alone in there, facing the back wall, as if mesmerized by his photo of Skip Terry at sixteen.

I stepped up behind him. "Hello, Rex. Nice to see you again."

His eyes never left the photo. "He was the most remarkable young man, don't you think?"

"Yes," I agreed quietly. "He certainly was." And after a long, awkward lull, I left.

Out at the curb, the hunky valet, Liam's new boyfriend, handed me my keys and complimented the car again. When I reached for my wallet, he wagged a hand, informing me, "No tipping tonight. But thank you."

"Thank *you*," I said as I got into the convertible. He closed the door for me.

I was about to drive off when my phone buzzed with a text. It was from Ben at the Sunny Junket office: "Can you handle a VIP Check-In tomorrow? Indian Wells at two." I typed: "No problem."

Setting the phone aside, I grinned at the valet, who responded with a bashful smile. Then I pedaled the clutch, shifted into drive, and pulled away.

Above the open car, dusk had faded to dark. The balmy evening hinted of cooler days to come, when locals could brag again about living in paradise. That summer would soon fade, reduced to a scorching memory—of Skip and murder and my own brush with death.

Onward, I thought.

Tomorrow, Saturday, I would be back from Indian Wells in plenty of time to primp and preen for my dinner date. Months earlier, when I first suggested it to my neighbor Isandro, he sounded indifferent, claiming his irregular schedule at the hospital made it difficult to make plans. I assumed this was a brush-off, signaling he wasn't interested—beyond our occasional quickie at dawn.

But then, a few weeks ago, he lucked into a new assignment with regular hours and weekends off. Tomorrow would be our second Saturday dinner together. When we planned it, he said, "And afterward, maybe you could spend the night."

Maybe I would.

Heading home under the stars, I recalled a morning when I heard another neighbor, Zola, singing softly in her apartment—something about youth, wasted on the young. Something about new beginnings.

Her wistful words now drifted on the breeze as I sped along beneath the arching palms.

■

ACKNOWLEDGMENTS

The novel *Desert Getaway* is based on my short story "VIP Check-In," which appeared in the anthology *Palm Springs Noir*, published by Akashic Books in 2021. I am highly grateful to Tod Goldberg for initially suggesting my inclusion in the project, as well as publisher Johnny Temple and editor Barbara DeMarco-Barrett, who placed me in the company of more than a dozen talented writers contributing to that volume.

While developing the short story into this novel, I received invaluable assistance with various plot details from David Sirek, Kevin Hickey, Thomas Johnson, and attorney David Grey. First readers of the manuscript included Larry Warnock and Barbara McReal, whose keen attention to the words on the page helped produce a more polished narrative.

Crime novelists John Copenhaver and Michael Nava generously contributed early endorsements of the manuscript, and then Mitchell Waters, my agent for some twenty-five years, secured a home for the project with Brash Books.

At Brash Books, co-founder Lee Goldberg proved to be an enthusiastic and collaborative editor whose guidance shaped *Desert Getaway* into a tighter and more compelling story, for which he has my deepest gratitude.

And finally, as always, my husband, Leon Pascucci, has been a steady font of patience, support, and good cheer.

My sincere thanks to all.

ABOUT THE AUTHOR

Michael Craft is the author of eighteen novels, four of which were honored as finalists for Lambda Literary Awards. His 2019 mystery, *ChoirMaster*, was a Gold Winner of the IBPA Benjamin Franklin Award. He is the author of two produced plays, and his prizewinning short fiction has appeared in British as well as American literary journals.

Craft grew up in Illinois and spent his middle years in Wisconsin, the setting for many of his books. He holds an MFA in creative writing from Antioch University, Los Angeles, and now lives in Rancho Mirage, California, near Palm Springs, which provided the setting for *Desert Getaway*.

In 2017, Michael Craft's professional papers were acquired by the Special Collections Department of the Rivera Library at the University of California, Riverside. A comprehensive archive of his manuscripts, working notes, correspondence, and other relevant documents, along with every edition of his completed works, is now cataloged and made available for both scholarly research and public enjoyment.

Visit his website at www.michaelcraft.com.

Made in the USA
Middletown, DE
26 April 2022

64456609R00165